WICKED NEED

(The Wicked Horse Series)

By
Sawyer Bennett

All Rights Reserved.

Copyright © 2016 by Sawyer Bennett

Published by Big Dog Books

This book is a work of fiction. Names, characters, places, and incidents either are products of the author's imagination or are used fictitiously. Any resemblance to actual events, locales or persons, living or dead, is entirely coincidental.

No part of this book can be reproduced in any form or by electronic or mechanical means including information storage and retrieval systems, without the express written permission of the author. The only exception is by a reviewer who may quote short excerpts in a review.

ISBN: 978-1-940883-44-1

Find Sawyer on the web!
www.sawyerbennett.com
www.twitter.com/bennettbooks
www.facebook.com/bennettbooks

Table of Contents

Prologue	1
Chapter 1	9
Chapter 2	18
Chapter 3	28
Chapter 4	38
Chapter 5	50
Chapter 6	61
Chapter 7	71
Chapter 8	84
Chapter 9	95
Chapter 10	108
Chapter 11	119
Chapter 12	132
Chapter 13	143
Chapter 14	156
Chapter 15	169
Chapter 16	181
Chapter 17	192
Chapter 18	204
Chapter 19	216
Chapter 20	228
Chapter 21	242
Chapter 22	255

Chapter 23	265
Chapter 24	277
Chapter 25	288
Chapter 26	297
Epilogue	306
Other Books by Sawyer Bennett	309
About the Author	309

Prologue
Rand

I WALK THROUGH The Silo, turning off the lights behind me as I go. Normally, this would fall to Bridger or Cain, but neither is around tonight. Bridger is attending a party out at the compound for the Mayhem's Mission motorcycle club, which translates into fucking some free pussy unassociated with The Silo. While this is Bridger's baby, I get the feeling that his "duties" here wear on him sometimes.

There are times it seems he actually hates "servicing" some people, but maybe I'm trying to read something into the situation that isn't there. Regardless, he's not here and neither is Cain.

He just flew back from Tennessee today, and he's shacked up with Sloane. I'm sure he's still hammering out the necessary apologies that woman deserves from him.

Cute couple though. I figured out of all of us dudes, he'd be one of the last to drop given his history with Rachel, but what the fuck do I know? I'm definitely unlucky in love, but I'm okay if it never comes my way again. I've got friends, a great job, and all the kinky fuckery I could ever imagine.

I snicker to myself, thinking about that.

Kinky fuckery.

Some chick said that the other night while Logan and I were both doing her, and we thought it was hilarious. She said it was a term in one of her favorite books, but whatever.

It totally describes what happens within the walls of this circular building.

I make my way down the short hallway to the exit, flipping down the switch of the sconce lighting and pushing open the door. The air is crisp and smells refreshing. Cleans the soul kind of good because sometimes when I walk out of The Silo, I feel like I'm tainted by the things I do.

But again, whatever. I might feel dirty at times, but some of the shit I dip my wick into also feels fucking amazing.

I pull the door closed and ensure the lock is engaged. Security's become more important now than ever given that fuckwad Colton Stokes blabbed his mouth. Of course, on one hand, you could say it was a good thing because it brought Sloane Preston to our neck of the woods. Not only was she a fantastic fuck, and I hope Cain lets me in on that again, but it's also made my buddy super happy. So maybe Colton just deserved an ass whipping instead of the murder I'd like to dole out to him for threatening our existence.

The parking lot is nearly deserted, The Wicked

Horse having closed about an hour ago. The Silo is technically open twenty-four/seven for any members who want to get debauched, but the bartenders go off duty at the same time The Wicked Horse closes down at two AM. I'm the last to leave after getting a last-minute cock suck from Carol, one of the lovely purveyors of fine drinks. She toddled out not fifteen minutes ago with a tart goodbye. I should have returned the favor to her, but she owed me the blow job because she lost a bet last week on the Yankees' game. She's a transplanted New Yorker and I hate the Yankees, so I always bet against them, no matter the price of the potential loss.

My eyes zero in on my Suburban parked up near The Wicked Horse in the space closest to the slate path that leads from the back door over to The Silo. I click the remote entry fob and the lights flash, indicating the doors are unlocked. I reach for the handle, pull it open, and just as I'm about to step in, my gaze falls on a white Mercedes coupe sitting two rows back and three spaces over. I start to turn away and then do a double-take as I realize it's Catherine's car.

I know she left The Silo probably about half an hour ago after giving everyone a show tonight. Since her husband died last week, she's been at The Silo every night, indulging in every wicked sex act you can imagine. Not that she didn't indulge before, but for some reason, since the old fart's death, she seems a bit more free-spirited in her pursuits. Maybe even doggedly determined to outdo herself every time.

Tonight, my tongue was hanging out of my mouth while she occupied a room all to herself and played with a variety of electrical and mechanical toys Bridger's been collecting. She got right up against the glass wall and made sure everyone could see what she was doing. I bet I watched her come at least six times before she finally fell into a heap on the floor, panting with sweat-soaked skin and drowsy eyes. After she collected herself, she got dressed and sauntered out the door, waving goodbye over her head. I was so fucking horny after that, it took no time at all for Carol to wrench an unbelievable orgasm out of me. And strangely... I was imagining Catherine sucking my cock at the time, which is a bit weird.

It's not like there's any mystery there. Catherine's deep throated me on a few occasions before, and I've fucked her on even more occasions than that. Didn't think she was really anything different from all the other sexual encounters I've had, but for some reason, it was her dark hair I imagined clenched in my fist rather than Carol's strawberry-blonde curls.

Perhaps Catherine left her car here and went home with someone else. That must be it.

Just as I start to turn my eyes back to my vehicle, I see movement within the darkness of the interior of her car. I peer harder, willing the light from the nearest security post to reveal the inside, and if I'm not mistaken, the seat is leaned back and someone's lying down, perhaps having just turned from one side to the other.

What the hell?

I close my door and walk quickly across the lot to her car, my head tilted in curiosity. As I get closer, I can see better, and it is indeed Catherine lying in the driver's seat reclined all the way back. She's on her side with her hands curled up by her face, her back to me. Those long, dark locks are spread out over her back and shoulder.

I tap gently on the window, knowing I'm going to startle her but not being able to help it. She jerks upright, looking at me with frightened eyes. When she recognizes me, I can see her give a sigh of relief. She raises the seat up and rolls the window down. It's then that I notice her car is running.

"Hey," she says, her eyes darting around the parking lot.

"What are you doing?" I ask, completely perplexed to find her sleeping in her car. I know she's not drunk because Catherine doesn't drink.

At all.

That's because she does some crazy shit in the club, and she doesn't want anyone to ever think it's not of her own free will. She owns her kinky fuckery… and owns it good. I don't think she does drugs, so it's very confusing to find her here like this.

"Um… I just…" Her voice trails off and her gaze falls down to her delicate fingers, which are intertwined tightly with one another.

"Catherine… were you going to spend the night out here?"

She lets out a huff of frustrated air. Looking back up

to me with resignation in her eyes, she admits, "Yes."

Nothing more.

I cock an eyebrow at her. Catherine and her late husband reside in Vegas permanently, but he has a luxury cabin just outside of Jackson that they spent a lot of time at since he got her a membership at The Silo.

"Is your car broken down or something?"

She shakes her head and looks back down at her lap.

"Then what the fuck?" I ask, exasperated and also damn worn out from the night's activities. I want to get home and get some shut-eye. Work comes early and I cannot miss it. I have to open the tattoo shop I work for at ten in the morning, and I need the few hours of sleep I can squeeze in.

She's silent and I think she may refuse to answer me, but then her small voice reaches my ears and it stuns me. "I don't have anywhere else to stay."

"What do mean? You have a seven-thousand-square-foot home not thirty minutes away."

She shakes her head, that dark hair falling in a veil to hide her face. It's a gorgeous face, too. High cheekbones, with an exotic slant to her liquid brown eyes. It's a face that should be in movies or on magazines. A face beautiful enough that it landed her a wealthy husband on death's door and should have left her swimming in riches.

"Catherine," I prompt, pulling on the handle to her door. It's still locked so I reach my hand inside, find the lock, flip it, and then pull the door open. I step in, squat down, and place my hand on her thigh. "What's going on?"

She pulls in a shaky breath, lifts a hand to tuck her hair behind her ear, which exposes her face again, and then turns to look at me with bleak eyes. "He didn't leave me with anything. Just this car, which he had titled in my name."

"Excuse me?"

"Samuel left everything to his two children. Of course, I knew he would leave them with something. But he always promised me he'd take care of me. I'd always have a place to live. An attorney showed up at the Jackson house two days ago telling me that I had to vacate. I was allowed to pack up my clothes, and that was it."

My breath hisses out from between my teeth, and I wish that creepy fucker was still alive so I could pound his withered, crippled ass into the ground. That goddamn motherfucker.

I stand straight after giving a quick pat on her thigh. "You can crash at my place tonight. I'll help you figure something out."

"Seriously?" she asks, her eyes wide and her lips trembling. "I mean… we don't really know each other."

"I've been balls deep inside you a time or two, Catherine. I think I know you a little bit," I say with a teasing smile.

She blushes, and fuck… that's pretty. I've never seen Catherine blush, and she's done some things to make even the kinkiest of motherfuckers go red in the face.

"Are you sure?" she hesitantly asks.

"Positive. You can follow me to my place."

"I'll be glad to pay you," she says earnestly. "You know… in sex or something. I've only got about fifty dollars in cash left to my name."

My cock leaps at the thought, because yeah… although I'm tired, I would not say no to fucking her tonight. But instead, I decide to be a gentleman. "You don't owe me anything. Let's get you to my place so you can get a good night's sleep. We'll talk about it more tomorrow and try to figure out how to take care of you."

She blushes again as I put my hand on the door to close it for her. Just before I do though, she whispers, "Thank you, Rand. You're a lifesaver."

Hmmmm… I like the sound of that.

Chapter 1
Rand

I TRY TO be as quiet as possible as I creep past the couch where Catherine's sleeping. My tiny apartment can be walked from end to end in about five seconds. Roughly 475 square feet of efficient living. I've been renting this apartment from my buddy, Jake Gearhart. It's situated over the garage of his modest ranch house in the town of Jackson, Wyoming.

It's nothing but a large square that has a semi private foyer/mudroom as soon as you enter. When you round the corner, you have the kitchen and living room to the left, and my bedroom to the right. The bathroom sits adjacent to the foyer.

While I can certainly afford bigger and better, I don't see any need to spend my money on my living conditions as I'm rarely here. Over the last several years, I'd gotten used to sleeping in small quarters or hotels, so I'm comfortable as is.

Jake's different. He has a family that includes the pretty wife who's a local, an adorable two-year-old daughter, and another kid on the way, although you can barely see Lorelei's baby bump at this stage.

As I try to creep past a sleeping Catherine, I wish I had bigger digs so I could have offered her a guest room so she could get some rest. I actually did offer her *my* room when we got to my apartment last night, but she refused.

Staunchly.

Said she didn't want to inconvenience me and she was already feeling like an imposition.

I assured her she was not and tried to push my room on her.

Her eyes immediately turned warm, and then sizzled with blooming sexual heat that made my dick start to get hard. "I'll only take your room if you let me pay you, and well… you know the only thing I got to offer at this point is my mouth or my pussy. Want it?"

Fuck yeah, I wanted it. I've had both before and they're fucking fantastic.

But not last night.

Last night, Catherine was in a bad spot. I wasn't about to take advantage of that offer. I wanted her to see she could get something from someone without the expectation of needing to give something in return. It's called friendship and that's what friends do.

And I think Catherine and I are friends.

Maybe.

Fuck, not really sure.

So even though I really wanted to fuck her, I saw the stubborn pride bubbling low beneath the sensuality in her eyes, and I knew my dick was going to bed alone.

Since she wouldn't take my room without feeling the need to basically prostitute herself in return, I conceded and fixed up the couch for her complete with pillow, sheets, and a thick quilt. I also offered her up a t-shirt and a pair of my sweatpants, of which she accepted only the t-shirt. It swallowed her whole and made her look even more vulnerable than I was already considering her to be.

She doesn't stir as I walk behind the couch that sits perpendicular to the mudroom wall and essentially creates a living area that opens right up into an L-shaped kitchenette that houses my stove, refrigerator, and enough cabinet space to barely hold my dishes. A small, round table with two chairs completes the set up.

As quietly as I can, I start making coffee, but the minute I open a squeaky cupboard door, I can hear Catherine starting to stir on the couch. After I fill the pot, measure the coffee, and start the brew cycle, I turn to find Catherine now sitting up with the quilt pulled demurely over her lap. She must have slept fitfully because her hair is a tangled mess and she has mascara smeared under her eyes, which reminds me of something.

"Your bags and stuff in the trunk of your car?" I ask her.

She blinks at me once, grimaces, and rubs a finger under one eye. She pulls it away, looks at the black smear, and wrinkles her nose. "Um… yeah."

"Give me your keys. I'll go get them so you can get cleaned up and changed," I tell her.

"Yeah," she says as she stands from the couch, her voice still rough with sleep. "I should get out of your way."

"I didn't mean it like that," I tell her as she pulls her purse from the coffee table and reaches inside. "There's no rush for you to leave."

Her face clouds over, almost as if she refuses to believe someone could be nice, before tilting down so she can look around inside her purse. I take the brief opportunity to appreciate that even with tangled hair, mascara smears, and a baggy t-shirt on, she's still one of the sexiest women I've ever seen. Hell, she may be the absolute sexiest, and I'm only judging this by the fact that, in this moment, I seem to be more attracted to her than ever before. I'm not sure if it's her vulnerability or my white-knight complex, but I've seen Catherine dressed in any number of sexy outfits with perfect hair and makeup, and I never wanted to fuck her as bad as I do right now.

When she turns to me with car keys in hand, I hope she doesn't notice the hard-on I'm sporting. Not that I'd be embarrassed about it because Catherine's gotten me hard before and she knows it, but because I don't want her to think that's all I'm interested in from her. I especially don't want her thinking she has to pay me in that way.

I take the keys from her and head for the door. "Mind pouring me a cup of coffee? I take it black."

"Sure," she murmurs, but I don't look back at her. I

need to get my dick under control.

In the trunk of her car, I find a large suitcase, a carry-on, and a duffle-type bag, all done in the classic brown leather and gold lettering of Louis Vuitton. I'm totally not into fashion, but I'd bought my fair share of that designer for both my mom and Tarryn, so I know how expensive this shit is. I can't help but think that Catherine might find herself in a situation where she has to sell her fucking luggage to get some cash, and that's a shitty place to be.

I cart the bags up the outside staircase to my garage apartment with my hard-on back under control. I find her sitting at the small kitchen table, a cup of coffee in her hand. My cup is poured and sitting by the coffee pot.

"Listen," I tell her in my most casual voice so she doesn't feel like a charity case. "Why don't you stay here for a few days until you can get your bearings?"

"I couldn't—" she starts to say, and I knew she'd rebuff the offer.

"Come on, Catherine," I cut her off sternly. "We're friends. That's what friends do."

"It's Cat," she says.

This throws me off because I'd been expecting an argument. "Excuse me?"

"Cat. The name I prefer to go by is Cat."

I blink at her, stunned for a moment by the change in subject. "I didn't know that."

She shrugs nonchalantly and lowers her gaze to her cup. "No one ever bothered to ask. Catherine is what

Samuel insisted on calling me. It's how he always introduced me."

Fuck.

Just… fuck.

I can almost see her identity disappearing right before my eyes. What did this asshole do to her? He left her destitute after already stealing who she was right out from under her.

Taking my cup from the counter, I walk over to the table and sit opposite of her. I make a command decision, knowing it's the right thing to do in this moment. I know Jake will tell me I'm slipping into my savior role, but fuck him. Cat needs help and I don't think she has anyone else to turn to right now.

"Here's what we're going to do," I say in a firm, take-control voice. Her eyes immediately snap up to mine. "You're going to stay here in my apartment with me. If you want to remain stubborn and stick with the couch, that's fine. No argument from me. That will let you get your feet underneath you. You can take a bit of time, figure out what you want to do… or where you want to go."

"I don't have any money—"

"If it's that important to you, you can pay me back when you get some." I don't even consider trying to talk her out of just accepting my generosity because I can see Cat has pride. I can see that's about the only thing she has of value to her name, and I'm not about to steal it from her. "How's that sound?"

She turns slightly away from me, letting her gaze roam over the tiny space of my apartment. It takes her two seconds before returning to me. "You don't have a lot of room here. I wouldn't want to get in your way."

"I'm not here a lot," I tell her as I stand from the table with my cup in hand. "I have a full-time day job. Between that and being at The Silo, we probably won't run into each other that much."

And why do I feel a crushing sense of disappointment over that thought?

"I'd want to pay you rent once I maybe get a job or something," she says, her chin lifting higher. Christ… the sexy seductress looks just adorable right now, all bowed up with dignity and determination.

"What kind of work would you want to do?" I ask her, thinking I've got contacts in this area. Maybe I can help her out that way too.

"I've only ever done two things to get by in this life, Rand," she says softly with just a trace of bitterness. It sucks to hear that tone the first time she calls me by my name. "And that's dancing and fucking."

"Dancing?" I ask, because I can't bear to think of her prostituting herself to make a living. Although really… wasn't that what she was doing by marrying an older man?

I mentally curse at myself for letting my head go there.

"I was an exotic dancer in Vegas," Cat says with a grim smile. "That's where Samuel met me."

I've seen Catherine naked many, many times and yeah… she has a dancer's body. Long limbs, soft curves in just the right places, and breasts that are spectacular. I bet she put on a fucking fantastic show.

But that wouldn't benefit her here in Jackson as there aren't any titty bars and the thought of her returning to Vegas isn't all that appealing to me either for some weird reason. So I point her in the next best direction for now.

"I suggest you work on finding out more about your legal rights," I tell her with a pointed look before lifting my cup to my mouth for a sip.

"My legal rights?" Her eyes blink in confusion.

"Well, yeah. I mean… you thought Samuel was going to take care of you, then some attorney shows up and tells you to get out of your house. Did he even show you a copy of the will giving him that authority?"

Cat shakes her head, cheeks turning red with embarrassment. "I didn't ask. He was pushing me hard to get my stuff packed and to vacate."

Even though I may not have gone to college and only have a degree from the school of hard knocks, I know enough to know that doesn't sound right.

"You need to go to that attorney's office and ask for a copy of Samuel's will," I tell her. "As his wife, you're entitled to see it. I seriously don't think they can just kick you out like that. I'm sure there's some long process they have to go through or some shit."

Cat's cheeks turn even redder. "I didn't even think to ask for a copy. God, I'm so stupid."

Before I can stop myself, I take one step to her chair, grasp her chin with my hand, and squeeze slightly to get her attention. "You are not stupid. You're in a bad place and that attorney took advantage of that. But now you're on solid ground and I'll help you figure this out. Okay?"

For a moment, I think she might cry on me, and I brace myself for it. I don't do well with tears. I'm a sucker for them. If I see one drop spill, I'll pull her in my arms. At that point, I'll really have to take shit from Jake that I can't seem to help myself when it comes to a lost woman.

She surprises me though and nods against my grip. "Okay."

Though I'm loathe to release her, I do it anyway. "Okay then. I think your goal for today is to go to that attorney's office and ask for a copy of Samuel's will."

"Just show up without an appointment?" Cat asks with hesitation.

"Yup. Just walk in and ask for it. You shouldn't need an appointment for that."

I think. Fuck, I don't know, but it's a start.

"I can do that," she says as she stands from the chair.

For the first time since last night, I actually see a glimmer of hope in her eyes that perhaps things will turn out okay. I don't know that they will, but I know for sure I'm not going to abandon her.

Jake's going to give me so much shit.

Chapter 2
Cat

SO I HAVE a plan.

A temporary one, but at least I have a plan.

I also have a roof over my head for the time being, and since Rand told me to help myself to anything in the apartment, I will also have food in my belly. While he takes a shower, I make use of the carton of eggs in his refrigerator and scramble some up for both of us. I have a plate waiting for him when he emerges from the bathroom, wearing nothing but a pale blue towel wrapped low around hips.

I know that body well. It's tall and lean with just the right amount of muscles gracing a broad chest and strong arms. I happen to know when he flexes his abs, they'll tighten into a six pack, just as I know his pierced tongue feels good between my legs. I know well those green eyes that will stare at me with frenzied lust and the soft brush of his blond beard against my skin.

Rand is a beautiful package, no doubt. He's edgy with his golden hair shaved on the sides but long on top. He often brushes his fingers through it, pushing it away from his face. I find it amusing that he always seems exasperated by the length, but he never cuts it any shorter. Add in a multitude of tattoos over his chest, back, and upper arms, a silver ring through his left nostril and a matching one through his left eyebrow, and you have a man who's edgy, cool, and sexy all at the same time.

So I feed him scrambled eggs while he sits at the table. I try not to stare at the gap in the towel that rides up his right thigh and instead focus my attention on his apartment.

It's small in and of itself, but it's cramped with so much clutter that it feels like you're in a closet. Not the type of small clutter like unwashed cups left on tables, but rather his mudroom has at least four pairs of ski boots shoved under a bench along with a pair of snowshoes in the corner and puffy ski pants and coats hanging on hooks on the wall. In his living room, two corners have various skis and poles leaning in casual stacks. A bookcase holds trophies and glass-encased medals I briefly noticed last night as he was making up the couch. So many, in fact, they appear just haphazardly jammed on the shelves, not to display but merely to just put them somewhere out of the way.

I was so exhausted last night I didn't take a very close look, but while Rand was getting my luggage out of my car, I went to the bathroom and my attention was caught by a framed photo. It was pushed into the back corner of the second shelf from the top. It caught my attention because of one of the most recognizable logos in the world displaying prominently in the background.

Five circles.

Three on top. Two on the bottom. All interlinked.

Each a different color. Blue, black, red, yellow, and green.

I halted as I recognized the Olympic rings, but more importantly, I recognized Rand standing on a tiered podium, right in the middle and on the highest dais. Both arms were raised high in the air in victory, with one hand clutching a bouquet of flowers and the other raising his index finger pointed upward to the sky.

Around his neck, a large, round gold medal hung on a thick white ribbon.

I was stunned.

Rand was an Olympic medalist?

My eyes roamed around his small living room again, taking in the ski equipment. Back to the photo where he was wearing a heavy, puffed overcoat on the stand done in pristine white with the American flag patched over his left breast.

Holy fuck. Rand won an Olympic gold medal.

I didn't say anything when he came back in as he dropped my luggage next to the couch and said he had to jump in the shower and head to work. So I made eggs, my gaze flicking periodically to the shelves of trophies and medals, wondering what else was in there.

Now I look over Rand's shoulder as he hunches over his plate, shoveling the food in, which makes me suspect he might be late for work. My eyes come to rest on the photo I studied earlier.

"You won an Olympic gold medal?" I blurt out, dying to know more about him. I mean... he's always just been Rand. A gorgeous, sexy man who's tremendously talented with his cock, mouth, and fingers, but past that, I know nothing about him.

His eyes rise up to meet mine as he finishes chewing the eggs in his mouth. After he swallows, he swipes his lips with the paper towel I laid next to his plate and gives me a wolfish smile. "That was five years ago in Vancouver. Won the gold in the Super Combined as well as two silvers in the Super G and Downhill."

My mouth hangs slightly open in astonishment. "Three medals?"

He nods, gives me a wink, and takes another bite of his eggs, seemingly not interested in touting his accomplishments to me. But I'm amazed I didn't know this about him. "Did you compete in last year's Olympics?"

I can't say he gives me a look of sadness. It's not even bitterness. Maybe just a fondness for what will never be again, but he lays his fork on his plate, wipes his mouth again, and says, "I was going to. Made the U.S. Ski Team, but about a year prior to the start of the Games, I took a bad fall at an event in San Sicario. Injured my right knee pretty badly. Tore three of the four major ligaments in my knee."

"They couldn't repair it before the Olympics started?" I ask, feeling terrible he lost such an amazing opportunity.

Rand shakes his head and stands from the table. I get a flash of the golden skin covered in coarse hair on his thigh with rippling muscle, and for the first time, I notice scars on his right knee.

"Wasn't the first time I injured that knee. I competed in the 2006 Games when I was nineteen. Took a bad spill on my first run on the Super G. Knocked me out completely. So I had surgery to repair the damage and built myself up for the 2010 Games. Luckily, my knee held strong and I picked up a few medals along the way."

I stand up from the table as well, taking my plate and following Rand to the kitchen sink. Before he can start to rinse his own, I take it from his hands and say, "I'll clean up. You go get ready for work."

Our fingers touch as he gives up the plate and I swear I can feel the touch down to my toes. So innocent yet so powerful. When Rand turns toward his bedroom, I can't help but ask, "You don't seem all that bitter about losing out on those opportunities."

He turns to me with a wide grin. "Yeah, well, I guess I choose to focus on the successes I had while I was competing. And I always knew it was a fleeting career that could be cut short at any time. It's too dangerous and was bound to happen anyway."

"Do you still ski?" I ask, even more curious about this man.

He nods. "Sure I do… for pleasure only. And I don't get crazy or anything. You stick around when the snow starts falling and I'll take you out. You ski?"

I shake my head. "Never been."

"Then we'll have to do it," he says, and it almost makes me believe he means that. As if he expects me to be sticking around long enough to see the snow. Granted, the weather is getting colder and there have even been some scattered flurries, so it won't be long, but I have no clue where I'll be come wintertime.

In fact, I know absolutely nothing and it scares the shit out of me.

"I don't even know your last name," I murmur, pathetically aware that I know Rand is an Olympic medalist, but I don't know something as intimate as his complete name. I've let this man fuck me and I've sucked his cock, but I have no clue what his last name is. That makes me feel small and filthy.

"Bishop," he says softly, his head tilted to the side. "Rand Bishop. It's a pleasure to formally meet you, Cat Vaughn."

Shaking my head, I correct him. "Lyons."

"Lyons?"

"My maiden name. It's Lyons. I'd prefer not to have Samuel's last name attached to me anymore."

He nods with an understanding smile. "Cat Lyons. There's a redundant name for you, right?"

The small laugh that pops out of my mouth is unbidden and feels strange. It makes me realize I haven't had a genuine laugh in quite some time.

Without another word, Rand turns toward his bedroom and shuts the door behind him. I've seen him naked many times, but it doesn't feel weird for him to seek privacy to get dressed either. I use the opportunity to riffle through my bags where I find a pair of clean underwear, a bra, and a pair of jeans, as well as a lightweight cashmere sweater. Standing up with the items in my hand, I take two steps toward the bathroom, and then change my mind. If I'm going to see the attorney who has this supposed will that kicked me out of my home, I need to look more like the wife of a dead billionaire.

I go back through my clothes, choosing a black wool pantsuit with flared legs and double-notched collar on the jacket. Grabbing a pale blue silk blouse to wear underneath, I leave my black Louboutins in the duffle bag. I'll grab those before leaving.

In the bathroom, I'm momentarily shocked by my reflection in the mirror. My hair is a disaster, and I look like a raccoon with the mascara ringing my eyes. I have to laugh at myself. A silent laugh that I'd dare let anyone see me looking so wretched. Samuel always demanded I appear my best, even insisting I attend to my beauty ritual before I came downstairs to the kitchen for a morning cup of coffee. This meant shower, shave, full-blown makeup, and artful hair designs, as well as my designer clothing with the appropriate accessorized jewelry in place. It was the only way I was allowed in his presence.

I take a moment to appreciate that I just sat through breakfast with Rand, probably looking my worst, and yet not once did he even seem to notice. In fact, several times when he gazed at me, I could see that look in his eyes that he liked what he saw. I didn't miss the hard-on he was sporting either. I wanted to do something about that, yet for some reason, it seemed important to Rand that I not feel beholden, and it was equally as important to me that it not feel like a job. He knew that about me even before I did, and I appreciate it more than he'll ever know.

Sadly, my beauty ritual takes an extraordinarily long time. While I think I have a great body and amazing bone structure, it still takes a lot of work to apply the perfect makeup and dry my thick hair before curling or flat ironing it to get the crazy frizz out. By the time I'm polished and groomed, stepping out of the bathroom in a mild cloud of designer perfume Samuel gave me last Christmas, the apartment is silent and empty but for me.

My eyes drop to my purse on the table, taking in the white note sitting on top. I grab it and read, squinting and even stumbling over Rand's messy scrawl. I think it says:

Cat,

After you get a copy of the will from the attorney, come see me at the shop, Westward Ink. It's at the corner of Cache and Pearl. I want to see what it says.

Rand

Several things about this note hit me at once.

Rand works at a tattoo shop? By the name alone, it could be a print shop, but I know it's a tattoo shop because I've walked by it several times. It sits right in the heart of town, just a few blocks off the main square. Whenever Samuel brought me to Jackson so he could get his rocks off by watching me in The Silo, I'd have plenty of free time in which I was desperate to escape the house and proximity to his cold, leering eyes. So I wandered around Jackson and came to know a great deal about all the shops here.

I'm having a hard time wrapping my mind around this. Does Rand run the tattoo shop? Or does he just work there? And why? How come he doesn't work in the ski industry, which is absolutely booming around here in the snow months?

The other thing that hits me—almost with a warm, tingly sensation in my belly—is that he wants to see the will. That means his interest is deeper than just letting me crash on his couch, and the warm, tingly sensation flares a bit. I can't remember the last time someone took care of me or wanted to see me safe and secure. In fact, outside of the initial illusions Samuel gave me when we first got married—that he was my salvation, ha!—there's never been another person in my life who worried about my welfare.

I'm inherently distrustful nowadays, especially after Samuel roped me into a sham marriage and abused me in every way possible. This was only fortified when I was kicked out of the Jackson home and turned out in the street.

It would be very easy for me to suspect Rand's motivations, yet for the life of me, I can't help but believe he's a genuine person. As such, after I visit the attorney, I intend to visit him at his shop and let him read the will with me.

Chapter 3
Rand

I GOT INTO work right at ten, which is what time the doors are supposed to open at Westward Ink. I'm not a tattoo artist. My reasons for working here are varied, in no particular order, and really don't define who I am.

After getting knocked out of competitive skiing two years ago, I decided to make Jackson my permanent home. I'd spent a great deal of time here, skiing the double-black diamond slopes as part of my training. I liked the locals and the atmosphere. I also liked the powder that was always in abundant supply. In addition, Jake Gearhart, one of my closest friends, made this his permanent home and opened up a ski shop, so I figured… why the fuck not? This was as good a place as any to settle down.

What I did not want to do was work in or around the ski industry. It's not from sour apples or bitterness over my injuries and the early end to my career. I wasn't lying to Cat this morning. I choose to glory in the fact that I had a great career while it lasted. She didn't ask about it, but there's more to competitive skiing than just winning races. And I'm really talking about endorsement deals and sponsorships. Like I said before, I could afford much bigger and better than the tiny apartment where I live as I made a fuck of a lot of money during my heyday. But I don't need more, so my money is banked, along with my gold and silver medals, in a secure lockbox. I spend my money if I want something, and I still buy my mom Louis Vuitton and my dad expensive cigars.

Most of my early training was done on the East Coast, as I'm a native Vermonter. I attended prep school with Jake at the famous Carrabassett Valley, which is a private alpine skiing, snowboarding, and freestyle academy that has produced many Olympic and World Cup champions. It sits at the base of Sugarloaf and I cut my teeth there, but after I turned eighteen, I moved to Park City, Utah to train with the U.S. Ski Team. In between training for competitions and recovery of my injuries, I lived a great deal of time in places like Tahoe and Jackson where I'd spend weeks, sometimes months, working my way back up to championship level.

I met my buddy and Westward Ink owner, Pish Malden, here in Jackson when I got my first ink during one of my numerous stays in the area. He was someone I'd grown close to over the years. After I moved into the apartment above Jake's garage, Pish and I were casually talking one day as he was working on some ink on my arm and he ended up offering me a job. Not as a tattoo artist, mind you, but really just helping to run the shop to start out. I also took a part-time job bartending at The

Wicked Horse last year, which then earned me a one-way ticket to my role as a Fantasy Maker at The Silo, but I'm content helping Pish out here for now. It keeps me busy and I like busy.

While I'm not a tattoo artist, I am an artist of sorts. In fact, in my late teens, my parents were proud to see I excelled at two things. Skiing and drawing. I had mad skills at both. But they gently pushed me toward skiing, since honestly, there was just more opportunity there. So I became a competitive alpine skier who drew and painted in my spare time. When Pish learned this about me, he would often take some of my doodles and designs and put them in his tattoo template book. So yeah… I might not actually do the ink, but there are many people who walk around with one of my designs on their bodies.

Pish offered to teach me how to tattoo, but I'm just not interested. For one, it takes a long time to get good at it and, honestly, I don't know what I want to do with my life. I'm pretty sure it's not working at a tattoo shop forever. Besides, I end up spending a lot of time at The Silo and I'm not interested in working more hours at Westward. So Pish settled on me being sort of a manager of the shop, coordinating schedules of the other artists and keeping things running smoothly. I'm in charge of opening every day except on weekends.

In his spare time, he taught me how to do piercings. That isn't hard at all and while Pish did my tongue, I'm proud to say I did my own nose and eyebrow. So if someone walks in and wants a piercing and the other artists are busy, I can do that in a pinch.

Right now, however, the shop is dead. Pish is off today and the other artist, Josh, is finishing up a small piece at his station. He'll head out to a late lunch after, and I'll hang here until he gets back to handle any walk-ins. I'm scheduled to work all day today, but if it's really slow in the afternoon, Pish won't care if I take off a bit early.

About every five minutes, I've been looking at the front glass windows and door of the shop that look out over Pearl Street, expecting Cat to come walking in any moment. It's nearly two and I haven't heard a word from her. I don't even have her fucking phone number as it wasn't something I thought to get before I rushed out this morning. I just assume she saw my note, got dressed, and went to the attorney's office. Frankly, I expected it to take no more than a few minutes to obtain a copy and then she would come to the shop. I thought she'd be here a long time ago, and I'm wondering if she packed her stuff up and left.

It's a possibility I'm not liking at all.

I hear Josh's southern twang as he walks out of his cubicle. He's a transplanted southerner who came out this way about ten years ago to work at Yellowstone and never left. Josh is giving his customer post-care instructions, and then he's walking out the door to lunch while I handle the payment. Just as I'm counting out change, the front door opens with the clang of a large cowbell, and I see Cat walking in.

She's a stunning vision of elegant wealth. It's how I know she probably dressed most days of her married life to Samuel—in designer clothes and expensive jewelry. I've never seen her this way because whenever Samuel brought to her The Silo, she was dressed in leather, vinyl, or hardly anything at all. It didn't really matter what she wore through the doors, she was usually naked not long after that. Looking at her now as she walks toward me with a large, black purse slung over her shoulder and her sunglasses perched on top of her head, I'm having a hard time even imagining that this woman and I have ever fucked. Or done some of the really fucking dirty stuff we've done together. It's almost surreal.

She waits patiently while I finish with the customer, her arms casually folded in front of her and looking at some of the design options framed on the wall. Once the dude leaves complete with his bandaged biceps because he had barbed wire inked around his pale, skinny arms, Cat turns to me.

"Did you get the will?" I ask.

She reaches into her purse with a grimace. "That asshole attorney made me wait for almost two hours."

Cat pulls the thick document out. It is folded into thirds. She opens it as she steps up to the counter.

I walk out from behind and ask, "Why did you have to wait so long?"

She practically growls when she says, "I was being given the run around. At first, his secretary said he wasn't in, but I told her that was fine. I didn't really need to see him, just needed a copy of my late husband's will. Then she admitted he was in and would need to approve it, but was in a meeting and I'd have to wait. When he finally came out to the lobby, a fucking hour and a half later, he admitted he didn't have a signed copy on him. Just an unsigned copy that Kevin had given him."

I come to stand beside Cat at the counter as she flattens the thick document out before us. Before she starts to read, she flips to the last few pages and sure enough, there are no signatures there.

"If it's not signed, then it has no power, right?" I ask.

"Supposedly, but the attorney said the signed copy's in Vegas."

"And he never asked to get a signed copy before forcing you out?"

Cat shrugs. "Guess not."

We stand beside each other, our shoulders touching, and lean over the document. It's long and cumbersome, but within the first few paragraphs, we see the offending language.

> *I, Samuel P. Vaughn, being of sound mind and body, do hereby will, devise, and bequeath my entire estate, including all real and personal property, in equal shares, to my sons Kevin Vaughn and Richard Vaughn, share and share alike.*

The next few paragraphs direct what do with his property if his sons predecease him, including distribution to his grandchildren as apparently, his younger son

Richard has two kids. The real kick in the teeth is the next paragraph that states:

> *I specifically make no provision for my wife, Catherine Lyons Vaughn, in this Last Will and Testament, other than her clothing and other personal effects accumulated throughout our marriage as well as any jewelry I have bought her through the course of said marriage.*

Cat makes a sound of disgust low in her throat and flips through the rest of the thick document. We can't see any other provisions that really apply to her and again, the last few pages are conspicuously bare of signatures.

"This document means nothing," I say as I stand straight and turn to face her. "Without signatures."

"Agreed," Cat says with loathing. "I'm thinking about calling Richard who lives in Vegas. Even though he's the youngest, he's the more 'reasonable' of the two brothers."

"Where's Kevin?" I ask.

"I think at the Jackson house. That's what the attorney said when he kicked me out. That I had to vacate because Kevin was coming to stay."

"So he essentially told you to leave your own home without having a valid copy of a document giving him the power to do so, probably only on the word of Kevin Vaughn telling him one had been signed?"

"Pretty much," Cat admits.

"Yeah, that doesn't fucking work for me," I mutter as I grab the will off the counter and fold it back up. Handing it to her, I say, "Listen… you really need to hire an attorney. That's the best thing you can do at this point."

Cat shakes her head, grim resignation evident. "I can't do that, Rand. I just don't have the money it would take. Maybe if I could get a job, I could save up or something."

Well, fuck. She's between a rock and a hard place.

Ordinarily, I'd see the damsel in distress, particularly one as lovely and alluring as Cat, and I'd step in to save the day. Jake teases me mercilessly because I have this inherent need to nurture, care for, and develop others. Not sure where that comes from, but it's something I can take to the excess sometimes.

I should offer to loan Cat the money to hire an attorney, or maybe take it upon myself to do that. But I don't make those offers because, frankly, I don't think Cat would accept. She seems to have the art of "stubborn pride" down to a science if the fight over her sleeping on the couch is any indication.

Besides, there is something I could do that's more behind the scenes.

"You should feel free to go hang back at my apartment, or whatever," I say as I lean my elbow on the counter. "I've got about another hour here and then I'm heading over to The Silo. If you don't have any objections, I'm going to talk to Bridger about this and get his take on it."

"Why Bridger?" she asks, her head tilted curiously to the side.

"Because he's one of the smartest dudes I know. Plus, he's well connected. He'll probably know something about this attorney who forced you out of the house. If not, maybe Woolf will. Do you mind if I tell them about this?"

She doesn't hesitate as she sticks the document back in her purse. "No, not at all."

"Okay, good then," I say with a smile, reaching out and touching my hand to her shoulder, where I give a reassuring squeeze. "We'll get it figured out."

As I start to pull my hand away, I'm stopped by hers coming up to latch onto my wrist. Her grasp is delicate, barely touching me, but it holds such power. Cat steps into me, her soft brown eyes shining with gratitude. She goes to her tiptoes, which isn't much more of a stretch given the sky-high heels she's wearing, and leans into me. Placing her lips against my cheek, she kisses me just barely and pulls away. "Thank you, Rand. For everything."

Christ, she smells good. And that body is just inches from mine.

She releases her hold, and my hand falls away from her shoulder. I want to grab her back to me and... what?

Hug her? Fuck her? Tell her it will all be okay?

Tell her to suck my dick?

Please Cat, suck my dick?

Instead, I turn away from her and walk behind the counter. "I probably won't be home until really late tonight, so I guess I'll see you then."

"Okay," she says with a smile and starts to turn away.

"Unless you're coming to The Silo tonight?" I throw out, hoping my voice doesn't sound anything more than casual.

She gives a small shake of her head. "I don't think so."

The weight of crushing disappointment hits me again. While I've firmly made up my mind I am not touching Cat while she's at my apartment because I've invited her there out of friendship, I'd reasoned in my mind that she was still fair game at The Silo. I mean, if you walk in those doors, it means you want to fuck. No-strings-attached sex to be precise.

Right?

So, if Catherine Lyons were to walk into that door tonight, technically she would be fair game.

I think.

But that apparently isn't happening.

Chapter 4

Cat

I CAN'T BELIEVE I'm here.

I promised myself I wasn't coming back. Not after Rand found me sleeping in my car in the parking lot last night.

Not ever again.

Yet here I am, nervously smoothing down a simple black, form-fitting strapless dress as I stand outside the entrance door to The Silo.

One of the most truthful things I've ever admitted to myself is that my feelings for The Silo are complicated. It's a place I've loved and hated at different times.

It's made me feel beautiful and ugly.

Needed and abhorred.

Powerful and weak.

The times I've felt good walking out those doors were fleeting, the buzz and adrenaline of great sex already a cold, distant memory. The lingering happiness that filled me from being desired and needed by others soon fizzling into nothingness.

But those times I've felt bad walking out... those stuck with me a lot longer. Usually through a scalding hot shower to wash away the sweat of others, while I sat on the tiled floor and chanted over and over again that this was what I needed to do to survive.

Oddly enough, The Silo helped me survive the sick perversion Samuel was intent on forcing me to endure. It was the lesser of two evils, and so I made sure I put on quite the show whenever my husband brought me here so he could watch me get fucked and debased because that made him happy. He watched with clouded eyes from his wheelchair, his mouth twisted into a feral grin, and I made sure he believed I loved every bit of it, because it was one of the few ways I could assert my independence from him. It was also how I could hurt him, if even only a tiny bit, because he'd much rather believe I hated it.

Sadly, sometimes I did love every bit of it. My lips curve upward as I realize, many of those times involved Rand. He's an amazing lover and he's adventurous. He is wide and varied in his kink, and even if he wasn't fucking me, I loved watching him get off with others.

And that is the reason I'm here.

Rand Bishop.

A man I've fucked and sucked several times in the past.

A man I am immensely attracted to.

A man who has provided me unparalleled kindness in the last twenty-four hours.

I want him, and I want him tonight. It has to be here because I get the sense he's deemed me to be off limits in his apartment. He wouldn't accept my body as payment to him for his generosity last night, but that's not what The Silo is all about. It's about people making free choices to get their rocks off in an environment with like-minded people. It's about sex with no strings or expectations, and pleasure as the only end goal.

Taking a deep breath, I reach into my little clutch purse and pull out my security fob. I punch the digital code it provides me into the wall panel, and the door unlocks with a soft click.

The Silo is the brilliant brainchild of business partners Bridger Payne and Woolf Jennings, although Woolf recently sold out. It's a round concrete building with a white-domed top that looks just like an authentic silo. It sits just off the back of Bridger's nightclub, The Wicked Horse.

While it might look like a colossal bin to store grain in from the outside, the inside is a massive round space with glass-walled rooms around the perimeter. It's a sex club and all kinds of kinky, nasty, sexy stuff goes on inside this place. It's a no-holds-barred type of club and anything goes as long as it's consensual. Some of the things I've done in this club would make the devil blush.

As I exit the short hallway that leads me to the center, I immediately spot Rand standing up at the round, black-lacquered bar that takes up the middle of The Silo. I ignore all the other activity around me as I've seen it before. Fully dressed couples mingle with cocktails in their hands. Naked couples in the glass-walled rooms, fucking in every way imaginable. It's all almost passé to me, because I've not only seen it all, I've done it all.

Just last week, I let Bridger lock me in a stockade, effectively securing me around the neck and wrists, and then I invited several men to fuck me. Pussy, ass, mouth… didn't matter. Luckily, it was one of those nights that was a good one. I enjoyed it. I came several times, and when I walked out, I didn't feel degraded. That's because it was my choice to be there, not Samuel's, and I did what I wanted. I also called a stop to it all when I was done. And trust me, after the seventh guy, I was done because I was sore and my neck ached. My wishes were immediately granted, and I was treated with kindness and reverence by the men around me. Bridger was there to cover my body with a robe and lead me off to the bathroom where I could get cleaned up and dressed in privacy.

Yeah, that was a good night.

I'm hoping tonight will be better.

As I take in Rand, I see he's wearing the same clothes he had on at the tattoo shop today. Faded jeans with a small rip in one knee, a thick, black leather belt, and a black *Rage Against The Machine* t-shirt that fits his chest extraordinarily well. His blond hair falls across his forehead and he pushes it back in what I recognize as a habit now, causing me to smile.

He's talking to a woman, and I take a moment to size her up. I don't think I've seen her in here before, but honestly, I don't pay much attention to the women. I like cock, so the women never interested me much. Although one time, Bridger strapped me to the St. Andrew's cross and invited people to come in and eat my pussy. A procession of men took up his challenge, except one lone woman who came in as well. I don't remember much about her other than her lips were so soft, and frankly, she worked my clit better than any man ever has before. I'm going to have to assume she was a lesbian and damn... she really knew what she was doing.

The woman Rand is talking to is pretty. Very pretty, actually, with caramel-colored hair streaked with golden highlights. Her skin is tanned and she looks to be about my age. I immediately figure either she's a bartender from The Wicked Horse with a limited membership here, or she's a lot like me... here with a rich sugar daddy of some sort.

Rand doesn't look away from her. He seems to be totally interested in what she's saying, which I can tell is something flirty by the way she's standing in close to him and holding her drink so that her cleavage is squeezed for maximum display. She even leans in closer, goes up on tiptoes, and whispers something in his ear while resting a hand on his chest. My fingers curl inward, balling to tight fists when I see his hand drop to her hip. His fingers splay wide and while he does nothing more than grip her there, he does nothing to dissuade her from stepping in closer until her breasts brush against him.

I don't hesitate a second. I walk through the minglers, sidestepping and nodding greetings here and there.

I'm well known and get smiles from everyone. When I reach Rand and the woman I don't know, he turns to look at me, his eyebrows rising first in surprise, then with a welcome smile on his lips. His eyes roam down my body, lighting up with appreciation. It makes me immensely happy to see his hand fall from the woman's hip.

She also turns to me, her lip curling in disdain while she shoots daggers at me from her eyes. I don't spare her another glance. Instead, I reach for Rand's hand that is closest to me. His fingers immediately thread with mine and he tilts his head in question.

"Let's fuck," I murmur, turning to start pulling him away from the woman.

He doesn't hesitate in the slightest, and I try hard not to laugh as the girl makes a loud sound of disgruntlement that she's being left so abruptly by a man she clearly had her sights set on.

I lead Rand back across The Silo, down the short hall that heads back toward the door I had just entered in through. But rather than leave, I turn right into the hallway that runs the perimeter of the round building, behind the glass-walled rooms. Rand follows behind, his hand holding mine tightly, but not saying a single word to me. He doesn't need to say anything, but I know he's feeling what I'm feeling. The sexual tension is so thick that I can feel it coating my exposed skin like a blanket.

"Which room do you want?" I ask as I walk in front of him, my hips swaying provocatively. I know… can just feel those green eyes pinned to my ass. "The black room… we can fuck on a bed of black silk and that woman you just left behind can watch your cock sliding in and out of me?"

Rand doesn't say anything, but I know if I were to let go of his hand and reach backward, I'd find him hard as a rock.

"Or how about one of the rooms where you can restrain me? Maybe the St. Andrew's cross, or even the stockade. Lock me up and do what you want to me."

I think I hear a low growl of need in Rand's chest, and it fills me with euphoria that he wants me so badly.

"Or maybe one of the rooms with toys," I suggest silkily as we walk slowly along. "So many things you could do to make me come with toys."

Rand moves so quickly, I give a startled yelp of surprise. His hands come to my shoulders and he spins me toward the outer wall, which is nothing but cold, gray concrete staves. I open my mouth to say what, I don't know, but then his tongue is twirling against mine while he presses me back into the wall.

And I can't recall… has Rand ever kissed me before? I'm not sure. I think I'd remember something like this… so possessive and animalistic. Necessary. That's what it feels like… absolutely needful to him.

We may have fucked before, but I don't recall kissing him, so I'm thinking we haven't. Such a personal act and one I don't do often. Usually it's because a man wants it and I oblige, no biggie.

But this kiss with Rand?

It causes my legs to go weak and my heart to skitter out of control. It makes me want to sag in relief over the warm feelings it produces in me, and I want nothing more than to stand in this hallway with Rand and just make out with him all night long. I think I'd be completely satisfied with just kissing him. It's that damn good.

Yet, he has other ideas. Pulling his mouth away just enough to growl against my lips, he says, "None of the rooms. Gonna fuck you right here… keep you all to myself."

He gives me no opportunity to respond because he steals my breath away with another fast but deep kiss before he's jerking my skirt up around my hips and then my panties down my legs. Squatting before me, he taps against the outside of my right ankle. I raise it so he can slip that leg free.

"Other leg," he mutters. I lift that one, and then he's standing up with my panties in his hand. He orders me, "Get my cock out, Cat."

I don't hesitate. I work his belt buckle with expert hands, only stumbling once when he pushes a hand between my legs and drags a finger between my folds. I can feel how ridiculously wet I am, but that was a given. Rand's take-charge ways are turning me on like nothing else ever has.

When I get his belt freed and his zipper down, I push at the jeans a bit until his thick cock comes in to view. I reach my hand in, circle it around the girth, and gently pull it free. I'm confident this didn't hurt him and that the hiss of air that rushes through his teeth is merely because my hand on him feels good.

I want him to feel better so I start to stroke him, causing Rand to groan in response and his body to stiffen all over with trembling need.

"Enough," he says gruffly, pulling my hand away. "Now open your mouth."

I grin for a moment before I open my mouth, expecting him to push me to my knees so I can suck on that beautiful hardness sticking straight out between us, but he surprises me when he shoves my panties in instead. My eyes flare wide with shock as he gives me a devilish grin. "Don't want anyone to hear you scream. Don't feel like sharing this tonight."

He doesn't want to share me tonight? Meaning he doesn't want anyone else to watch?

And yeah... he stopped me in the darkened hallway lit only with soft sconces and relative privacy unless someone decides to go in or out of the rooms. Good chance that will happen, so I know Rand doesn't have complete expectation we won't get caught, but it makes me even wetter knowing he wants something with me that I've never given another man here in this building.

Just myself.

I hum in my throat, letting him know I approve of his methods, and he doesn't waste any time. He bends his knees, pushes his hands between my thighs from the front, and lifts me. As he extends his arms wide, my legs spread obscenely before him and Rand gazes longingly at my pussy. I don't look down at what he's looking at but rather at his face, watching the way he licks his lips.

"Guide me in, baby," he whispers hoarsely, still never taking his eyes away. I circle a hand around his dick, feel it jump in response to my touch. Then, along with a flex of Rand's hips, guide the tip right to my entrance.

The fat head of his cock pushes into my slickness easily before meeting with some resistance. The only foreplay we had was dirty words, so even though I'm wet, I'm not relaxed. In fact, I feel strung tight with tension and need, and even though I know that first push is going to sting, I want it so bad my mouth waters, which is immediately soaked up by my panties.

Rand finally lifts his gaze as his hands tighten their grip under my thighs. He has me firmly in his hold and his cock is wedged in just the right place, so I let the base of it go and bring my hands to his shoulders for leverage.

Our eyes lock together. We just stare for a brutally clear moment where nothing else exists but a man who wants a woman, and vice versa. There is no sex club and nothing overly kinky about what we're doing.

Just a man and a woman who want each other with a raging passion.

Rand gives me a smile before leaning his head toward me, tilting slightly, and placing a soft kiss at the corner of my mouth. I moan against the panties because the gentleness of that move touches me.

When he lifts his head and looks at me again, there's

a possessiveness in his eyes now that I've never seen before in my life. Not from any man before who has claimed my body and certainly never from my husband. It's a look I didn't know existed until this very moment, and once I realize what it is, Rand takes it upon himself to thrust into me hard.

My head falls back, and I groan against the invasion. The sting, and then the melting of my pussy around him. He doesn't even give me a moment to adjust, just starts thrusting in and out of me with bruising force. He's a large guy, thick and long, and he hits that spot deep within me that makes my toes curl and my eyes threaten to roll into the back of my head.

"Look at me, Cat," Rand demands of me.

It takes all of my effort to raise my head up so I can comply.

His eyes glow with that same possessiveness and now a spark of triumph as he pounds into me, every punch of his cock into my pussy bringing me closer and closer to orgasm.

"Feel good?" he asks, although he knows I can't answer. So I smile at him with my eyes and nod my head.

"Yeah... feels damn good," he mutters and thrusts faster. "Always loved fucking this pussy. Dream about this pussy. Jack off to thoughts of this pussy."

Oh, damn... those filthy words and his hips slapping against me rhythmically while he holds my gaze the entire time make me feel in this moment that Rand Bishop owns every part of me. Surprisingly, I'm okay with that.

Samuel once told me he owned me and that he could do whatever he wanted with me. And he was right about that. I hated him and his ownership.

But not this with Rand.

If he can make my body feel this good and make me feel this needed, then I'll sign away the rights and title to my body right now.

My orgasm catches me off guard and bursts within me after a brutally hard thrust deep into my body. My muscles clench and grab onto his cock, rippling with pleasure around him and causing Rand to finally lose eye contact with me. His eyes flutter closed and he thrusts into me one more time before going still and muttering in staccato bursts, "Coming. So. Fucking. Hard."

He grinds against me. My pussy clamps hard on him, and he groans as he spurts inside of me, "Goddamn… that greedy fucking pussy can milk my cock any day of the week, Cat."

I laugh against the silk in my mouth when he says, "And twice on Saturday."

Dropping my head to his shoulder, I try to remember every single detail of this experience. I'm betting it was a one-time only thing, but I think I just had the best sex of my entire life.

Chapter 5
Rand

CHRIST… THAT ORGASM.

That motherfucking amazing orgasm that just rocked my world and made my knees go weak, which sucks because I already have a bum knee. My hands grip harder under Cat's thighs and I shift her up a bit, my cock still wedged deep in her. Her forehead is planted on my shoulder and her back is rising and falling with labored breaths.

I broke a few rules tonight, the biggest being that I promised myself I wouldn't touch Cat. The nature of our relationship has changed by virtue of me bringing her into my home and offering her sanctuary. The minute I offered her safety, her pussy should have become off limits to me… or at least, to my gentleman's way of thinking. So that was the first rule I broke.

I'm also here tonight as a Fantasy Maker. I'm essentially working for Bridger. While that means I can fuck whomever I want within the round walls of this building, it means it needs to be done in a way that makes me useful to the clientele. Obviously, there's the pleasure of the person I'm fucking to take into account, but there's also the viewing pleasure of the other patrons. I took Cat in the privacy of the hallways because I wanted it to be private. I didn't want to share her, myself, or what we were doing together with anyone.

Lastly, I broke a major rule and one I've never broken before. I just shoved my cock into a pussy without any protection. I wanted Cat so badly… wanted her all to myself without anyone sharing in the experience… that I held no regard for the consequences of such actions. I'd even like to blame it on the heat of the moment or that lust fogged my senses, but it would be a lie. I knew damn well what I was doing and wanted to feel that tight, slick pussy against my skin. Wanted to come inside of her and coat every inch of her.

I wanted it, and I didn't give a damn if I knocked her up doing it. While I went with gut instinct that she was safe and I knew I was safe, I still knew the risk.

Cat and I operate in a world of multiple sex partners, which means we are people who understand safety and consequences. Unless you're in a committed and trusting relationship with your partner, everyone in The Silo wears condoms, so I'm not so much worried about that with her, and she should feel secure that I'm safe too.

But goddamn… I didn't care one shit that I could get her pregnant, and even now, I just can't feel bothered to worry. Maybe because I'm still flush off probably the best orgasm of my life, because she feels damn good in my arms, or maybe because she's appealing to every single molecule in my body that feels the need to help her lost soul, but I just don't give a fuck.

Still… I have to ask, "Cat… you on the Pill?"

She moves in my arms, lifts her head from my shoulders, and pulls the panties I'd stuffed in her mouth free. Swiveling her jaw, she licks her lips once and says in a raspy voice, "Yeah. I'm protected."

"You okay I didn't suit up?" I ask, not needing to elaborate.

"I am if you are," she murmurs.

I totally am. I'm so fucking okay with it and how amazing that just felt, that if she gives me just a few moments and wiggles her hips just right, I'll be good to go for round two without ever pulling out of her.

But then I pull a dick male move and speak without thinking, totally ruining the moment. "But let's agree… we fuck anyone else, we still wear protection, okay?"

I know it's a mistake even before she stiffens in my arms. I know the words were wrong the minute they left my lips. It wasn't that I was thinking about screwing anyone else, or that I wanted anyone else. I just wanted her to know that she was different, and I meant that in a good way. But she clearly didn't take it like I meant it, and I know this for sure the minute she literally pushes out of my embrace and drops her feet to the floor. My dick slides out, and I almost curse over the loss of her warmth around it.

Cat's head drops and her hair falls forward so I can't see her expression, but I watch, mesmerized, as she takes her panties and swipes them between her legs, cleaning my semen away. When she straightens back up, she shoves the panties toward me and my hand automatically goes out to grab them. I note the wetness against my palm and watch as she pushes the hem of her dress down her thighs.

When she finally looks at me, she levels me not with anger but with a brilliant smile. She even reaches out and pats me on the chest. "Well, that was fun, Rand. Thanks a bunch. Now I think I'll head back into the main room and see what other fun there is to be had."

I have no clue if she's mad at me or serious about wanting to go back in there and fuck another man, but some sort of caveman-like DNA inside of me becomes active and my free hand shoots out to grab her by her upper arm as she turns to walk away. "You are not going in there to fuck someone else."

I cannot believe I actually just said that to her.

Even as I cannot believe I actually said those words of possession, my grip tightens on her arm. She looks over her shoulder at me with wide eyes as her lips part in surprise. "But you just said—"

"I know what I said," I snap at her, angry with myself for even saying something so insensitive, and angry with her for even thinking of fucking someone else even though I apparently gave her carte blanche to do so. Taking a deep breath, I tug on her arm so she turns to fully look at me. I let it out slowly and try to explain myself. "Cat… let's go back to my place."

"Why?" she asks, her tone heavy with suspicion. I

know it's because I've confused her. But fuck... I'm confused myself.

"Because I am not done with you by a long shot," I say without further explanation.

"You can have me here," she counters.

"I don't want you here," I tell her, deciding to go with brutal honesty. I don't know the reason why, but I can't stomach the thought of us fucking out there for everyone to see. More than that, I really want her spread-eagled on my bed.

Her eyes flick back and forth between mine for a moment before she gives me a tiny nod of acquiescence. She merely whispers, "Okay," and nothing has ever sounded sweeter to me before.

THERE ARE A million different things I want to do to Cat in this moment. I knew she'd look lovely naked on my bed, her arms raised above her head and her legs spread wide for me. Gorgeous breasts that are full and heavy looking with dark brown nipples and that pretty pussy trimmed tight and drenched inside with my jizz from our fucking at The Silo not but an hour ago.

Million things to choose from... suck on those nipples, finger her ass, or suck on her clit until she screams. And yet I'm obsessing about my cock in her cunt, bare, with no walls between us.

Like I really can't let the thought go.

I followed her to my apartment from The Silo, focusing on the taillights of her Mercedes as we drove the thirty-odd miles in the dark, but all I could think about was every glide of our flesh against each other. It vaguely reminds me of the first time I ever fucked a woman... fifteen years old and the giddy rush of feeling the ultimate pleasure for the first time. But that was a horny kid who took almost a full five minutes to put on a rubber and almost came the moment I sank into Beverly Bay's non-virgin but not well used seventeen-year-old pussy.

But fucking Cat bare was infinitely better. It was wondrous, new, and I'm not sure can be replicated, but I'm obsessing about it, so I'm pretty sure her clit, nipples, and ass are going to get ignored right now. I'll give them attention later.

As I kneel on the bed between her knees, my dick hard as fucking concrete and throbbing to get into her, I can't help but wonder at the look on her face right now. It's guarded, for sure. Her eyes are heavy with lust, but there's a touch of skepticism there too. Perhaps like me, she's wondering if what we had in the back hall of The Silo was a fluke or not.

Only one way to find out.

Putting my hands under her knees, I raise her legs and spread them wide. Her pussy literally blooms for me, right before my eyes. Cat reaches a hand out, grasps me by the base of my dick, and pulls me to her.

To fucking heaven, I groan internally as I sink inside of her.

"Mmmmmm," she moans when my pelvis is pressed

hard to hers.

"Goddamn," I mutter as sweat beads on my forehead just from the overwhelming pleasure of her surrounding me. "Is it just me or does that feel fucking amazing?"

"Never felt anything like it," she whispers. A shiver actually runs up my spine over the awe in her voice.

I'm a base creature. I like to fuck hard and fast, never really needing to prolong the rush to climax because I know there's another one on the horizon waiting for me. But with Cat right now, legs spread wide and that pussy belonging solely to me in a way I'm betting it's never belonged to another man before, I want this moment to last for-fucking-ever.

So I release my hold on her legs and urge her to wrap them around my waist. I lower myself over her body and press my elbows into the mattress at her ribs, lowering my mouth to hers.

And while we kiss without a care or rush in the world, I fuck her slowly and without needing anything more than this moment.

⭐

"We really should get some sleep," Cat gasps as my finger lightly circles her sensitive clit. I'm kneeling between her legs again, having just eaten her pussy and given her an orgasm, but intent on giving her another. That sweet bundle of nerves is swollen and darkened pink with not only the rush of lust but also because I've been playing with it all night. It might even be a little painful. But she doesn't push me away, even though she just suggested we get some sleep.

It's late.

Or rather, early morning, and I have to open the tattoo shop in about six hours.

But fuck... I cannot stop touching her.

Making her come.

Slipping my cock in that piece of wet perfection that I think I might be slightly addicted to right now.

Filling her up with what may be buckets of my cum by now. Thank God, she's on the pill because otherwise, she'd be so knocked up right now just by the sheer volume of sperm I've shot into her.

"You sore?" I ask as I dip my finger into her, pull out her juices and my sperm, and swirl it around her reddened clit again.

She moans with her eyes partially closed, her hips lifting a bit, even as she nods, "A little."

"Hmm," I muse as I study her pussy. I want back inside bad. You know, the addiction and all. But I don't want to knock her out of commission either because I plan on a repeat of this tonight after work. In fact, I might just live my life working by day, and sweetly fucking Cat by night. We'll eat, of course, for nourishment, but it sounds like a damn perfect life to me.

"Want me to stop?" I ask her, my eyes dragging up her body to her face.

Her lips tilt upward mischievously. "I can take whatever you got."

This I know, I sourly think. I've watched her fuck multiple men in one session. Hardcore fucking where lots of lube was needed because a woman can only take so much.

But she didn't need that lube tonight now, did she? This will be our fourth time and she's still just as wet, slick, and inviting. We're both a little raw, but we both have mileage in the tank. Of that, I'm sure.

Still, the thought of lube… has me thinking.

"Turn over," I tell her suddenly, rolling over her to the side of the bed. As Cat moves to her stomach without question, I reach into the drawer of my nightstand and pull out a bottle of lube.

When I turn back to her, she has her cheek lying on my pillow, her eyes facing me. Her gaze travels back and forth from the lube to me before her tongue peeks out and swipes at her lower lip. "What are you going to do with that?"

"Going to give your pussy a break," I tell her ominously as I flip the cap open.

Cat has a great ass. I've fucked it before, even once while her mouth and pussy were full of other guys' cocks. My own cock starts dripping at the memory of that, and I crawl back over her body until I'm kneeling behind her.

She needs no encouragement because I know Cat loves anal as much as I do. Her ass goes up in the air and she spreads her legs to give me access.

While I'm horny enough I could happily drive into that snug hole, I take my time with her. I make excellent use of the lube, pressing my thumb in her ass while I stroke her clit softly with my other hand. By the time her body starts shaking with an orgasm, I've got three fingers in deep from behind and she couldn't be more ready for me.

She sighs deeply with pleasure when I sink my cock in her ass. I bite the inside of my cheek so that I focus on pain, and this is so I don't blow a nut right then and there.

And Christ... I'm glad she just came because I'm not going to last long at all. The gentleman in me has to remind myself that she's come numerous times tonight and it's okay if I race quickly to the end this time. Besides... I know she needs sleep.

The first swivel of my hips against her has my balls already tingling. My hands go to her hips. Latching onto her hard, I start a rhythmic thrust. Cat groans and thrashes below me, which turns me on even more to know she loves my dick in her ass. I squeeze my eyes shut and pump in and out, not so hard I can hurt her, but quickly enough that my balls quickly pull up tight with an unbelievable need to explode.

And I do... quick and viciously inside of her, planting myself in deep so I can fill her up from this end too.

Suddenly, my body becomes utterly exhausted. The hours of fucking we've just done becoming almost unbearably too much to comprehend. Cat's body sags underneath of me to the mattress, and I follow right along with her. I immediately roll us to the side and wrap my warms around her. She snuggles into me, wiggling her ass, which is still gripping my dick inside of her.

I'm content and well sated, and I wonder if when we both wake up tomorrow, we'll still want each other this way.

I'm pretty sure I know the answer to that as far as I'm concerned, but I have no clue how Cat feels.

Chapter 6
Cat

SAMUEL'S HEAVILY LINED face leers at me, hovers over me so close I can smell his breath, which is sour from the rot of decaying teeth. His blue eyes have a milk-like glaze over them because he's mostly blind, but they still see me clearly enough.

"It's time to pay up, Catherine," he sneers at me before letting out a demented cackle of a laugh.

I roll hard to my left, so fast that I dislodge something heavy lying across my stomach, but it does nothing to hold me back. My terror-filled need to get away from Samuel fuels me with a burst of adrenaline, and I launch myself right out of the bed.

Straight onto my knees... where they thud painfully, but then I'm standing up and looking to bolt to the nearest door.

"Cat... what's wrong?" I hear from the bed. For a split instant, I think it's Samuel.

But then just as quickly it registers... that rich, deep voice... the smell of sex heavy in the air that is definitely not Samuel's rotten breath.

I spin back to the bed and see the outline of Rand's

body sitting up in the bed, then his legs are swinging over the edge. I can't see what he does, but I hear the snick of the lamp switch as the room is bathed in a soft glow.

He stands, swiveling his face to look at me. It's filled with concern, even as he's walking around the bed to me as he repeats. "What's wrong?"

My hand comes up, resting over my chest, and I can feel the mad pounding as I realize I must have been having a dream. I try to force myself to calm down, thinking of Samuel's body lying in his casket so that I remember he's dead and can't hurt me anymore.

Rand's large hands come to my shoulders, feeling steady and comfortable as they hold me. He's completely naked, yet I don't really see that right now. All I see are his blond lashes framing those green eyes, which are filled with worry for me.

For *me*.

I'm almost lost as to what to say to him because no one ever worries about me. I don't think I've ever had anyone in my life ask me "what's wrong". Maybe a teacher, but I really can't recall a specific instance. Certainly not my mother. Don't know my father. And definitely never Samuel.

No close friends who fretted over my feelings or safety.

Not even co-workers where I danced in Vegas had ever asked me if something was wrong.

Not one person in my life cared enough, and yet here

Rand stands before me, holding me steady and asking me a very simple question.

What's wrong?

"I had a nightmare about Samuel," I say, my voice hoarse with sleep, but I'm pleased that it's steady with the truth.

Rand's eyes get soft with understanding. Before I know what's happening, he's picking me up in his arms, depositing me back into bed and crawling in behind me. We lay on our sides, facing each other, and he puts an arm around my waist to pull me in closer to him.

"Want to tell me about it?" he asks, his gentle voice putting me at ease.

"I think I do," I murmur, tilting my head back so I can look at him.

He surprises me by giving me a kiss. Not a sexual kiss but just a sweet one that validates he's here to listen and support me. "Lay it on me, Cat. I've got you."

And he does. For the moment anyway. Eyes shining with support and a steady arm around my waist. This man who has been nothing in the past to me but a mindless fuck has very quickly become perhaps the nicest person I've ever encountered.

So I barely stumble over my words when I tell him why Samuel visits me in my dreams. "My husband never had sex with me. Not once in the time we dated, nor in the time we were married."

Rand blinks at me in surprise. "Come again?"

I know why he's surprised. Who in the world didn't

look at Samuel and me together and not whisper to their friend with judgmental looks, "Well… we know why he married her."

Everyone thought Samuel pulled me away from topless dancing so that he could have a beautiful young wife who would fuck him day and night and that perhaps he'd regain his youth that way. He was certainly rich enough to get any beauty he wanted, and he was powerful enough in Vegas that no one would dare laugh in his face over the disparity in age.

But that's not the way it was with Samuel. So I try to explain him to Rand. "I thought when he asked me to marry him that he wanted a conventional marriage. I mean… don't get me wrong… I didn't love him and his money enticed me. I was tired of taking my top off and having men stick their grubby hands down my panties when they tipped me. I saw his mansion and imagined myself living there. I swam in the designer clothes and expensive jewelry he bought me while we dated. I thought I knew what he wanted in return. In exchange for him giving me a stable life, I'd be a wife to him in every way, and I was prepared to do that. But he never did anything more when we were dating other than give me kisses on my cheek and hold my hand. I thought he was old fashioned and sweet. It was charming to me."

I stop for a moment, trying to gauge the look on Rand's face, because I can't begin to imagine what he's thinking. But he clues me in quick enough when he says, "You were trying to survive life."

I lower my gaze and can't help the tiny smile that comes to me… because he gets it. He understands me without even knowing me.

"I left home not long after I'd turned seventeen. Mom was a bitch—an entire story unto itself I'll tell you about some time. Lived on the streets for a while, practically starved to death at times. I learned to hustle and dealt some petty drugs to put food in my stomach. Gave a blow job or two so I could crash on someone's couch rather than sleep outside."

"Cat… you were surviving," Rand says, arm loosening from my waist and his hand coming to my hip where he gives it a squeeze.

"Yes, but with Samuel, it was different. It wasn't just survival. I saw a way to better my life."

"You did what a lot of women in your position would do," he says, his tone matter-of-fact.

"I married him," I agree. "And after he put that ring on my finger, he made my life a living hell."

Rand's body stiffens and his fingers dig into my hip a bit. It doesn't hurt, but it tells me he's immediately on edge, so I bring my hand to his chest and lay it over his heart, stroking his skin with my thumb. Then, I proceed to tell him what a monster Samuel was.

"At first, he didn't do anything. For a few weeks, he sort of ignored me. I moved into his house and had my own room. I started to think that perhaps he was nervous to be with me, or maybe even had physical problems and couldn't, but he was never around for me to talk to about it. And then… well, I got comfortable living a solitary but rich life. I had my own credit cards and could shop whenever I wanted to. I spent hours in spas and salons, having everyone cater to the hotelier Samuel Vaughn's new wife. I thought that was the way my life would be, and I was really okay with that. I mean… Samuel was old and I wasn't looking forward to those duties as a wife even though I was prepared to do it if he wanted."

"Yeah, I could never imagine you and him together," Rand says with a thoughtful smile.

I give a small laugh in agreement, but he won't be smiling for much longer. "One day, Samuel sent word to me from his assistant that he was having a business dinner at the house and wanted me to join him. I thought it was awesome. Boredom was getting to me. I thought I could at least be a wife to Samuel in some ways by letting him show me off to people he wanted to impress."

"I get the feeling this is going somewhere I'm not going to like," Rand says hesitantly. He knows it's bad if I have nightmares about Samuel, and it is bad. Best to rip the band-aid off and all.

"When I walked into the dining room that night, it became clear pretty quickly that I was what was being served on the menu. There were five of them… all business associates, I think. I heard bits and pieces of conversation while they were all fucking me that led me to believe that. My husband conducted business right there in the dining room while those men took turns with me. He watched from the end of the table and egged them on, encouraging them to do whatever they wanted to me."

"Son of a fucking bitch," Rand growls as he rears upward. My hand immediately goes to his shoulder, and I push him back down.

"You need to listen so I can get this all out," I urge him gently.

"That fucking bastard prostituted his own wife out as a business incentive?" he demands furiously.

"He prostituted me out to *anyone* he wanted a favor from," I clarify, and his eyes go darker with rage. "He once didn't have cash on hand to tip a driver he hired to take us to the airport, so he had me suck the driver's dick in payment."

"What the fuck?" he hisses and again tries to sit up in the bed. I try to hold him back, but he's stronger. Besides, I don't think this conversation lends itself to snuggling so we both come up into sitting positions. He turns to me and braces himself with one arm on the mattress. His other reaches out, touching the tips of his fingers to my jaw as he whispers. "I'm so sorry, Cat. No man should ever do that a woman, much less his wife."

I give a little shrug and try to make light of it. "It didn't happen all the time. I tried to reason to myself that it was what I needed to do for this 'so-called' better life I wanted."

Rand's fingers slide from my jaw, past my ear, and

then curve around the back of my neck. He pulls me a little closer to him and looks at me intently. "The Silo... that wasn't something you wanted, was it?"

And yes... Rand doesn't know me all that well, but he does get me. "The Silo is complicated for me, but no... joining was all Samuel's idea. Like I said, he didn't let his friends and associates have me all that often, and what I came to quickly realize was that Samuel got off on watching me debased. Sure... it garnered him favor with his friends, but really... he gave me to those men because he liked watching me suffer."

"The Silo... you mostly did gang bangs," Rand mutters as his gaze drifts a bit to the side in contemplation. "We all thought... I mean... we just assumed that was your thing. You liked multiple guys. But it was Samuel who insisted on it."

"Yes," I say simply.

His eyes come back to me filled with guilt. "I'm sorry," he whispers hoarsely. "I wouldn't have... I don't think anyone there would have done that to you if we knew you didn't like it."

I can't stand to see him feel guilt over something he had absolutely no knowledge of, so I need to make sure he understands that nothing about me is simple. "Rand... you couldn't have known. No one did. And like I said... it's complicated. There was a part of me, deep down inside, that sometimes liked what was being done to me. Sometimes, I'd be getting drilled by one man with another one waiting and I'd look at Samuel...

and rather than see that smug satisfaction on his face, I'd sometimes see a kernel of jealousy. Another man was fucking his wife while he couldn't. He'd sit there, limp dicked and unable to get off on the spectacle, and I swear to God, Rand… I'm not sure if it makes me a monster or what, but that would make me get off. Thinking of that sadist suffering while I was getting fucked raw would give me mind-blowing orgasms."

"Jesus Christ," Rand growls again, and then he's pulling me roughly into his arms. He wraps himself around me, pressing me into his chest.

I manage to turn my face to the side so my cheek is resting over his heart and tell him, "It wasn't all bad. All the guys at The Silo were really nice."

He makes a sound deep in his chest. I'm not sure what it signifies, but his arms wrap around me tighter. "If that fucker wasn't already dead, I'd kill him for you, Cat. I swear I would."

I smile over his declaration, but I know he doesn't mean it. I'm not worth killing someone over.

"Is there anything else I need to know?" Rand asks without loosening his hold on me.

"Isn't that enough to give me nightmares about Samuel?" I ask, sort of tongue in cheek, but also as a means of perhaps avoiding one other ugly truth I'm thinking might be best left untold.

Rand's silent for a moment, but then he says, "You trusted me with something deeply personal, but I need it all, Cat. How can I chase away your demons if I don't know what they all are?"

My body goes utterly still, and then a phenomenon happens to me that has never happened before in my life.

My heart literally fucking melts within my chest.

I blink my eyes hard to chase away the sting of tears I feel forming over a man I barely know who is telling me he's my champion. It's unbelievable to me.

"Cat," Rand prompts me. "Anything else?"

Giving a cough, I clear my throat and pull back so I can look him in the eye. I tell him perhaps the worst of it. "His oldest son, Kevin. He shared me with him quite a bit. Favorite son and all."

He doesn't say a word to me, but I can feel the fury vibrating off him. Rand's eyes turn practically red and his jaw locks so tight that the muscle jumps violently. But because he has shown he cares for me, and doesn't want to make this more upsetting than it already is, he keeps his silence and merely hugs me in commiseration.

A hug.

How novel.

How soothing.

I may not have much experience with them, but I'm finding they're warm and secure, and I feel like I could sleep without nightmares if Rand's arms are around me.

Chapter 7
Rand

It's barely seven in the morning. I don't need to open the shop for three hours, but I have important shit to do. I slip quietly out of my apartment, leaving Cat sleeping in my bed. I hope she continues to sleep for hours to come because I know she's exhausted. Not only did I completely wear her body out last night, but also after she told me about that shit with her motherfucking-dead-but-want-to-kill-him-again husband, we stayed up and talked. Eventually, I settled us back down and pulled her close to me. Her body fit against mine naturally, and it felt better than right.

I may spend a lot of time at a sex club, but I'm not one of these guys with emotional barriers who uses no-strings sex as a way to keep women at arm's length. I'm an actual snuggler to the core. I don't care if it's a one-night stand or the love of your life. After sex, there's nothing better than spooning and drifting off to sleep.

So tucking Cat into me felt natural. I didn't give it a second thought. I just held her tight and we talked until she could get it all out.

Have to say, I admire the fuck out of that girl. She

didn't shed a tear even though I could hear in her voice how disgusting it was for her to relay that stuff to me. She's tough as nails and it's true what I said… she did what she had to do to survive.

As she opened up more to me, it practically killed me to hear her own self-loathing for getting herself caught in Samuel's web. I asked her—because I had to or it would kill me not knowing—why she stayed with him, and it boiled down to fear and doubt. Samuel preyed upon the perfect woman for his sick plans. He showed Cat how good it felt to live with the comforts we all take for granted. A soft bed, a warm home. Food in her stomach. She told me he'd often go weeks ignoring her, and during those times, her life was fine. She lived it as she wanted, so she reasoned to herself it was a penance she could handle.

I thought penance was an interesting word for her to use, and I had to wonder why she thought of herself as a sinner. Personally, I think she's an angel. And while she never came out and said it, I got the feeling that Cat was fearful of Samuel. Not sure if he threatened her, or implied he'd do something, but Cat had said something to the effect of "for my safety, it was best to just toe the line".

Regardless, our talk came around to The Silo again, and I gently prodded at her as to why she continued to go there once Samuel died. "You were free," I told her. "Why come back to the place he made you do those things?" Where he got his fucking saggy nuts off—

metaphorically speaking since he couldn't get his little dick up—watching his wife get fucked over and over again by multiple men.

Burns me the fuck up. Don't get me wrong… a good gang bang when a woman is consenting and receiving pleasure from the depravity of it all is awesome, but the thought of Cat doing it and not enjoying it… not sure I can handle that thought.

What she told me about that left me unsettled. Not sure if I'm supposed to feel good or bad about it, but it's weighing on my mind.

When I asked her why she still came back after Samuel died, she was quiet a moment, and I wondered if she was remembering back to a few nights after his death. She was at The Silo and told Bridger that Samuel was dead. He, in turn, let a select few of us know. We circled her protectively, wondering what she wanted and how we could help ease her sadness. She ended up choosing several men to fuck her—present company excluded. This wasn't all that unusual, as there are, after all, many men from which she could have picked.

At any rate, she went into one of the rooms that housed a stockade Bridger had built. After she was locked up tight, she took cock after cock with a satisfied smile on her face. It was one of the hottest things I'd seen and I thought she needed it to take her mind off her sadness.

Turns out… she was celebrating, and she told me as much in answer to the question I had posed.

"Because sometimes I liked it," she admitted in a soft

voice.

I think she was ashamed, so I validated her. "There's a lot to like about The Silo, babe," I told her in a firm but gentle voice. "Sex there can be exhilarating and beautiful. There's nothing wrong with what we do there."

I felt the movement of her nodding in agreement. "Many times, I loved it… loved the rush and the feeling of being wanted. I don't fake my orgasms, so you know I'm turned on by much of that stuff. But I also hated a lot of stuff."

"I can imagine," I consoled.

"But if you really want to know why I went back," she continued. "It's because Samuel loved those gang bangs. His favorite thing was to watch me take it over and over again with no ability to say no to any of those men. He liked me stripped of control. But that night… even though I was locked in the stockade, it was my choice to do that. I chose which men fucked me, and then I said when it was over. I had all the control. I hoped Samuel was rolling over in his grave, looking up at me from the burning pits of hell when I called a stop to it all."

I was blown away by those words, and haunted at the same time that something as simple as being able to say "no" could have such a big impact on a person's self-worth and security.

So again… no clue how I feel about all this. Cat's emphatically said that her feelings about The Silo are complicated, and that's a fucking understatement. She's loathed it and loved it, and I get the feeling it's in equal measures.

I did ask her because my ego was bruised a bit, "Why didn't you choose me that night you were in the stockade?"

Cat didn't answer me directly, but in a roundabout way told me what I wanted to hear. "Rand… I think Samuel ended up conditioning me to be a woman who knows nothing but submission. I do as I'm told because I'm afraid to do otherwise."

I thought this was an odd observation and wasn't sure how it applied to my question, but then she made it all clear. "But with you, I never felt fear. Never felt I was in danger from you. Always felt safe and no matter how dirty we got, I felt cherished. I knew if I said "no" to you, you were a man who would respect it immediately. I didn't have anything to prove to you or myself by bringing you in that room. It was about confronting my fears and taking back control, and that's not something I've ever needed to do with you. It was unnecessary to choose you that night."

Yeah, those words right there pretty much sealed my fucking fate. I was going to do whatever I had to do to get Cat on her feet with a permanent smile on her face, as well as the knowledge in her soul that she could do whatever the fuck she wanted and no one was going to hold her back.

This is exactly why I left her sleeping in my apartment and left for work almost three hours before it started. Even though I live only a few blocks from Westward Ink, I needed to drive out to The Wicked Horse and that was an hour round trip.

After I start up my Suburban and begin to navigate my way out of town, I dial Bridger up on my phone. I know he's awake because he always gets up early despite the late hours he keeps. I doubt if the dude sleeps more than a few hours per night. He usually gets into his office at The Wicked Horse no later than eight AM.

He answers on the second ring. "What's up?"

"On my way to The Wicked Horse to see you," I tell him without any lead in. "Hope you got a few minutes before you get going for the day."

"Not there," he responds in that gravelly voice that's typical Bridger. "At the Double J getting ready to help Woolf with some stuff."

Not surprised. Bridger and Woolf are best friends and while Woolf may no longer be involved with The Wicked Horse or The Silo, those two are still thick as thieves. Bridger's house actually sits on Double J property. As if the guy doesn't have enough to do as it is with running a nightclub and sex club, he often helps Woolf out at the ranch.

Woolf is the CEO of JennCo, a massive conglomerate comprised mostly of cattle and oil, but it makes him one of the richest motherfuckers in the USA. You'd never know it though by talking to him. Unassuming and unpretentious, he's just one of the guys so to speak.

Hate that he's no longer involved in The Silo or Wicked Horse, as the gang doesn't get to see him enough as it is. But love does funny things to people and he's clearly happier keeping Callie happy, so good for him.

"I'll be there in half an hour," I tell him, not asking if he minds me taking up his time. I disconnect the phone and step on the gas once I get out of town.

It ends up taking me almost thirty-five minutes because of a minor traffic jam caused by rubbernecking tourists. Dozens of cars pulled haphazardly off the road, some with their ass ends still in the lane of travel. People jumping out of their cars without a care that there's still traffic on this two-lane rural road that will flatten their asses.

But that's part of living in Wyoming, and I slow to a crawl as I navigate my way past travelers who are standing on the side of the road in a large group. I recognize a park ranger's truck and while we're technically outside of the Teton National Forest, they'll respond to dangerous wildlife calls. And I see immediately as I creep by what the hubbub is about. About two hundred yards into a pasture covered with sagebrush and dried grass, a grizzly bear is lying on top of what is probably an antelope carcass. He's massive and appears to be gnawing on the neck of his kill. It's the park ranger's duty to keep the tourists at a safe distance because there's always one moron in the group who wants to sidle closer for a better picture opportunity. Once I make my way past the minor traffic jam, I fight the temptation to speed to make up the lost time. It's not worth the cost of a ticket or the extra time that would be lost if I'm stopped.

When I pull up to the Double J office, I park in between Bridger's red Corvette and Woolf's black Range Rover. Grabbing my phone off the seat beside me, I get out of my truck without locking it up. Nothing of value in there to steal and no one would anyway. That's not the way we do things in Wyoming.

I trot up the steps and push open the door to the ranch office, which is actually an old homestead on the ranch. I think it might have even belonged to Woolf's grandpa or something.

The sounds of Bridger and Woolf's voices pull me down the hall, and I find them both in Woolf's office. Woolf is sitting in his chair behind his desk, booted feet propped up on the scarred, wooden top. Bridger sits in a large chair done in cowhide on the opposite side and sips on a container of coffee.

"Morning, sunshine," Woolf says with a big grin on his face.

"Good to see you, man," I say with a laugh as I take an identical chair next to Bridger. He tips his chin up at me and grumbles, "What's so important you needed to see me first thing this morning?"

I know Bridger and Woolf's time is valuable—far more than mine is, as all I have to do today is run a tattoo shop—so I don't beat around the bush. "Cat's in trouble and I need some advice. Maybe some direction."

"Who the fuck is Cat?" Bridger says with his eyebrows furrowing in.

"Sorry," I say quickly. "Catherine."

"Vaughn?" Bridger asks for clarification.

"Lyons," I say automatically, and his eyebrows draw inward again.

"Who?"

Shaking my head, I hold up a hand for him to let me speak and start again. "She goes by Cat, her maiden name is Lyons, and she prefers to be known as that. I found her sleeping in her car in the parking lot of The Wicked Horse two nights ago and found out she's homeless."

"What the fu—?"

I cut him off because again… time valuable and all. "Local attorney showed up at the house in Jackson and told her she had to vacate. That the will left her nothing and his son was demanding she leave. She was allowed to leave with nothing but her clothes, jewelry, and a little cash. All credit cards shut down."

"You're fucking kidding me?" Bridger growls as he sits up straight in his chair. I quickly see he's taken as much offense to this notion as I have. While Cat is but a member of The Silo, Bridger takes care of his own. I also know he has a soft spot for her and worries about her at times.

"She went and got a copy of the will, but here's the kicker… it's not signed. The attorney insists the signed copy is in Vegas. Cat's thinking about calling one of the sons and asking for a copy with the supposed signatures, but she'll probably get the run around."

"Who's the attorney?" Woolf asks.

"Harlan Grables," I tell him. "Know him?"

"Yeah," Woolf says. "Small-town lawyer, does a variety of stuff. Mostly speeding tickets and stuff. Kind of sleazy actually."

"Which means there's no way in hell he drafted the legitimate will of a billionaire hotelier from Vegas," Bridger concludes.

"You think the attorney's lying?" I ask incredulously. "But why?"

"Could be the son paid him to draft the bogus document to get her out of the house," Bridger says with a careless shrug to his shoulders. "Could be Samuel's real attorney drafted it, the signed one *is* in Vegas, and the son had a copy here. He asked the attorney to enforce it, and the lawyer did so moronically without seeing the signed copy."

"I'm betting there's not a signed copy," Woolf chimes in. "The mere fact she's been given the run around... I bet they're just hoping she gets tired of waiting for an answer and will go away."

"Well, that's not happening," I say with a growl as I lean forward in my chair. "No fucking way."

I don't miss both Bridger and Woolf's eyebrows rising as they shoot each other a smirking look. Ignoring them, I ask, "Any bright ideas on what I should do? I'm letting her crash at my place until I can get her on her feet."

"Taking up her cause, huh?" Bridger asks slyly.

"Something like that," I mutter, but then I get distracted as my phone starts ringing to the tune of Maroon 5's *Wake Up Call*. I roll my eyes without bothering to look at caller ID as that song tells me all I need to know. I press the decline button, sending Tarryn to voice mail.

"Seems to me you still have your hands full," Woolf says with a sly grin, looking down at my phone gripped in my hands.

"I've got Tarryn handled," I assure him. Because the only thing to do with her is ignore her. She'll eventually get bored and move on.

Temporarily at least.

"I'll give Cat a job off the books as a Fantasy Maker," Bridger says. "Under the table, of course."

My head immediately shakes back and forth in denial. "She's taking a break from The Silo. She needs a job far away from that shit."

"Come on, dude," Woolf says as he swings his feet off his desk and sits up in his chair. "Catherine was born to be a Fantasy Maker."

Maybe my personal fantasy, I think for a brief moment before anger over Woolf's innocently callous words overtakes me.

"That shit's off the table," I snap at him, and he blinks at me in surprise. "And clearly you two don't have any helpful advice."

I surge up out of the chair and mutter to Bridger, "Catch you later."

I storm out of the Double J office but even as my own feet hit the dirt outside, I can hear Bridger saying, "Wait up."

Turning, I see him trotting down the steps toward me. "Cut Woolf some slack," he says gruffly. "He doesn't know."

"Know what?" I ask him, confused and slightly skeptical.

Bridger's head turns slightly, and he gazes out over the open range that stretches for miles with the Teton Mountains standing tall on the horizon. When he looks back at me, he scratches at his chin. "Cat... she forced by her husband to go to The Silo?"

He worded it as a question, but I can tell he's actually laying it out as a statement he wants verified.

"Yeah."

"That motherfucker," Bridger snarls, aiming his cowboy booted foot at Woolf's front tire. It slams into the tread and bounces off as he curses under his breath.

"Not your fault," I tell him just loud enough to penetrate his curses. I know what he's feeling right now and it's guilt, plain and simple. That Cat was forced to do something she didn't want to do. "And her experience isn't all bad there. It's complicated."

So fucking complicated.

"She want a job at The Wicked Horse?" Bridger asks.

I shake my head. "Still too close."

"Let me think on it," Bridger says. "And I'll also check into this attorney, but I'm betting he was just paid to enforce a document that may or may not be legit. Now, can I front Cat some money?"

"I've got her covered," I tell him, because fuck if I'm going to allow him to ride in and save the day for Cat. I'm not sure why I have this overwhelming need to protect her and help her. I mean, I feel for her. I really do. And she's a great fuck, and it's been awesome to have her right there in my apartment… but still, I can't figure out why I have this strong of a connection to her cause.

Bridger nods in understanding. "Alright, man. But I'll help in any way I can."

"Appreciate it," I tell him and turn toward my Suburban. While I might not want Bridger being Cat's personal champion, I'll gladly take any help he and Woolf can give me until we can figure out what's best for her future.

Chapter 8
Cat

Opening the oven, I take a quick peek at the meatloaf I have baking and then glance at the timer on the microwave I had set. Another ten minutes and it should be done.

Rand had texted me a few hours ago letting me know he'd be home from work by seven. We had our first minor disagreement after I responded back to him that'd I'd cook dinner.

His response was almost immediate. *I'll pick up pizza.*

I wasn't sure whether to be offended that he was perhaps distrustful of my cooking or he was being an overly gracious host, but I sent him back a firm response. *I insist. I want to do something nice for you.*

No need, he wrote back quite succinctly.

I wasn't so succinct. *I'm cooking dinner and not arguing about it. I'll have it on the table and ready to go at 7PM. If you can't let me do something to show my gratefulness for your generosity, then I'm going to have to make alternative plans to stay somewhere else.*

His response was still just as short, just as quick, but it made me smile. *Look forward to your cooking.*

It's my hope he appreciates my efforts, although knowing Rand, that's sort of a given. The more I come to know him, the more I admire the type of man—no, human—that he is. In all my dealings with him before at The Silo, I never looked past the exterior. He's a glorious package and was one of my select favorites there. But let's be honest... he was fucking a shell of a woman then. I closed off everything on the inside and would only let my body feel. With all the things that make me uniquely human shut down, there was nothing available by which I could see inside someone else. Not that I wanted to since it never occurred to me I could have a life outside of Samuel. That I could have someone truly care for me. I never even hoped for such a thing because you can't hope for something that you don't even understand.

That you don't even know exists in the world.

So without that knowledge, there was never any need for me to look past the exterior of any man who had me. I was nothing but a vessel to them, and they were nothing but a few moments of physical pleasure that hopefully outweighed the shame of what was happening to me.

After our text exchange, I drove to the grocery store and put a dent in my meager funds, coughing up $9.63 for some ground bison, an onion, and some milk. The milk was for the box of macaroni and cheese I found in a cupboard. He had butter, ketchup, eggs, and spices, so I had everything else I needed for meatloaf and macaroni and cheese. Very simple and basic. I considered throwing in a green vegetable too, but I actually got sidetracked in the grocery store when I started thinking about Rand and how perfectly he was able to play my body last night. Which is weird. I never think about sex in general, but I seem to be obsessed with Rand and how he makes me feel in bed. Out of bed too, so to speak, as he got me to easily open up to him. Telling him my secrets and shames last night was freeing. The fact that he listened without judgment speaks volumes.

So yeah… I got sidetracked thinking about Rand and walked out of the grocery store without a veggie. Rand doesn't have any vegetables among his canned goods, which leads me to believe he probably doesn't like them anyway.

I think I'm a decent cook, and it's something I enjoy doing. Granted, I haven't had a lot of opportunity to experiment, but I can hold my own with the basics. Growing up, I had to fend for myself so I could get pretty damn creative. Once I left home, I took whatever food I could get, and it was often just a stolen candy bar or something. With Samuel, we had a chef when we were in Vegas. In Jackson, I did get to cook for us, although he'd never hand down a compliment to me even if he thought it was the best food ever. Not going to say I didn't think about poisoning him a time or two, especially when he'd farm me out to others, but I just don't have that in me, I guess. Samuel's food remained healthy and poison free, even though I hated him enough that I hoped his advanced age would get him sooner rather than later.

Or that he'd choke on a chicken bone, it being fortuitous that I did *not* know how to do the Heimlich maneuver.

The macaroni is done boiling, so I go about fixing the cheap box of Kraft, adding in extra butter because that makes everything taste better. By the time the meatloaf is done and I'm pulling it out of the oven, I hear the door to the apartment open. My entire body goes on hyper-alert, and a rush of giddy excitement runs through me.

Rand's here.

The sensation is so startling that it takes a moment to realize the heat from the glass dish of meatloaf is starting to sting through the towel I'd grabbed it out with. I hurriedly set it on the stovetop.

"Smells amazing," Rand says from behind me. I turn to him, feeling my cheeks get warm from the praise and the anticipation of seeing him.

God… I've never felt this before. It's how I imagine children feel on Christmas morning when they wake up and are beside themselves with excitement to know what Santa left them. I've never had that experience, but I had friends at school who did, so I could easily envision it.

I've most definitely never felt it for another man because I never really had a serious relationship before. I've made attempts, but I always picked poorly. When you're sometimes homeless and occasionally stripping to pay rent, the choices for "good guys" are relatively lacking. I guess that's why Samuel seemed like such a godsend at first when he showed interest in me.

Rand's eyes flick from the meatloaf to me. His gaze lingers in a long, slow slide up and down my body. The giddiness ramps up as I feel a rush of dampness between my legs. Normally, when I feel the signs of lust coming on, my body and persona tend to take on a life of its own. I know how to work my assets and incite the same lust in someone else with either a particular look or a sway of my hips.

But right now, I'm not feeling the need to do that with Rand. In fact, I feel a little off kilter. Rather than give him a sensual look of invitation, because let's face it—I would not say no if he wanted to have sex right now—I blush even deeper if the heat in my face is any indication.

Rand notices this because I don't miss the quick flash of amusement on his face but rather than make me feel uncomfortable about it, he merely gives me a boyish smile and asks, "Do I have time for a quick shower before we eat?"

"Sure," I say, because the food isn't going anywhere.

"I'll only be about five minutes," he says as he turns toward the bathroom. I figure I could use the time to set the table, but then I see him peel his shirt over his head as he walks away from me and all thoughts of plates, utensils and napkins evaporate.

And this time, the dampening of my panties is enhanced by a cramping need of want low in my gut. Just looking at his naked back roped with lean muscle and colored with tattoos incites me to near madness with desire for him. I look back to the meatloaf, and figure it's safe enough where it is. I look back to the bathroom, where Rand has shut the door. Noticing it is not quite shut all the way, I wonder if it's an invitation.

I look back to the meatloaf and consider my options.

Rand originally made it clear that there were no expectations of sex in exchange for his generosity in letting me stay here. But that didn't mean there wasn't sex, as evidenced last night by the repetitive and stellar sex we did have. I've had that beautiful man in my body before at The Silo, but last night was different. Last night, it was personal and moving. It was in the sanctity of his home. It was within a caring embrace. He saw me as more than just a vessel, and I literally felt the difference in the very marrow of my bones.

So last night had nothing to do with paying him my share of the rent. That was because he wanted it and I wanted it.

The meatloaf is definitely a gesture of my gratitude, but if I were to walk in that bathroom right now, would he know it's because I want him and that it doesn't have a damn thing to do with payback?

Only one way to find out.

I drape the towel in my hand over the warm pot of mac and cheese before walking to the bathroom door. I can hear the water running and the unmistakable sound of hot spray against skin. Before I can talk myself out of it, I push against the door and slip inside.

Rand's bathroom is small, but it does have a tub against one wall with a navy blue shower curtain that completely hides him from my view. I can only imagine what he looks like on the other side… maybe rubbing soap all over the planes of his body, or maybe his eyes are closed and face serene while he washes his hair.

But before I can wonder any further, I hear a low groan issue from the other side of that curtain. I recognize the nature and tone of that sound because I've heard it often before, and I know exactly what he's doing now. Without hesitation, I step forward and peel the curtain back a bit near the foot of the tub.

And oh my God… it's better than I ever imagined. Rand has his face tilted to the ceiling to let the hot water hit him on the top of his head. His eyes are indeed closed and his lips slightly parted.

And a soapy hand is wrapped around his hard cock while he slowly strokes himself, twisting his wrist just a bit when he reaches the head.

I pull the curtain back further and the slide of the shower rings against the bar is loud enough to disturb Rand. His eyes open and his neck straightens.

He looks at me with lazy eyes and never misses a stroke. "Sorry. Took one look at you when I walked in that door, saw the way you blushed, and it made me incredibly horny. Had to jerk off before dinner."

I can't help but laugh, pulling the curtain back all the way. "Rinse your dick off."

"Excuse me?" he says with wide blinking eyes, his hand still working himself.

"Rinse the soap off. I don't like the taste of it."

"Oh," he says in understanding and immediately turns his body into the spray to do as I ask. When he's squeaky clean, he shuts the water off before turning to face me.

He's spectacular. Wet and muscled. Thick cock hard and standing straight up, just begging for my attention. I indulge and wrap my hand around it. He groans again and then rasps out, "Get naked, Cat."

I shake my head with a smile before lowering my knees to the tiled floor. Rand steps to the edge of the tub, and he's within perfect striking distance for my mouth. I wrap it around the head of his cock with both my hands to his ass, pulling him in deep. Over the last few years, I learned how to deep throat by virtue of all the cock I've had in it. Samuel loved to watch me choke on it. He'd get most excited when I'd gag and slobber all over. I hated the fucker for that. So I was determined to learn how to take it like a pro and not give him the satisfaction of it. With nothing but determination and a driving need to take something away from Samuel, I can now take a cock all the way down without even missing a breath or a stroke.

Rand knows this, of course, because I've given him head a few times. But he's never had this reaction to me before as he shouts out when my nose presses into his pelvis and his hands come to my head to grip hard.

"F-u-u-u-c-k," he curses as he literally pushes me off him but I make sure to give a measured suck once he's out of my throat. "Fuck, that's good."

Yes. It. Is.

The taste of Rand in my mouth, the feel of his soft skin stretched over what feels like forged steel. The way he goes crazy when I take him back down deep again.

"Cat, you need to pull off right the fuck now before I come," he growls at me, once again using his hands to push against me. I let him do this, leisurely sucking on him, but I have no intention of stopping.

When Rand walked back here and I felt that mad rush of desire for him, I thought I wanted him to fuck me. Yet what we have going on right here is something far and away different from the other times we've been together. It's like we were in black and white, but now we're in Technicolor.

In this moment, I realize that I don't care if I get off. I want him to have the best damn blow job in the world, and I want him to remember that it's from me.

So instead of releasing him as he commands, I relax my throat, open up, and pull him in deep again. It's a clear message to him that I'm not stopping. I raise my eyes, looking up at him with his cock wedged down deep inside me, and he returns my look. His eyes are swimming with need and perhaps a question to me as to what I want.

I answer by pulling back before immediately sucking him down deep again. Repeating the move, I take a quick breath in between. Then once more, and he gets the message.

I want him to fuck my mouth.

I know he gets this because his hands grip me just a little harder but instead of pushing me off, he holds me still.

Finally, his hips start moving and Rand takes every bit of pleasure that I offer up.

He doesn't last long at all, shouting out my name on a backward pull before shooting all over my tongue. I drink it down while staring up at him, savoring the warm, salty flavor. His eyes are closed and he has the most peaceful, blissed-out look I've ever seen on a man. His hands shift so his thumbs stroke my temples.

Opening his eyes, he looks down at me with a soft smile. "That was unbelievable."

"You should have just asked me to do that to begin with," I say with a grin.

"I didn't want you to think—"

"I know… and I get it. But I wanted to do that for my own pleasure as well. That had nothing to do with owing you anything."

"I'd really love to return that favor right now," he says as he bends over and helps me off my knees.

Shaking my head, I step away and give him room to exit the tub. "We have dinner to eat first. After that, you can have your way with me."

Reaching over to the towel rod, I grab the one I know is Rand's and toss it to him. He catches it and starts to dry off. When I turn to walk out of the bathroom, he says, "Cat."

I look over my shoulder at him. "It's going to be another all-nighter, just so you know."

Oh, God... I squeeze my legs together to alleviate the ache that just formed.

Maybe we don't need to eat dinner just yet.

Chapter 9
Rand

"DAMN, THIS IS good," I say before taking another bite of meatloaf.

"We should have at least heated it up," Cat grumbles as she takes a tentative bite herself.

Turns out, she went ahead and let me return the favor to her right after that fucking unbelievable head she gave me. She appeared to weigh her options carefully when I told her we'd be up all night again. I could literally see the wheels turning in her brain and imagined her balancing needs against wants.

On one hand, an immediate and satisfying orgasm from my tongue on her clit.

On the other, cold food that could be reheated.

She chose the orgasm, and I, in turn, tossed her on the bed and ate her out so thoroughly, I think she actually had two orgasms. A big one and then a smaller one right on the heels of that when I nipped her clit with my teeth as she was coming down. She shrieked in surprise and her back arched off the bed, and I was so fascinated by her response, I pressed two fingers in her wet pussy and felt the tremors of that release from the inside. Made me start to get hard again, but I figured we needed to eat and get some sustenance for what I had planned for her.

So I pulled a weak-kneed Cat from the bed and tossed her a t-shirt from one of my drawers. After I pulled on a pair of jeans, we stumbled into the kitchen where I fixed us up two plates. Because I was starved and horny for her again, I didn't bother heating the food. The look on Cat's face right now tells me she's not a fan of cold grub.

"The sooner we eat, the sooner I can fuck you," I tell her in a matter-of-fact manner.

"You're insatiable," she says with a grin, then pokes her fork into the mac and cheese.

"You're a bad influence," I tell her with a return smile full of mischief, but then I feel the smile slide right off my face when I hear my phone ringing from the bathroom where I left it with my clothes.

Wake Up Call.

I ignore it and stab at the meatloaf, pissed that Tarryn's calling me again and that she can't take a hint. Even more pissed that she's ruining my hard-on.

"Do you need to get that?" Cat asks softly.

I look up at her with a shake of my head. "Nah. We're eating, and this is fabulous by the way."

Her eyes light up from the praise. Thankfully, the phone goes silent.

Sadly, it starts ringing again.

Wake Up Call.

I lock my jaw and make busy work cutting up the rest of my meatloaf. Cat doesn't say a word.

Finally, the phone stops ringing, but within just a few seconds, it's starts again with that vile song I used to love but now hate because it reminds me about the worst of Tarryn.

"Christ," I mutter, dropping my fork to the plate and rubbing the bridge of my nose in frustration.

Raising my face, I see Cat looking at me with her head tilted and faint worry in her eyes.

"Maybe you should get that."

The phone stops ringing and for a blessed moment, I think maybe she's done. I even reach back for my fork, but then it starts back up again.

"Son of a bitch," I curse as I push up from the table and stalk to the bathroom where I'd left my phone before I got in the shower. I stab at the *Accept* button and growl, "For fuck's sake, Tarryn."

"I was worried since you hadn't called me back from this morning," she says in that clipped New England accent that hasn't faded much after living several years out west.

"Here's a fucking hint," I tell her as the anger continues to rise within me. "I didn't call you back because I have nothing to say to you."

"Come on, Rand," she says in a soothing voice. "You don't really mean that. Regardless of you being angry right now, we shared too damn much for you to just disregard me."

Closing my eyes, I drop my head in resignation because she is right about that. I could never disregard Tarryn. In fact, my problem was always that I regarded her too much. One of the reasons I tried to avoid her now was because she always seemed to say the right thing to suck me back in. My need to nurture and develop inherently kicking in. It makes it hard to completely let go sometimes. It is also probably proof of why she has a specialized ring tone to alert me to her call, so I have the choice to talk to her or not versus just blocking her number completely.

And as if to prove that sentiment, she strikes fast and hard. "I've started training again. Going to take a shot at the giant slalom. There's an event at Copper Mountain in November."

Gritting my teeth, I hold back the flurry of curses I want to spew at her. Instead, I force myself to say in a calm voice, "That's great. I'm sure you'll do great."

She's silent a moment, but then she prods. "Could use a good coach."

"Plenty around this area," I say.

"Interested in the job?" she asks with an awkward chuckle.

"You know I'm not, Tarryn," I say quietly, sneaking a peek toward the kitchen. Cat's eating silently, her face lowered in an attempt to give me privacy, I think, but that's impossible in an apartment this small.

"Come on, Rand," Tarryn cajoles. "No one knows my skiing better than you. No one pushes me the way you do."

I try hard not to snort at that because there was a time in the not so distant past that she hated the way I pushed at her. In fact, the way memory serves, and according to Tarryn, I pushed so hard that she fell right into the arms of another man.

At least that's the way she tried to excuse her infidelity.

My eyes flick to the bathroom mirror, and I take a good look at myself. I'm not the same man I was eleven years ago when I started dating Tarryn. Not the same man I was four years ago when we broke up.

My gaze focuses in on Cat's reflection at the kitchen table behind me.

Hell, I'm not the same man I was two nights ago when I found her sleeping in her car.

"Look Tarryn," I say with a firm tone as I turn and walk out of the bathroom toward Cat, who looks up at me. "I've got company, so I need to get off the phone. But if you're looking for a training coach, check in with Jake. He'll hook you up."

"But I don't want—"

"Sorry, but I really have to go. Take care," I say into the phone just before I disconnect.

As I reach the table, I look down at Cat… her big, brown eyes swimming with focused curiosity.

"Ex-girlfriend… Tarryn," I say by way of explanation. "She has phases where she gets lonely and reaches out to me."

"How long did you date?" she asks hesitantly. Possibly feeling the need to explain her question, she adds on, "When you meet people within the confines of The Silo, it's sometimes hard to picture them in real relationships."

I laugh and sit back down at the table, picking up my fork. Food wasn't getting any warmer, but I was still hungry. "Seven years. Started when we were seventeen. We met at prep school. She was a competitive alpine skier too."

Cat's eyes flare wide in a *holy shit* type of way. "Seven years is a long time. Which begs the question… how old are you?"

"Twenty-eight," I tell her before taking another big bite of the meatloaf. It really is pretty good. "And you?"

"Twenty-four. I was twenty-one when I married Samuel."

"And you've got the best of your life still to come," I tell her.

Cat gives me a faint smile, pushing some macaroni around on her plate before asking, "Why did you two break up? That's a long time to be with someone."

"Well, if you ask Tarryn the reasons, she'll say it's all my fault," I tell her with a wry grin.

Cat's eyes go round and she dips her chin in mock astonishment. With an exaggerated gasp, she teases, "What? No way. Rand Bishop has faults?"

I laugh because she's cute as all get out. Now that I think about it, I never saw Cat smile very much at The Silo. Damn sure never saw her make a joke, but she's a fucking natural.

"I'm not without faults," I tell her, pushing my empty plate away. I contemplate a second helping, but she's touching on a fairly serious subject even if it's with some levity. Because even though Tarryn is the one that cheated on me, and it was ultimately the demise of our relationship, I did help drive her there. That's a tough pill to swallow sometimes.

"Everyone has faults," Cat says simply. "It's called being human."

"Well, to make a long story short, since I'd really rather take you back in the bedroom, I've got a white-knight syndrome. Or, at least that's the definition my best friend, Jake, has labeled me with."

"A white-knight syndrome?" she asks skeptically with a cocked eyebrow.

"I'm the type who likes to rescue the damsel in distress. Or so Jake seems to think."

"But you don't think that?"

I shrug. "Tarryn has her fair share of issues. She didn't have an easy life growing up, but her natural talent on the slopes got her a full ride to Carrabassett Valley, which is how we met. I saw her skiing as a way for her to have a different life, so I tried to help push her along."

"Encouragement is good," Cat points out.

"Yeah… it wasn't just encouragement. I mean, I really pushed at her. Pushed her to train, lead a clean lifestyle, and work harder than she ever has in her life. Because that's what I did to be at the top of the game, and I wanted the same for her. It was her ticket out of a mediocre life. It takes hardcore training to compete at the Olympic level. Tarryn's a great skier, but she's not a great athlete. I wanted her to follow me in my path, and really... she just wanted to be a regular girl. She didn't want the gold medals the way I did, and I just couldn't understand it."

Cat's face softens with understanding. "You wanted it bad for her, but she didn't want it for herself."

"Exactly," I say pointing a finger in her direction. "The last few years weren't great before we broke up. I was traveling, and she was living here doing some ski instruction. She started seeing someone else, and when I found out about it, I wasn't all that broken up. I think it all just sort of withered up and died from neglect, but I recognize my part in that for sure. I pushed her so hard that she became bitter. On top of that, I was traveling a lot for competitions, and we were apart most of the time because she wasn't skiing at my level. So, the way she looks at it is that I pushed her right at someone else."

"That doesn't excuse cheating," Cat says hotly. "If she didn't respect the relationship, she should have ended it."

Again, I shrug. She's not telling me anything I haven't thought about more than a time or two since we broke up almost four years ago. "I agree. But I've let it go. And I learned from it."

"That you shouldn't rescue damsels in distress," Cat says, and I can tell by the pointed look on her face she's talking about herself.

"No, that's not what I learned," I tell her with a censuring look. "A good man always helps a woman if she needs it. But I learned that sometimes my definition of who needs help is different from others. In Tarryn's case, she didn't need what I was pushing on her, and since I can practically see that beautiful brain of yours trying to work out how this means I view you, let me assure you, two nights ago, you needed rescuing. You needed a hand up, so I gave it to you. That's all it was, Cat. Plain and simple."

"So none of your attraction to me has to do with the fact that you see me as lost and needing rescued?"

"I was attracted to you long before I found you sleeping in your car, Cat. Hell, I've even fantasized about you when I was getting my dick sucked by another girl." I lean forward and put my forearms on the table, staring at her hard so she understands what I'm saying. "But I'm not going to lie either. I couldn't stand to see you hurt and alone. If that's my white-knight complex, so fucking be it. It brought me into your life on a deeper level. But most assuredly, the reason I was jacking off in the shower to you, and the reason I think I'll be fucking you repetitively tonight, is that I find you fascinating and attractive on more than just a physical level. If it was just physical, I'd be at The Silo right now instead of my mouth watering to get back on your pussy again."

Cat sort of rears backward in her chair and blinks at me in confusion. "You find me fascinating?"

"You're smart, tough as nails, and resilient. You have a wicked sense of humor, although I'd like to see more of it. You cook a pretty damn good meatloaf and survived an intolerable situation with plenty of grace intact. Oh, and you give the best blow job I've ever had in my life."

She giggles over that last part, which is exactly what I was hoping for. It wasn't a lie about it being the best blow job ever, but I knew it would lighten the seriousness of what I was saying.

"Look, Cat," I say, causing her giggles to dry up, but she looks at me through smiling eyes. "I like you. I think you like me. I think we sure as hell like fucking each other. You've got a place to stay until you get on your feet, so the pressure is off. Let's enjoy this and see where it goes, okay? I could totally be on board with us going at it with each other every night."

"Are you saying you want to be exclusive?" she asks hesitantly, the smile dying instantly and her lips flattening out.

Well fuck... maybe I was reading her wrong. Maybe she can't give up the gang bang or something.

"Well, if that's not something you're interested in—"

"Okay, let's do it," she blurts out.

"Be exclusive?" I ask, just so I make sure we're on the same page. I know what it's like to be on the very opposite page from where you think someone is.

"Yes," is all she says.

"What about The Silo?" I cautiously ask.

"That was never really my thing," she says sadly, and

it makes my heart squeeze in pain that her asshole husband made her do that. "I only went back after he died because it was at least something I knew, and I didn't feel so alone there."

"Then it's agreed… we take a break from The Silo," I reassure her. Of course, I'd have to get with Bridger and explain to him that I was taking a hiatus. I'm only a part-time Fantasy Maker there, so I won't even be missed. Plus, I know he won't begrudge me this.

Whatever this is, but I'm rolling with it.

Cat stands up from the table and picks up both plates. I stand as well, quickly taking them from her hands. "You cooked so I clean."

"Not going to argue there," she says smugly and sits back down.

I intend on making quick work of the kitchen because now that I've disclosed my baggage with Tarryn—which admittedly pales in comparison to hers with her dead husband—I really, really want to get back to the business of sex with this gorgeous creature.

"Why does she call you now?" Cat asks, and it takes me a moment to realize she's shifted back to Tarryn.

I don't bother to turn to look at her, working at filling the sink with soapy water. "I have no clue, but it's been a pattern since we broke up. She'll get involved with someone, and then I won't hear from her. Sometimes for months. When she's single again, she calls me. Or sometimes, she shows up on my doorstep to talk, or she'll ask me for a favor that is seemingly innocuous, but she tends to think if I help her out, I'll want to get back together with her."

"Maybe it's because you're not competing anymore, so now she thinks you're more ideally suited at this point in your lives," Cat points out.

I scrape the tiny bit of food left on Cat's plate in the garbage and stick both plates in the suds before turning my attention to packaging up the leftovers. "Just because I'm not competing anymore doesn't change who I am. She's still the same person who gave up because things got too hard, and I just can't respect that. What that really tells me is that no matter how hard I might have pushed her away, she wasn't the right one for me anyway."

"It's fascinating to me that you've had this whole other life outside The Silo," she says almost in awe. "You just never think about the people you come in contact with there outside of that building."

"The Silo is about fantasy, not reality. It's easy to leave your real life at the door."

"Except that was my real life, inside The Silo. There was no fantasy for me," she says, and my gut clenches hard.

I grab a towel, give my hands a quick dry, and turn to Cat. "That's over with," I tell her softly. "The day Samuel died is the day your real life started."

I watch her carefully. The way her brown eyes look at me blankly a moment, as if the words bounce off, and then a small flare of hope sparks as she swallows hard.

Finally, a small nod of her head while she murmurs in agreement with me, "Yes… my real life has just started."

Good.

She understands.

Now I wonder what she's going to make of it.

Chapter 10
Cat

"All right," Rand says as he turns the ignition of his Suburban off and unlatches his seatbelt. He turns to look at me in the passenger seat beside him. "I'm going to go hang out with my buddy, Jake, while you do your thing. Just come find me there when you're done."

"It could be a while," I remind him as I also take my seatbelt off.

He just gives me an amused smile before his left hand shoots out to grab me behind the neck. Pulling me across the expanse of the front cab, he presses a hard, swift kiss to my mouth before letting me go. I actually go dizzy from the unexpected move, but mostly from the display of affection he just laid upon me. I have to restrain my fingers from touching my lips, hoping to savor the tingling he left behind.

"It's Teton Ski and Snowboarding," Rand says as he releases me, and then points over my shoulder. "Two blocks down East Broadway. And take your time. I've got nothing else going on today."

"Okay," I murmur as I grab my large satchel purse from the floorboard. In addition to my wallet, lip gloss, my sunglasses case, and a handful of pens, it also now carries a copy of a resume Rand helped me type up this morning. It's pathetic and small, and we couldn't put all of my "work" experience on there, but I did do some waitressing in addition to dancing, and I served on the board of a charity in Vegas that Samuel asked me to do. I'm hoping my youth and eagerness to learn will make up for my pathetic work history.

One of my goals today is to walk the town square and see if anyone is hiring.

When Rand asked me last night just before we fell asleep what my plans were today, I told him I intended to find a job. He offered to drive me to the town center as he was taking his ski equipment into his buddy's shop for a tune-up with ski season fast approaching, or at least that's what he said was the reason. I suspect he just wanted to offer gallant services to me, and it warmed me so much that he wanted to do that, I graciously accepted. I hope to cover most of the businesses surrounding the town square with my resume. Maybe something will come through.

Before I committed to staying in Jackson, there was a moment last night when I thought about just heading back to Vegas, even though I didn't have any money to get there. I knew I could get a job stripping pretty quickly. I'd have immediate cash by which to live, so it was a decent option if I could just make my way back home.

But then I took serious stock of where I was in that

moment and realized I didn't want to go to Vegas. I wanted to stay right there, in that bed with Rand, with his arms wrapped tight around me and his beard tickling my neck. I wasn't ready to give up the security he was temporarily providing me, nor these new and delicious feelings blooming inside my chest whenever he looks at me. It was my very own Christmas every time he touched me or smiled at me. I was soaking it up like a greedy sponge.

We both exit his Suburban, me taking a bit longer as I carefully use the running board to step down in my Fendi heels. I look at the shoes that cost $750, wishing I had that cash in my pocket rather than the designer label on my feet. Hopefully, that won't be an issue by the time I meet Rand over at the ski shop after I finish all my errands.

"Good luck," he says with a smile at me over the hood of his vehicle. "Call me if you need anything. I'm just going to be hanging out."

"Will do," I say, hitching my purse up as Rand turns toward the rear of his Suburban where he has his skis stashed. Apparently, a tune-up is nothing more than getting the skis repaired of any damage from the season before, such as nicks and stuff, as well as getting them waxed. Again, I suspect this is not something that had to be done right now, but was rather his excuse to drive me to the center of town, which I find almost unbearably sweet because I don't understand what I've done to deserve that consideration.

I step up onto the sidewalk that borders the town square, which is nothing more than a small park with large shade trees that are still full and green, a few benches, and a small walking path. I head in the opposite direction of Rand, with no intention of job hunting right away. Tucked inside my purse is all the jewelry Samuel bought me. Well, I actually bought it myself, but it was with his money. Even my engagement ring I picked out and bought, at his insistence and with him pushing his own personal credit card into my hand since my limit wasn't enough to cover the three-carat rock.

Rand has no clue I'm doing this, and I suspect he'd try to discourage me from something so rash, especially since I have a roof over my head, food in my stomach, and his amazing cock fucking me every night. But the one thing Samuel taught me, and taught me well, is that no one is truly looking out for me but myself. I can't rely on Rand to be there for me, and while I'm fairly confident he wouldn't abuse the trust I've placed in him the way Samuel did, I still have to be ready to jet out of here at the first sign he's something less than I hope him to be.

That means I need money.

I'll sell my jewelry, or at the very least, I'll pawn it. After that, I'm free, mobile, and I won't be beholden to anyone.

I won't be owned again.

Except… I have that nagging feeling like I want to be owned by Rand or something, but that's just crazy.

Samuel owned every part of me, and I hated it. There's no way I could possibly want that from Rand.

Right?

I glance over my shoulder at Rand receding in the distance as I continue to walk away. He's already got his skis pulled out and the door shut, standing at the corner waiting for a light to turn green so he can cross. He doesn't look back at me as I turn right onto South King Street, which houses Libertine's Jewelry just half a block down.

I decided to start with actual jewelry stores, independently owned and small. I figure they would be the most likely to buy from me. I actually purchased a piece here last summer, so I hope the owner remembers me.

With my gaze lowered to the sidewalk to make sure I don't lodge my spiked heels in a crack or something, I'm almost knocked sideways by my shoulder colliding with someone.

"I'm sorry—" I start to say as I turn toward the person, but I come to a dead stop with my mouth hanging open and my blood turning to ice.

Kevin Vaughn stands there leering at me.

I can tell by the mixture of contempt and challenge in his eyes that he had seen me coming down the sidewalk and purposely ran into me. He's not surprised to see me the way I am him.

"Hello, Catherine," he says as he takes a step toward me.

My eyes take in his appearance. Samuel was old and

practically withered with the slew of medical problems he had, but I could always see in his face that he had once been a good-looking man. His sons both have the same bone structure and look.

Kevin Vaughn keeps his blond hair perfectly cut, styled, and sprayed. Fake tan that is so well done it looks real. Thousands of dollars of veneers that make his teeth almost neon white. Dressed in designer labels. He loves money and he loves spending it. As the director of operations for Samuel's hotel empire, he makes a lot of money.

He also has a small dick and a large problem with premature ejaculation, so I always think of that whenever I'm in his presence. Otherwise, he'd skeeve me out too bad just by the way he looks at me.

It tore me up to admit to Rand the other night that Samuel let Kevin have me. I'm not sure if the offer was ever made to Richard or not, but he and I never fucked. In fact, Richard was unfailingly polite but reserved around me. He was married to a nice woman, had two kids, and managed Samuel's investments, seeming to enjoy a much quieter life than his plastic brother.

The first time with Kevin was my first Christmas with Samuel, which was just an ordinary day to me. Samuel and I ate breakfast together in almost total silence—the only sound interrupting us was the doorbell ringing.

I found Kevin there when I opened the door. He told me he was just dropping by to give a present to his father, but I knew it was a lie. I knew it because as he said those words to me, I could see him undressing me with his eyes. He was also empty handed.

Samuel wheeled himself into the foyer. The minute Kevin stepped in and I shut the door behind him, he made it clear that I was actually Kevin's Christmas present.

"Catherine, darling," Samuel said in that weak voice made so by congestive heart failure. "Be a good girl and wish Kevin a very Merry Christmas."

I only spared a moment to stare at Samuel in completely stunned disgust, but I saw the resolve on his face. When I turned back to Kevin, he was already undoing his belt and breathing shallowly as if he hadn't been laid in months. I suspect that was true because his wife looked a little uptight and they didn't have any children, so something wasn't working right.

"Get on your knees," Kevin ordered me, pushing his pants and underwear down, that tiny little dick popping free. I almost laughed, but I didn't because what I was getting ready to do wasn't the least bit funny.

I shudder over the memory and take an involuntary step backward, my ankles wobbling just a bit.

"I'm surprised to see you still in Jackson," Kevin says as he rubs a finger over his chin in a thoughtful manner. His voice is mildly polite, but I can sense an underlying vibe of distaste for me. While Kevin never had a problem fucking me, I knew he hated the fact his dad married me. Hated he had a stepmother younger than him and who would potentially carve into his inheritance one day. I know this because he would sometimes mutter that to me while he was banging me.

"Not sure why you're surprised," I tell him calmly. "You left me without a dime to my name when you had that attorney kick me out of my home and shut my credit cards off. Just how did you expect me to get out of town, Kevin?"

He shrugs dismissively. "Not my problem really. Figured you could fuck your way back to Vegas or something."

I have to curl my fingers inward and press the nails deep into my palms to restrain myself. It's almost impossible to hold myself back from kneeing him in his tiny nuts and following it with a right hook to his smug face.

But I decide to choose a different way to change his attitude. "I want a signed copy of the will, Kevin. Apparently, that attorney had only an unsigned copy. It seems a little suspect you'd have me evicted based on that alone."

"You weren't there for the actual reading in Vegas," he says calmly, that smug smile still in place. "That's where the signed copy is."

"I figured as much," I tell him with a pointed look. "That's why I'm going to call Richard and ask him to send me a copy with the signatures, so I can have my own attorney look at it."

And... there it is. That superior-than-thou attitude

melts as his lips flatten into a grim line. He has no clue if I'm bluffing, and I'm totally bluffing. I can't afford an attorney, but I am going to do whatever I can to see a copy of that signed will. I also have no intention of calling Richard because even though I think he'd be fair to me, I can't be sure. It's best not to trust either of Samuel's sons at this point.

"Listen," Kevin says in a conciliatory tone as he steps closer. His eyes are glittering with something I can't quite put my finger on but which sets off all my internal alarms. His arm reaches out and he grasps me by my shoulder. "If you need a place to stay, you can come back to the house here. I'll even give you some cash to help you out."

Twisting my upper body to dislodge his hand, I laugh at him. "And let me guess… in return, you want me to fuck you?"

His eyes light up with the prospect. "I wouldn't be averse to that."

"Well, I would," I sneer, surprising him by taking a step forward into his space. I poke a finger in his chest while molten rage fuels my words. "I wouldn't let that needle dick you have anywhere near me. And if I find out you're lying to me about the will, you're going to regret the day you ever fucked with me."

Kevin's arm shoots up and he grabs my wrist, squeezing hard and pushing my hand from his chest down his stomach. "Come on, Catherine. You know you're good for one thing only, and I'm offering you an easy ride.

Jump on board, and I'll keep you here at the Jackson house. You'll be my little piece on the side."

Just as my knuckles brush against the edge of his belt, I rip myself out of his grasp. "You're a sick, fucking—"

He moves so swiftly that I don't have time to react. His arm wraps around my waist and he pulls me in tight to his body. His other arm comes up so his hand can grip me at the back of my head. It looks like a lover's embrace, even though I manage to get my hands to his chest in an attempt to push him away. But he's stronger than I am and he holds me rigidly. Tourists are walking by, oblivious to what's going on.

Kevin leans his head toward me, puts his lips near my ear, and in a low but deadly serious voice, he says, "*You* do not fuck around with *me*, Catherine. You can either walk away intact or in pieces. Your choice. But I seriously suggest you forget about that will."

He pulls his head back so he can look down at me, his eyes flicking back and forth to see if what he's said has sank in. I don't respond, but I don't break eye contact either, gritting my teeth together in anger and some fear.

"I can see you understand me," he says confidently, releasing his hold. I take two stumbling steps back.

Kevin merely tucks his hands into the lightweight jacket he's wearing and says, "I'll make these two offers, and then I'm done with you. I'll give you five thousand in cash and you move on with your life. Stay away from my brother and me. Or move back into the Jackson house—I'll give you a monthly allowance and you'll be at my beck and call when I come to visit."

Straightening up to my full five-foot-seven—thank you, Fendi—I stiffen my spine and lock my knees in figurative battle. I forget about the fact that not only does Kevin disgust me, but he also slightly scares me too. But I don't get caught up in that. Instead, I tell him with as much sarcasm as I can muster, "As tempting as those two offers are, I'm going to decline."

Kevin's eyes harden, his lids lowering until I see just tiny slits of brown irises peeking out at me. He inclines his head at me in acknowledgment of my position and says in what can only be taken as a clear threat, "So be it. But don't say you weren't warned."

He takes away my ability to walk away from him, making a casual turn on the sidewalk and meandering off in a carefree saunter. I can tell by the set to his shoulders and the almost jaunty step that he's not worried about me at all.

But he should be.

Because I just learned something very important.

There is no new will where Samuel cuts me out. If there were, Kevin would have offered up the signed copy to me without hesitation. Instead, he tried to buy me off, relying on his faulty instinct that I am still a woman who can be owned.

It's a mistake to underestimate me, and I know exactly what I need to do.

Chapter 11
Rand

"I CAN'T BELIEVE we essentially live in the same house and I only get to see you when you have a few minutes to pop into my place of business," Jake says as he walks into the back breakroom of his ski shop.

I've been here for almost two hours waiting for Cat to finish up her job hunting visits, shooting the shit with some of Jake's employees or other locals who stop by for some sporting equipment needs. Although his shop is named Teton Ski and Snowboarding, it's actually morphed over time into a sort of one-stop shop for all of your Wyoming outdoor needs. He runs guided fishing trips in the summer, hunting trips in the fall and winter for big game such as elk and moose, as well as black bear in the spring. He even has guides who will just drive you around and show you where you can see all the wildlife. Jake sells everything from skis to guns to fishing lures to sporting apparel, and he's been quite successful at it.

I don't respond directly but throw a teasing jab while looking at my watch. "Must be nice to have a job you can roll in at close to lunch time. Wish I had as easy a life as you."

Jake laughs. As well he should, because he's one of the hardest-working men I know, and he knows I'm joking. He's normally in the shop at least an hour before it opens, and while he may go home so he can have dinner with his family, I know he works in the evenings too to stay on top of things.

"Lorelei had an ultrasound this morning," he explains as he walks over to the coffee pot on the counter and pours himself a cup.

"And how is the little niblet?" I ask, leaning back in my chair so the front legs come off the ground a bit.

"Looking like a chip off the old block," he says before taking a chair at the table opposite of me. "He's got the look of a snowboarder for sure."

"It could be a girl," I point out since it's still too early for the ultrasound to show that.

"Nope. Gonna be a snowboarding boy. Amber's going to be the skier."

I laugh and shake my head, but, secretly, I'm a little envious of him. Beautiful wife, gorgeous kid with another on the way, and leading a spectacularly full life. Once I figure out what I want to do with my own, I'm hoping things shake out for me like they have for Jake.

"So what's up with you?" Jake asks. "Jimmy said you've been here a while."

Jimmy is one of his employees who is manning the store today. He also doubles as a fishing guide, but the trip he had set this morning got cancelled. It rained like hell last night and the rivers are too muddied to make it worthwhile.

"Just waiting for a friend who is doing some errands around town; thought we'd go get some lunch after she's done."

"She?" Jake asks, an eyebrow cocked and with a quick lick to his lips.

"Yes, a she," I affirm. "I've been known to like the opposite sex, you know."

It's no wonder Jake has a healthy dose of skepticism when it comes to me making any type of plans that sound like a date with a woman. He's the one person who knows firsthand how turbulent my relationship was with Tarryn. He also knows that when it ended, I sort of swore off relationships for a while. While he has no clue about The Silo and what I do there, he's also observed me for the past four years and hasn't seen me date anyone. I've been to dinner at their table, gone out with him and Lorelei on many a weekend, but they've never seen me with a date.

And why would I?

Even though I truly understand what happened to our relationship, Tarryn left me a little jaded by her infidelity. Besides, there was no shortage of tourists and locals to fuck once I settled here in Jackson. Once The Silo opened, that pretty much sealed my fate as a bachelor because I could get off whenever I wanted with no-strings attached. It's not that I'm opposed to the strings, but it's just easier when they're not involved.

"This is monumental, dude," he says with a grin.

"It's about time you started dating again."

"We're friends," I correct him. "She's down on her luck and crashing at my place for a few days."

Friends who are fucking though.

"Friends my ass," he says without any qualms of dismissing my motives so quickly. "So when do Lorelei and I get to meet her? How about dinner this weekend?"

"Maybe," I say, not bothering to try to assert that this is a friends-only deal. He's not buying it. Not because he has any great insight into me, but because he doesn't want to. Jake's always been a romantic at heart, and he wants everyone to fall in love, get married, and pop out kids. "She's going to come here after she's done dropping resumes off, so you can meet her then."

"She's job hunting?" he asks before taking a sip of his coffee.

"Yeah, you hiring?"

"Not right now, but I will be in about two weeks to gear up for the start of hunting season. I'll need some extra help to keep track of all the expeditions and guides."

"How many are you up to now?" I ask curiously. Jake has never hunted or fished in his life that I know of, but he's become quite successful at gathering knowledgeable guides who flock to this area during peak tourist season to pick up work.

"I've got eleven," he says nonchalantly. "Seven returning from last year and four new that I'm hiring."

"Jesus," I say with a teasing grin. "Do you even bother with the snow sporting world anymore?"

"Still my one true love," he answers before pushing his chair back and standing up. "And I need to get to it as I have a shitload of stuff to do today. I'm already a few hours behind."

"Sure, man," I say, standing up as well and not wanting to hold him up… too much. But I have to ask, "Listen, this friend of mine… her name's Cat, and she's really in a tough spot. If you hear of any job openings, let me know, okay?"

"You know I will," he reassures. "But you know it's tough around here. Everyone wants to live and work in this area."

And that's the fucking truth. I've been all over the world and much of the United States, and there isn't much that's comparable to this area in the way of scenery and activities. Throw in the grandeur of Yellowstone just north of us, and the competition for work is stiff.

Movement over Jake's shoulder and beyond the open doorway of the breakroom catches my attention. I see Cat walking toward us. I'll admit that my tongue was hanging out of my head this morning when she came out of the bedroom wearing a slim-fitted skirt that came just down to her knees but with a slit up the side that showed just a tiny peek of her lower thigh when she walked in her high heels. It wasn't enough to be overtly sexy, but it was enough to get a man's attention and for him to wonder what else was up there. Luckily, I knew the answer to that question.

I smile at her, and she says hesitantly, "The guy up front said you were back here and that I could come on back."

Jake turns to the sound of her voice. Because he's a genuinely friendly guy and an extrovert on steroids, he sticks his hand out and says, "You must be Cat?"

She enters the breakroom and takes his hand, shooting me a quick smile before looking back to him. "And you must be Jake. I've heard a lot about you."

"And I haven't heard nearly enough about you," he says as he gives a quick shake and releases her hand. "But unfortunately I've got to get to work. So I demanded that your man set up a double date with me and my wife, Lorelei."

Cat's eyes cut to mine. While she doesn't need to say a word, I can read the look. It says, *He doesn't know we're just fucking?*

I shoot her back a look that says, *It's more than just fucking and you know it.*

She smirks at me before turning back to Jake. "That sounds like fun. We should do it soon."

And just like that, it looks like I might be having my first real date in well… for fucking ever. There's never been anyone other than Tarryn and shit… we were still kids when we started seeing each other. Dates back then consisted of making out in the school library or grabbing an ice cream in town. Once we got older and life got busy, dates were an uncommon occurrence.

"Sounds awesome," Jake says. He turns to look at me

with a pointed look that says, *Let's do this sooner rather than later before you chase her off.* Turning sideways, he slides past Cat while saying, "Nice to meet you."

"You too," she murmurs and then turns back to me. "Sorry that took so long."

"No worries," I assure her. "You hit all the places you wanted to?"

A slightly uneasy look crosses her face, but she nods. "Yeah… now it's a wait and see."

"What happened?" I ask bluntly. I can tell *something* happened in the last two hours that has her a bit rattled.

"What do you mean?" she asks, those large, brown eyes blinking at me in faux innocence. I don't buy it for a second.

"Come on, Cat," I say softly as I step into her. She looks up at me with her lower lip tucked in between her teeth, and Christ… that's sexy, but I move past that thought. "You've already told me enough of your dirty laundry that you obviously trust me to some extent. Tell me what's got that beautiful face filled with trouble."

That lip pops free as she gives a resigned sigh, her eyes lowering briefly as she takes in a breath and then looks back up at me. "I ran into Kevin on the street."

For a moment, I don't comprehend who that is, but then it hits me hard and my protective instincts arise. Reaching out, I take her by the upper arm and pull her a little closer. "Did he hurt you? Are you okay?"

She nods quickly. "Yeah… I mean, he was a creep as always, and he threatened me, but I think—"

"He fucking threatened you?" I snarl, and she jerks in surprise over the deadly tone in my voice.

"Not to fuck with him," she says timidly. "To forget about the will."

"You two discussed the will?"

"Among other things," she says as she steps backward and pulls her arm slightly to get me to release it. I'm not sure if she's seeking distance because I just scared her or she doesn't appreciate the caveman mentality, but I let it go for now. Instead, I cross my arms over my chest.

"Okay, how about tell me everything start to finish?" I command.

"It was short… we literally bumped into each other on the street. Well, actually, I think he ran into me on purpose to get my attention, but no matter. Anyway, I told him wanted a copy of the signed will and he wasn't happy about that. But then he propositioned me—"

I curse under my breath and that stops Cat's dialogue. She looks at me in question, and I wave an impatient hand at her. "Sorry… go on."

"He said I could move back into the Jackson house, but I told him I wouldn't let his needle dick anywhere near me. Then he told me not to fuck with him, reiterated the Jackson house offer, which was essentially to be his side piece, or I could take five thousand in cash and go away."

"Did he touch you?" I ask through a locked jaw and gritted teeth.

She knows by the tone of my voice that her answer

could be perilous, so she stiffens her spine and simply says, "Yes. He grabbed me and pulled me into an embrace just before he threatened me. But we were on a public sidewalk and he wasn't about to make a scene. When I pulled away, he let me go."

Blazing fury fills me as I think about that asshole taking advantage of Cat's body because he believed his dad owned her, and now trying to do so again. The thought he could think to take what I was fast starting to think of as mine pissed me off. That he would even think about trying to touch her again makes me furious, especially when he essentially forced himself on her before. She may not have fought him, but he damn well knew she didn't want her husband gifting her to his son whenever he felt the need arise.

"Something good came of that meeting though," she says quickly.

My eyes focus in on her, leaving my other thoughts about murdering Kevin behind. "What's that?"

"I know damn well that will leaving me nothing wasn't executed. Otherwise, he would have never threatened me or tried to pay me off. He was wigged out when I told him I wanted to see the signed copy."

"So what… you think the original will is still in Vegas?" I ask.

"I do," she confirms. "And I'm leaving tomorrow to find out if I'm right."

"What?" I ask in stunned disbelief.

She's leaving?

Maybe not coming back?

"I'm going to drive back to Vegas," she says with a gleam in her eye. She gives a pat to her purse. "I was able to pawn all my jewelry, so I have some money to help me get by. I'm getting into that house and Samuel's office, and I'm not leaving until I know the truth."

"You pawned your jewelry?" I ask in disbelief. "Why would you do that?"

"Because I need the money, Rand," she says with a little irritation in her voice. "I can't just live off you, you know. And I can't sit back and let that dickhead take advantage of me anymore."

I hate she has to make these tough choices, and I can't stand the thought of her being so desperate she pawned her jewelry, but I can understand her reasoning to do just that. Cat's done with taking a backseat to her life. She let Samuel dictate everything and now that he's gone, her backbone is starting to shore up.

"You should have at least tried to sell the jewelry to some reputable jewelry stores," I grumble.

"I did try," she says. "No one was interested, so I had no choice."

"Well, at least if you're owed some of Samuel's estate, you can get it all back," I concede.

Cat gives an unladylike snort and shakes her head. "I don't want that jewelry. It means nothing to me. I don't want anything reminding me of that man and what he did to me."

I smile in understanding and take a step back into

her. Putting my arm around her waist, I pull her in and give her a kiss to her forehead. "Okay, I get it. You're ready to charge into battle and nothing's holding you back."

She responds by wrapping both arms around my waist, her purse squished in between us. Squeezing me, she says, "That's right."

"You coming back?" I ask, bracing myself for the possibility that tonight might be the last time I ever see Cat again.

"I'm… well, I'm not sure," she says quietly with her cheek still pressed to my chest, and that's a better answer than I actually expected. Vegas *is* Cat's hometown. She can get a job there quickly, I'd imagine. Nothing here to pull her back this way.

"So what time do *we* leave tomorrow?" I ask, throwing caution to the wind and then locking my arm tight as I expect her to pull away.

She jerks slightly but merely tilts her head back to look at me. "You want to go with me to Vegas?"

"Fuck if I'm going to let you ride off into battle alone," I tell her with a charming grin. "I'm a white knight after all. Besides, I don't trust Kevin or Richard. If for some reason they're there, I don't want you handling them on your own."

"But your work," she points out.

"Pish won't care," I tell her confidently. But he'll so care. He'll be pissed because he'll have to get his ass up now and open the shop. He works late hours, preferring to do his inking at night, but I can't worry about him right now. This is more important—although why, I'm not quite sure. But I've decided to follow my gut, and if I lose my job, so be it. I don't need the money as my earlier sponsorship deals have left me financially secure. "Now how about we go grab some lunch and we can plan what we need to do?"

"No... I can't let you do that. I can't disrupt your life like that. This may be nothing more than a fool's errand."

Fool's errand.

Funny.

Am I a fool for getting involved like this? Am I just entranced by what an amazing fuck she is or is there something more with this woman?

"I'm going and that's the end of it," I tell her firmly, but then I try to emphasize that this truly isn't a big deal. "And you're not disrupting me. I wouldn't have offered if it did, okay?"

"Rand... it's too much—"

"Cat... I'm going so just accept it. It'll be a fun road trip. We can buy sugary soda and sour gummy worms to eat on the way, sing bad 80's songs at the top of our lungs. It'll be awesome."

I then give her my best and most charming smile.

The indecision and doubt on her face melts away, and she gives me a girlish laugh with a pat to my chest before releasing me. "Okay, fine. You can go."

I take her hand, relieved that today will not be our

last day together. As I lead her out of the breakroom and through the shop, we wind our way through racks of ski apparel, which is the most direct route to the door. Jake's behind the counter and throws us a wave.

I call out, "Later, man."

"This weekend," he reminds me with a pointed look.

I just nod. I'll have to call him later and explain this weekend isn't going to work as, apparently, I'm going to Vegas with this woman and we may or may not be breaking into a house that may or may not belong to her. Also that I may or may not be developing some feelings for a woman who may or may not be in my life for much longer.

Chapter 12
Cat

Although it was a nipple puckering forty-two degrees when we left Jackson at six this morning, I don't regret my decision to wear a loose, flowered skirt for the drive. This time of year in Jackson is amazing. The days are sunny and warm, but the nights get downright cold. The valley floor is thick with wildflowers just starting to fade but the alpine ones are peaking, which paint the mountains with color.

But we're headed south now and when I checked last night, Las Vegas was holding steady with temperatures in the eighties, so I know my choice of apparel is sufficient. Besides, when I kicked off my taupe-colored ballet flats and put my bare feet up on the dashboard of Rand's Suburban, I know he appreciated the way the skirt slid along my thighs and revealed my skin. I know this because his head immediately snapped my way for a moment. As he studied me, or rather my legs, his lips tipped upward. He didn't say anything, but he did place a warm palm on my knee and slide his hand along the same path my skirt took. He did this pushing inward slightly so the stroke of his skin against mine was along the inside of my thigh.

Sliding his hand slowly along, he pushed my skirt even further up legs until his hand was resting just inches from my panty line.

My heart felt like it was about to explode. I knew if he moved his hand just slightly, he'd feel the dampness of my underwear. Yes, I was horny for this man. He fucked me well last night, but it was only once, and then he proclaimed we needed to get to sleep because we had to get up early for the long drive ahead of us. With a man like Rand, I'm finding once just isn't enough.

But he did nothing more than squeeze my inner thigh with his large, warm hand and then pulled it away so it could rest casually again on the steering wheel. It took a good twenty minutes for my heart rate to go back to normal and for me to think coherently.

The rest of the trip is proving to be uneventful, however. We've been driving for almost eight hours with short stops to refuel and grab something to eat. I've offered to drive, but Rand's refused. Not sure if it's a macho, alpha thing, a gentlemanly thing, or maybe he just doesn't trust me with his vehicle, but I'm not averse to riding shotgun as long as he's not too tired.

It was my decision to drive versus fly, which is what Rand wanted to do. He felt the ten and a half hours it would take us to get there was a waste of time, and he's right about that. But my money's tight and it was cheaper to drive. I netted around $3300 from pawning my jewelry, which sucks since it was probably worth ten times that amount. But beggars can't be choosers, and I have to ration my money carefully. This meant I could budget money for gas to Las Vegas, but not plane tickets. Rand offered to buy the air fare, but I shut that conversation down quickly. I also reminded him that I didn't need him to go with me and that I was driving, and it was the end of the discussion. Except he did somehow convince me to take his Suburban rather than my small Mercedes, which would be more comfortable for Rand, and I felt that was a good compromise.

I smile over that word.

Compromise.

I've never been able to compromise with anyone before. It was flat out impossible with my mother, and with Samuel… well, there was no question I'd ever cross him.

But Rand has proven that he'll listen to me and give my wishes consideration. While I could tell he wasn't happy at all for me to be spending any of my meager money on this trip—and yes, he was incensed I only got $3300 for my jewelry—he also recognized it was important for me to be in control of how this was done.

I keep a running chatter of dialogue going so if nothing else we are semi-entertained. While I've intermittently put my feet up on the dashboard and other times curled them up under me in the big expanse of the Suburban's front passenger seat, Rand has remained a gentleman the entire time. I've kept the conversation light because we have some serious shit waiting for us in Vegas, which would be taking our attention soon enough.

"What about your family?" I ask him because we've been talking about the friends he's made over the years doing competitive skiing and how they became like a family because he was traveling so much.

Rand smiles while maintaining his concentration on the road. We're on I-15 south with nothing but flat desert valley with shadowy mountains in the distances to look at. Sometimes, the monotony of the landscape can almost be hypnotizing, and not in a good way.

"My parents are still back in Vermont where I was raised in a little unincorporated village called Quechee. My dad is a full-time novelist—true crime stuff—and my mom teaches middle school."

"No siblings?" I ask.

"Nope. Only child, and as such, I may have been doted on," he says with a grin as he watches the interstate before him.

My heart squeezes in what I think might be a very brief moment of actual jealousy. In those few words... in that smile he has on his face right now, you can see the genuine love for his parents.

"Sounds nice," I murmur as I glance out the passenger window at the desert landscape whizzing by.

"It was," he says pointedly and with no shame for having an amazing family. I turn to look at him to find him staring at me, just briefly before turning his head back to the road. "My parents are great. They sacrificed a lot by sending me to Carrabassett Valley. Not only in the money it cost, but also because it essentially took their only son out of their lives. It was hard on them to let me pursue my dreams. We only got to see each other occasionally, mostly on holidays, even though my parents only lived about four hours away. But between school and training, there was never any free time."

"They sound amazing." *Go away, jealousy.* Rand is the type of man who deserves great parents.

"The most amazing," he agrees. "When I started competing on a serious level, my dad started to travel with me because his job can really be done from anywhere. This, of course, took him away from my mom. So it wasn't a conventional family relationship, but it worked for us."

"Why live so far away from them?" I ask with curiosity.

Rand shrugs. "I don't know. I love Vermont. Its beauty rivals Wyoming. Ton of skiing, my family's there. Maybe one day, I'll gravitate back that way, but for now, I have the freedom to travel and live where I want to. I guess until I figure out what I really want to do, I'm fine in Jackson."

I wonder what it would be like to have that type of freedom. And I'm not just talking about financial freedom, as that's clearly part of Rand's ability to do what he wants. But to actually just take your time and figure out what you want in life. To have no pressures or worries hanging over your head.

To not have to constantly weigh pros and cons of

every action you take, or to be forced into something just because your very livelihood would depend on it. Another flare of jealousy burns within my chest for a moment, but I squash it. Rand's earned his right to have that type of life.

I haven't.

Not yet, anyway.

"What about you?" he asks, and it takes a moment for the question to permeate. I turn slowly to look at him—that stunning profile of his—and I wish desperately he didn't have his sunglasses on because I know that low afternoon desert sun would make his green eyes shimmer like spun glass, and he'd become an even more romantic hero than I was already building him up to be in my mind.

"What about me?" I ask hesitantly, although I know deep in my gut what he's inquiring about.

"Your family. What's your story?"

My gaze slides back out to the desert as we fly down the interstate. I've never felt a special affinity to Nevada, even though I was born and raised here. Right now, the shades of brown from the hard-packed dirt to the creosote brush feels a lot like my life. Dull, cruddy, and depressing.

I contrast those colors to the palette of Rand's life and where he lives. Vivid greens, cool blues, and sparkling whites.

"I have no clue about my father," I say as I bring my hands to my lap where I twirl my fingers together. "My mom wouldn't tell me anything about him other than he was an asshole. She didn't even put his name on the birth certificate."

"What?" Rand says in astonishment. "She didn't think you'd have the right to judge that yourself?"

"Guess not," I say glumly. I never knew what to think of the man who gave his sperm to my mom.

"Do you believe her?" he asks. It surprises me he would question my mother's character without knowing anything about her. But I suspect Rand is making some preconceived judgments based on what little he knows about me, and let's face it... he wouldn't be wrong to question her motives. I question them all the time.

"Probably not," I admit softly, still staring at my hands. "My mother wasn't a very motherly figure. It's hard to trust what she says."

"More," Rand orders, not in an autocrat type of way, but rather in a way that says he's not going to let me chintz on the gory details of my life. He's demanding to know my demons, because as he said, how can he slay them if he doesn't know what they are? "I promise I won't judge."

My head snaps up and swings to stare at him with my mouth slightly open. "I know you'd never judge me," I say vehemently. Not once in the entire time I've known Rand—whether it was while he was watching me get fucked by other men or while he was absorbing the wretched details of my relationship with Samuel—has he ever looked upon me with anything other than intrigue, lust, curiosity, respect, and most recently, with care.

"Then lay it on me," he urges softly as he takes a moment to turn his attention from the road to give me an encouraging smile.

I take a deep breath, pull my bare feet up from the floorboard, and put them on the dash again. I notice briefly it's time for a pedicure as the polish is starting to chip, then just as quickly remember I can't afford those anymore. I actually pull my skirt to my knees and hold the edges there with my hands.

"I'll give you a classic example of my childhood," I say after exhaling. "One night, I woke up really hungry—I was eight, I think. I was hungry because Mom sent me to bed without dinner. She said it was because I was a pain in her ass, but I think it was because she hadn't bothered to go grocery shopping. But I knew there was probably something I could get out of the cupboards, so I got out of bed and made my way down the narrow hall of our little desert trailer to the kitchen. The kitchen actually stood between the hallway and the living room, and I saw my mom in there with a guy—just some random dude, which was par for the course. They were sitting on the couch, smoking a joint together. There was a pizza on the coffee table. Mostly eaten, but there were two slices left. She saw me and asked what I wanted. I told her I was hungry and asked for some of the pizza. She told me tough shit and to get back to bed. She said it was hers, and she'd need it for the munchies that were sure to come on after they finished smoking their joint. Then they both started laughing hysterically."

"Unbelievable," Rand growls from low in his throat.

"My mother is irresponsible and selfish. She had absolutely no business having a kid. She didn't even care when I left home at seventeen. I know this because I came back after a few days to get more of my stuff and she was there. Didn't even ask where I'd been. Only wanted to know if I had any money, because I'd been working since I was fifteen, to make sure I at least had food."

"Was she on hard drugs or something?" Rand asks in wonder, because that would be a good explanation for her lack of care.

"Nope. I mean, yeah, she smoked some pot every once in a while, but she held a steady job. Worked as a secretary at an auto body shop. She had friends. She'd see a lot of different men, but she didn't really parade them in front of me. I think she was embarrassed she had a kid."

"What a fucking bitch," Rand mutters.

"It's funny," I say in reflection. "I left home when I was seventeen, didn't finish high school, and ended up on the streets for a bit. And still... it was better than what I had. I never had someone care for me before, and that didn't change whether I was in her house or sleeping on some strange dude's couch in exchange for a blow job. The difference is that when I was with her, I still always expected she'd care a little. As much as she let me down, over and over again, I always still expected it of her. And that means I was repetitively hurt when I didn't get it. At least on the streets, I had no expectations that anyone could smash."

Rand's hand comes out, and he takes mine. He pulls it across the cab, making me lean a little toward him, and gives a soft kiss to the inside of my wrist. "Your mom sounds like a vile person. I'm thinking one of the best things you ever did was leaving when you were young. You're in a much better place now that you're rid of her."

I give a cold, bitter laugh, and shake my head. "I'm not rid of her. That woman became a leech on me once I married Samuel."

"Come again?" he asks with a head tilt.

"She saw in the society pages that I got married. Not two days later, she's at our house, asking for money."

"Did you give it to her?" Rand asks.

"Yeah, I did," I admit to him, but without shame.

"Why?"

"Because it made me feel superior to her. Is that bad?"

Rand gives a chuckle and squeezes my hand. "You were already superior to her, Cat. That money didn't prove anything."

I squeeze his hand back. "Maybe not, but I couldn't say no. She was my mom, after all."

"Amazing," Rand murmurs as we fly down the highway. "That you would still have any empathy for a woman who treated you so badly throughout your life. I think that makes you absolutely and perfectly amazing."

"Or stupid," I mutter, and Rand laughs.

"Maybe a little foolish, but never stupid," he offers.

"I'll take that," I tell him with a grin. "Of course, she called the minute she heard Samuel had died. I'm sure she saw that in the paper. I figured I'd be hearing something from her, asking about my inheritance, and that's exactly why she called. You'd be proud. I put her off and told her I didn't have time to deal with her. Ironic it wasn't but a week later and I was all but homeless. Good thing she's not asking for money now, huh?"

"Yeah, well, you better not give her one dime of that money you got for your jewelry. You earned that the hardest of ways and that's for your future, not hers."

"Agreed," I say as I see a looming sign growing closer.

Las Vegas – 56 Miles.

Almost there.

And then I'll hopefully find out what my future really holds.

Chapter 13

Rand

"BIG STEP UP from my little trailer in the desert, huh?" Cat says on a low whisper as we stand before the front portico of one of the biggest houses I've ever seen in my life.

The house Cat shared with Samuel is monstrous. She had told me it was eleven-thousand square feet. To be that big, it comes in three chunks with a main center section and two wings that flank at a slight angle inward. Done in taupe stucco, brown brick, and red tile, it fits into the desert scenery well.

It's nine AM. We decided that if we were going to enter the house, we were going to do it as if she belonged there. Without really knowing what Samuel's will truly says, it's more than plausible that Cat has every right to be here. We thought it would look far less suspicious if done in the bright light of day.

Thus, we got to the hotel yesterday afternoon, a lower class, budget hotel Cat chose that sat on the outskirts of Vegas. Since she was insisting on paying, I had to let her choose. Rest assured, if it was in my hands, we'd be at the Bellagio, but I'm honoring her need to do some of this on her own. It's important to her pride.

"Ready to do this?" I ask as we stand side by side on the bottom step. Before us stands double doors made of solid wood, and either her key will work or it won't. Same for the security code.

"Ready as I'll ever be," she says firmly, and then reaches out with her hand to take mine. It feels natural. It makes me remember how much I missed being part of a unit.

Together, we walk up the steps.

Cat told me on the way here that Samuel bought this house about twenty years ago after his first wife died. Because she was the love of his life, he couldn't bear to stay in the family home where they raised their two sons. Since he moved in, Cat had been his fourth wife, the other two before her outliving their usefulness after they reached the age of twenty-eight. Cat told me she wondered if Samuel did to them what he did to her.

I didn't offer an opinion because I think we both know he did.

When we reach the front door, Cat releases her hold on me and digs into her purse slung crossways over her chest and resting at her hip. She pulls out a set of keys, flips through them, and chooses a gold-colored one that doesn't look much different from the others.

With a deep breath, she reaches out and slides the key in. Twisting her wrist, she lets out a huge sigh of relief when the lock turns. She looks at me, her lips peeling into a wide grin and her eyes sparkling with excitement. I smile back at her, relieved of course that her key still works, but knowing deep down that it doesn't mean shit. She may have still been cut out of Samuel's will, but the locks just haven't been changed yet.

Cat pushes the door open, and we both step into a cavernous foyer aglow with natural light from the huge, arched window above the door. A beep from the security panel beside the door catches my attention, and I watch as Cat puts in the code. It shuts the alarm off, and we both let out an audible sigh of relief.

The house is sparsely decorated—minimalistic. It would be easy to say that was so because Samuel was a bachelor for a long time and didn't care what his house looked like, but I'm going to guess it's because Samuel didn't get much pleasure out of life and didn't care what his house looked like. From what I know about the asshole, he derived pleasure from watching his wife be degraded, so I doubt fancy artwork and priceless knick-knacks would do much for him.

"Come on. His office is this way," Cat whispers, reaching back for my hand to pull me toward the stairs.

I immediately place my palm against hers, but ask, "Why are you whispering?"

"I don't know," she rasps back with a giggle. "I guess because I'm not sure if I'm actually breaking and entering, or not."

"Let's assume not and talk in our normal voices," I prod her. Although she's cute as fuck doing that, it's also setting me on edge a bit, making me feel like we shouldn't be here, and I'd rather take the optimistic route that we are definitely allowed.

Cat had assured me there was no full-time staff who lived in the house. While Samuel employed a chef, housekeeper, and an attendant for his personal needs, none of those employees lived in residence. As far as we knew, Kevin was still back in Jackson, probably never suspecting Cat would come here to search the house. Richard was probably oblivious to everything but we didn't know that for sure. Cat decided not to reach out to him, mainly because she figured he wasn't going to help her. He may not have any clue what Kevin was doing from Jackson, but then again, he might have full knowledge. We'd never know, so why alert him any further that Cat was questioning the validity of the will?

Now, it certainly can't be helped she let Kevin know she was questioning it, but we're sort of banking on his ego and his complete underestimation of Cat to keep him happily in the dark. So if we're lucky, he's probably on a fishing trip right now on the Snake River. Cat says that's one of the reason's he goes to Jackson, and if there's a God above, maybe he'll fall out of the fucking boat and drown.

Cat leads me up a curved staircase done in deep mahogany to a large second-floor landing. Hallways branch left and right… entryways into the wings of the house.

"My room was that way." She points to the right, and then back to the left. "Samuel's that way."

I find it interesting she referenced her room in the past tense. Not sure if that's because she doesn't believe this house is hers or that she doesn't intend to come back here regardless. I'll ask her about that later, but for now, I follow her straight ahead from the landing to a set of double doors that she pushes open to a huge office.

It's what I would expect of an egomaniac, billionaire hotelier. Expensively paneled walls, luxurious silk rugs, ornately carved desk, and the faint musk of cigars in the air.

"Samuel spent a lot of time in here," Cat murmurs in a grateful tone as she drops my hand and walks in. Glad he spent time in here and not bothering her, I'm sure.

She heads straight for his desk and pulls back the massive leather chair on wheels so she can sit down in it. Turning to a side drawer, she pulls it open and starts rifling through. I walk up to her and stand behind the chair to the side, watching her progress. She pulls out a thick pack of stapled papers and hands them to me, saying, "Our pre-nup. The will trumps anything in the pre-nup as best I can remember, but we should take pictures of this as well."

Before we came in here, we agreed we wouldn't take any documents with us. Our main goal was to verify if the will cutting Cat out existed, and to look at the current will if we could find it. Because there's not a copier in Samuel's office, we'll have to take a picture of each page with her iPhone.

I hold the pre-nup without looking at it. I don't care

what deal Cat made with her devil of a husband. I only care about her not getting screwed over right now.

"Bingo," she shouts with glee and pulls out another thick document. She lays it on the desk, and I step in closer to look at it over her shoulder. It's titled "Revocable Trust Agreement and Pour-Over Will".

"Quite a fancy name for a will," I mutter.

She nods. "Trust agreement... will... I'm assuming they're just different names for the same thing; how to distribute his estate."

Cat starts to skim through it, her finger sliding down the page as she scans and flips pages.

"Kevin is the trustee, but I knew that. Just means he'll administer the estate. Blah, blah, blah, blah," she says as she breezes past paragraphs entitled *Debts & Expenses* and *Administrative Powers of Fiduciaries*. My eyes actually start to cross when her finger stops and she says, "This is the paragraph."

I lean over closer and see the word *Residuary*. Cat reads out loud, "Upon my death, I direct my trustee to transfer five-million dollars to my wife, Catherine Lyons Vaughn. Pursuant to our pre-nuptial agreement, she will have no ownership rights or interests in any of my real property at the time of my death, with the exception of the house in Jackson, Wyoming. I further direct my trustee to ensure transfer of title and deed of said property to my wife."

"Did you know that was in his will?" I ask her.

She nods. "Not the exact details, but he told me he

would leave me with enough money to sustain me as well as a house. I didn't know it would be the Jackson house. I suppose that was his way of reminding me in death how much he loved taking me there."

I wince at the bitterness in her voice. There's no way she'd ever want to stay in a place that held such terrible memories for her.

Cat flips quickly through the rest of the document to the very end, where I can see the original ink of Samuel's signature as well as a notary public seal.

"He signed this two weeks after we were married," she says, still looking at the document.

"We need to go through the rest of his stuff," I tell her as I squat down at the drawer that's still open and start rifling through the contents. "If there's another will or trust agreement or whatever the fuck you call it dated after that one, you're screwed."

"But if there's not, Kevin's screwed," she says, and my head turns toward her because of the icy tone in her voice. She narrows her eyes at me and in a voice bristling with anger, she says, "That asshole kicked me out over five million dollars and a house? When Samuel's estate is worth billions? What a fucking douche bag."

I give her a wry smile. "I think it was more about controlling you than the money. The fact he wanted you to stay at the house tells me all I need to know. He was banking on you crawling to him for help."

"Bet he was stunned I didn't," she says quietly.

Nodding in agreement, I turn back to the drawer,

eager to get this over with and get the hell out. I start flipping through hanging folders containing tax returns, bank statements, and deeds of trust. Folder after folder of the story of Samuel Vaughn's wealthy life.

"Thank you, Rand," Cat murmurs. It's so soft I barely hear it, yet my entire body feels like it's been punched by the depth of emotion in her words. My head rises and turns to her as she sits in the massive leather chair that swallows her up. "If you hadn't have taken me in, I might have gone to Kevin for help."

"No way," I say with a soft smile. I don't reach out and touch her like I want to, because I don't want to give any credence to her suspicion of what she might have done. I know Cat. She's stronger than that and would have never given Kevin the ability to control her. So I stay reserved so she knows it's a ludicrous thought. "The Cat Lyons I know wouldn't have ever done that. You would have figured another way. Hell, you did figure another way. You sold your jewelry and you came to Vegas to find the truth. So fuck you very much, Kevin Vaughn. This woman doesn't need you."

Her beautiful, brown eyes crinkle and she can't help the deep laugh that erupts. "Yeah. Fuck you very much, Kevin Vaughn."

Now I laugh with her and totally can't resist reaching out to wrap my hand around her neck, pulling her forward. I kiss her hard and knock the laugh right out of both of us. When I pull back slightly, I nip at her lip and ask, "Would it be bad form for us to fuck in this house?"

She snickers. "I don't think I could get wet for you in this house."

"Then I insist when we leave here, we head over to the Bellagio. My treat. We're getting a nice suite with a view over the lake, and I'm going to fuck you on a bed stuffed with feathered down and covered in silk."

She sighs and her eyes are closed with a dreamy expression on her face when I pull all the way back. That look… right there. I want her to have that on her face all the time. Regardless of where this creature lands in life, be it here or back in Jackson, I want this woman to walk through the rest of her days with that look on her face.

I STEP UP behind Cat as she looks out the window at the Bellagio lake below us. It's timed water show set to music is quiet right now, and besides, it's better to see that stuff at night. Of course, she's from Vegas so she's probably seen it a hundred times before. But I'm glad we're staying here. It's a good way to celebrate.

Celebrate that we didn't get arrested.

Celebrate we found the signed trust agreement leaving her money and the house.

Celebrate we didn't find the one that supposedly cut Cat out.

Of course, it didn't mean there wasn't one, but it wasn't in Samuel's house. We had to figure out our next move, but we could do that later, and besides… I want Bridger's input on that. He always has a cool head and a chess-like mind, and this is all about maneuvering into the right spot at the right time.

My hands go to Cat's waist, and I press the front of my body against the back of hers. She didn't give me any argument about coming to the Bellagio for the night and letting me pay.

That's progress.

Her head falls back and my chin drops to rest on her shoulder. "You know, I think feathers and silk are overrated. I'm perfectly fine just fucking you up against this window right now."

Many women would laugh, blush, and coyly banter with me.

But not Cat.

Taking one of my hands, she drags it across her stomach and pushes it down in between her legs. She chose to wear a pair of camel-colored pants with wide legs and matching heels to our scouting mission at her house. Her ivory-colored blouse and pearls made her look every inch the rich wife, and she quipped that if she were going to get arrested, she was going to look damn good doing it.

I agreed. She looked damn good, but now I'm bemoaning the fact she's not wearing her simple floral skirt she had on yesterday for the ride. It would make things so much easier.

Still, I remain undaunted and because her hand insistently pushes mine right to where she wants me, I reward her with a hard press of my palm against the bottom of her zipper. I estimate her clit is right about there and I know I'm on the money when she moans and tilts her hips into me.

"How about we get these pants off you?" I ask her, but I don't wait for permission. Instead, I bring both hands to her button, where I easily open it and pull the zipper down. I push the material, making sure to grab her panties with my fingers on the way down and squat right alongside. Pulling past the smooth, silky skin of her thighs until it's pooled around her feet, which are still encased in four-inch heels.

"How far can you spread your legs?" I ask her.

She turns her head over her shoulder, eyes at half mast, and tries to kick one leg out, but the constraint from her pants doesn't give. My eyes slide to her bare ass and just a peek of her pussy below, and I know that's not enough for what I want to do.

"Lift your leg," I tell her, tapping her left calf. She lifts that one up, so I can pull the material of her pants and underwear free. Before setting her foot back to the ground, I kiss the inside of her thigh.

I don't worry about the other leg, because now she's free enough to spread wide. Cat doesn't even wait for my command but pushes her left leg out about a foot. Now her pussy opens up to me. I surge upward, bringing my hands to her ass and peeling her cheeks apart so I can have better access. Tilting my head back, I bring my mouth to her and slide my tongue in as deep as it will reach.

"Oh, God... Rand," Cat moans.

She's wet and tastes amazing. My tongue is drenched with her need, and while my thoughts were to get her off with my mouth, my cock is so painfully hard that I want to give it relief. So I pull my mouth free of her and stand up, my hands working at my belt, button, and zipper. Cat's ready for me as she bends forward, placing her hands against the window glass and tilting her ass outward.

"That's a good girl," I murmur as I pull my cock out.

Step right up to her.

Dip my legs.

Slide my way home.

"Mmmmmm," I groan through tightly closed lips and gritted teeth. Because fuck, that feels good.

She responds with a low moan of her own, rotating her hips... trying to draw me in deeper, but that's impossible. I'm rooted.

"Hard or slow fucking?" I ask her because I want Cat to start realizing she has choices. I might take control most times and lead the way, but I want her to know she has the right to choose otherwise.

The right to ask for something she wants.

"Slow," she whispers, and I have to smile. Usually when we go at it, it's as if we're in overdrive, both racing as fast as we can to the climax because we know we can do it all over again. But yeah, she's right. I think, for right now, we go slowly. We have all day and night, as we're not leaving until tomorrow morning to head back to Jackson.

So I fuck her very slow and while at times it's almost torturous to hold back on blowing, in the end, it's a fucking stellar orgasm that actually drops both of us to our knees when we come together.

Chapter 14
Cat

I PUT IN my earrings, the only pair I kept that are sedate gold hoops, and check my watch—which I also kept. I kept it because I'm constantly checking the time and will go nuts without it, but also so I could have something else to pawn should I need to down the road.

Walking back out to the kitchen of Rand's apartment, I look down once again at the note he left me when he jetted out early again before I even woke up.

Cat,

Stuff to do but make sure you're dressed casual and ready to go by noon.

Rand

Short, to the point, and totally not telling me a damn thing. But it's the lunch hour and I'm guessing maybe he's taking me out to lunch. Maybe like a date?

Which is a foreign concept for the most part. I mean... I went out on dates with Samuel. They were formal affairs where he'd send a stylist to me, who would dress and polish me up. Then a driver would pick me up at my crummy little apartment I shared with two other strippers. They'd jokingly say, "Have fun, Vivienne" as I walked out the door, an homage to *Pretty Woman*.

Samuel would then take me to a posh restaurant I couldn't even afford to work in and we'd make polite small talk while we ate.

So not sure that's really a date.

Not the type that a twenty-four-year-old woman should have.

Maybe we'll go to The Million Dollar Cowboy Bar for burgers, which is totally a tourist trap, but I'm not really a local, am I? Perhaps a stroll around town square afterward? That sounds fun—like a real date should.

The knocking on the door surprises me, and I flip my watch to look at it again. Noon on the dot, but that can't be Rand as he'd just walk right in.

I go to the door, put my eye to the peephole, and see two women standing there. Young, roughly my age. One a brunette, the other a blonde. I open the door and peer out at them. "Can I help you?"

"Cat, right?" the brunette says, sticking her hand out and not even waiting for mine to meet hers. She takes it and gives a quick handshake. "I'm Callie Hayes… Woolf Jennings' girlfriend."

I immediately turn beet red and almost start to hyperventilate. Woolf Jennings' girlfriend is shaking my hand? What the fuck?

I mean, seriously, what the fuck? I had sex with her boyfriend a few times at The Silo back in the day.

I furiously try to scrub some of those images from my

head as I desperately try to think of what to say, but then she's dropping my hand and the blonde—who looks vaguely familiar—steps forward, taking it. "I'm Sloane Preston. I think you know my boyfriend, Cain Bonham."

A strangled sound gurgles up from my throat, and I go dizzy. I think I might vomit for a moment, as I can only think these women are here to beat the shit out of me. I've been with both of their men, on more than one occasion, and in a nastier way than I'm betting these two beautiful women have been, and I just know I'm done for.

The blonde drops my hand, tilts her head to the side, and asks, "Are you okay? You look a little pale?"

"Um... I... um..." I stutter as I take a step back from them. My gaze flicks back and forth between the women, wondering if they have weapons and why in the hell I didn't slam the door in their faces.

The brunette—what was her name... Callie?—gives a nudge to the other with a knowing look on her face and takes a tentative step toward me through the doorway. "She thinks we're here to bust her chops about The Silo."

She says this to her friend, but her eyes are on me. I take another step backward.

"Well, reassure her we're not," the blonde—Sloane, I think—urges her.

"I'm here to offer you a job," Callie says, and I halt my backward momentum.

"Excuse me?" I ask, stunned at this weird turn of events.

"Bridger told Woolf you were looking for a job. Woolf told me. I happen to be looking for someone to help with my dad's campaign—"

"—he's running for governor," Sloane pipes in.

"—that's right. Things are starting to ramp up and I need help," Callie concludes.

Okay, now this is just too weird for me to comprehend. With all the peculiarity and stress in my life, I seriously cannot digest what these women are doing.

"Let me get this straight," I ask with hands on my hips and eyes slightly narrowed at Callie. I decide not to hold any punches. "You want to offer me a job on your father's political campaign?"

"That's right," she says with a bright smile. "I mean… you can do some basic typing, right. Address envelopes? Stick signs in yards? It's pretty basic, but it's a full-time position."

I ignore the requirements for the job as I'm more than qualified and decide to really address the elephant in the room. "I've been with both your men at The Silo. Why are you helping me? Why in the hell are you even here shaking my hand?"

My voice gets a little hysterical at the end, and Callie's eyes soften. She ignores the fact I haven't invited her in and takes two more steps toward me. Her hands come to my shoulders and she squeezes them. "Cat… I don't know you, but Bridger and Woolf both assure me that you are a very nice person. Sloane and I know all about The Silo and what our men did there before we came along. And that's where I want you to focus... you were with them *before* Sloane and I got involved, and we have no right to judge or be mad at something they did before we fell in love. So if we don't have a problem with it, I don't think you should."

I blink at her stupidly because although her words make sense, I know just enough about women to know they are jealous creatures. I also know no women who would want to be friends or co-workers with someone who had very kinky sex with their significant other.

"She doesn't believe you," Sloane says as she leans a shoulder against the doorjamb. "Figures."

"Well, we don't have time to convince you. I'm starved. We promised Rand we'd take you to lunch and discuss the job, so let's go," Callie says in exasperation and takes my elbow.

I'm still sort of frozen from the shock of all this, but my feet willingly move when she pulls me toward the door.

"Rand did tell you we'd be by, right?"

I shake my head, no words coming out. As I grab my purse on the bench in the mudroom as an afterthought, Sloane mutters, "Typical man. Forgetting the important things. Don't worry... we'll have a great time at lunch. Margaritas at The Merry Piglet make everything better."

Now that is something that's finally clicking with me. I could use a margarita.

Or five.

★

"So then everything spills out of my purse," Sloane says with a gasping laugh, "and a butt plug rolls out. Right to the foot of the waiter. He picks it up and just hands it to me with a red face. And Cain was dying laughing."

Callie wheezes she's laughing so hard, slapping at the table and nearly knocking over her third margarita. I look back and forth between these two women as I have been most of lunch… with my mouth hanging open.

Sloane looks up at me with tear-filled eyes and smirks. "Come on, Cat. That's funny, right?"

"She's still in shock," Callie affirms with eyes just as wet from laughter.

"Maybe we broke her," Sloane says thoughtfully, wiping a finger under her eye to push away the moisture. "Rand's going to be pissed."

I take another healthy slurp of my margarita, also my third, and mutter with a smile, "It's funny."

Then I take another slurp.

"So what's your take on anal?" Sloane asks me, and I start choking. "Like or dislike? Callie still hasn't worked up enough courage to take it all the way, but I love it with Cain."

"I… I…" I stutter as both of them look at me with mischievous faces. Eyes shining and happy, and truly, truly not in the least offended by the presence of a woman such as me. I mean, they seriously look like they're enjoying this company and discussion.

Almost like I'd imagine real girlfriends do.

Resolution strengthens my spine. I decide to accept the fact that they seem to like me and are not put out by my past relationships with their boyfriends. I decide to own it.

"Yeah... I like anal," I say confidently with my chin tilted up. "If it's done right. And let me tell you, Rand does it right."

Callie puts her chin in the palm of her hand and gives a dreamy sigh. "Maybe one day."

"Girl," Sloane drawls in exaggerated fashion. "You and I can compare notes later when Saint Callie isn't around."

"Hey," she exclaims, sitting up straight and glaring at Sloane. "I am not a saint. I'll have you know I've done a three-way with Woolf and Bridger."

My mouth falls back open again. I decide to fill it with more margarita.

"Please," Sloane scoffs and waves a dismissive hand at her. "Who hasn't had Bridger in a multiple before?"

My head snaps toward Sloane. I suck deeper on the straw until the last liquid is pulled up and the ice rattles in loneliness at the bottom of the glass.

"You've had Bridger before, right?" Sloane asks with a naughty sparkle in her eye.

"I would plead the fifth," I say resolutely, "but I feel like you two would berate it out of me. So yes... I've had

Bridger before."

"He's yummy," Sloane says.

"Totally," Callie agrees.

"And your dad's the governor?" I ask with comedic suspicion and a cocked eyebrow at her. "Because it's just so hard to believe with some of the things coming out of your mouth."

"It's true," she says solemnly, holding up her hand and placing the other over her heart. "Swear it."

"And you really want me to work for you?" I ask, not with any more doubt, but more in awe because I can't understand why this opportunity is being given to me. I did nothing to deserve it.

"I really do," she says with a genuine smile. "We help friends around here. You're Bridger and Woolf's friend, and so you are now my friend."

"And mine," Sloane chimes in.

Callie leans forward, pushes her margarita glass to the side, and says, "So I'm offering you the job and I think you should say, 'Thank you, Callie, I accept.'"

"Thank you, Callie," I say with a nod of my head in gratitude. "I accept."

Because I'd be an idiot not to.

"Excellent," she says, beaming me a huge grin, and then she's shouting across the restaurant. "Livvy, another round of margaritas."

"Oh my God," Sloane mutters. "I'm going to be so drunk. Cain's going to need to come get me."

"Yeah, I think our workday got shot to shit," Callie

agrees. "Good thing I'm your boss."

My head snaps to Sloane. "You're working the campaign too?"

"Yup," she says, sucking down the last of her third margarita. "Only until I can find something better suited."

Callie kicks Sloane under the table. I know this because the table rattles and Sloane yelps before glaring at Callie. "Ow. That hurt."

"Good, because that was a strike to my heart that you'd even imply you'd work somewhere else," Callie says seriously.

Sloane rolls her eyes and throws a thumb in Callie's direction. "I'm a journalist by nature, so I'm gladly helping Callie out until I can do something more suited to my degree."

"Gotcha," I say in understanding.

"So, listen," Callie says in a low, secretive voice as she leans forward. Sloane does the same, apparently eager for gossip. "I don't know any details, but Woolf shared with us that things with your husband were really bad. And he said that you'd been kicked out of your house, left with no money after he died, and that Rand was helping you out."

Sloane nods seriously in agreement. "What she's trying to say is, now in addition to Rand, you got two new peeps who will have your back until you can get on your feet."

"And you don't have to tell us any details, but if you

do need to talk, especially to another woman, you only have to call," Callie adds on.

Before I can respond, the waitress returns with a tray loaded with three margaritas and another basket of chips and salsa. We murmur thanks and when she leaves, Sloane reaches out to take a chip. How she can even fit any more food in her stomach is beyond me. She already killed a large chimichanga.

I take a moment to let not only what they just said to sink in, but everything that's happened in the last seven days. I've had apparently five people step up and go to bat for me, and they hardly know me at all. It provokes strange feelings within me because I've never even had those closest to me—mother or husband namely—care for me like this.

For the first time, I think I start to have a small glimmer of hope that there are good people in the world, and I don't just have to push my way through life in survival mode. I might actually be able to have fulfillment and happiness.

"I didn't marry for love," I say suddenly, looking up from my glass to first Callie's eyes and then Sloane's. "I'd run away from home at seventeen, spent time on the streets, and then eventually became a stripper. Marrying Samuel was my way out of destitution and back-alley blow jobs so I could afford to eat."

Callie and Sloane both wince, but their eye contact never wavers. Their gazes don't hold a speck of judgment but are full of empathy.

"He abused me," I continue on, and Sloane's hand shoots across the table to cover mine. She gives it a squeeze. "Not physically himself, but to make long, sordid stories short, he farmed me out to friends and business contacts. Even his son."

"Fucking douche-bag, evil asshole," Sloane growls, and Callie's eyes get moist again.

"He made me go to The Silo, and he made sure I became known as the woman who loved getting gang banged because that's what he got off on," I say, realizing I don't have any bitterness about it right now. It is what it is, and for whatever reasons these opportunities are being afforded to me, they landed me in a place with good people that I wouldn't have met but for The Silo.

"And if you're wondering why I just didn't leave," I continue, playing with my straw, "I berate myself over and over about my stupidity in not. But if I'm going to be honest with my new friends, I didn't leave because even though he did those things to me, my life was still better than what it was before. I wasn't handed out often, and I'll even admit, a lot of things that happened at The Silo I enjoyed to some extent. I don't know what type of woman that makes me... to let her husband treat her that way... which is why I still find it a bit hard to accept you want to be my friends."

"Cat," Callie murmurs. "We all make choices in our life that we are held accountable for later. I can't see that the choice you made to stay does anything more than label you a survivor. It's just that simple."

"And I'll add on to that," Sloane says quietly. "There's absolutely nothing wrong with liking your time at The Silo. Callie and I have both experienced it, and we love the freedom it provides. As women, we need to revel in our sexuality and accept that we are allowed to have desires and fantasies we want to be fulfilled. The Silo gives that to us. Find the right man on top of that—who understands and values your inner kinkiness—and well, hell… that's like the best sex ever."

"Yeah," Callie reiterates. "Don't ever feel ashamed about The Silo and what you've done there. Even with Woolf and Cain. Granted… we don't need details, but it's nothing that changes our opinion about you."

"So true," Sloane agrees.

My heart swells and grows warm. It settles in deep and a rush of joy pulses within me. These women… two amazing, non-judgmental, caring and confident women… actually seem to like me.

Accept me.

Want to help me.

Maybe my time at The Silo was nothing more than fate or pre-destiny. Maybe I had to meet and marry Samuel, have him debase me and ultimately lead me to The Silo, so that I could be in this very place at this very moment.

My thoughts turn to Rand, who has been equally as non-judgmental and caring as Callie and Sloane.

Actually more so.

I think about what Sloane just said… find a man

who understands and values my inner kinkiness.

That's totally Rand.

From the very start.

An idea strikes and it might even be fueled by the margaritas, but I know by the time I'm ready to act on said idea, I'll be sober. Reaching into my purse, I say, "I need to send a quick text to Rand."

"Oooohhhh," Sloane gloats with a knowing look in her eyes. "You're sexting him, aren't you?"

"Well, yeah," I admit with a sheepish smile as my fingers fumble across the keys. "Kinda, sort of."

Chapter 15
Rand

I'M NOT SURE I've ever had a day drag by more slowly than today has. It's been a long day. Agonizing actually.

It started off with me meeting Bridger to give him the trust agreement we took pictures of and that I had printed out early this morning. I left the copy with him and asked him to look it over, but I talked to him about what route we should take in the meantime.

On the way back to Jackson from Vegas, Cat agreed to let me talk to Bridger first. She wanted to call Kevin right then and there to confront him, but I wanted to take a bit of a more cautious approach. It might be better to hit up an attorney first for a legal opinion, but I knew Bridger always had great advice, so I figured we should wait it out just a day so I could talk to him.

I had already set up Callie and Sloane to take Cat out to lunch today. Woolf had texted me late Monday night after we got back to Jackson and Cat was already asleep, telling me he'd talked to Callie and she was going to ask Cat to work for her on the campaign. This was excellent news and was a job about as far away from The Silo as I could get her. Ironic since not but a few weeks ago, Sloane was digging around as an undercover reporter trying to connect the governor to the sex club.

So while Cat's apparently eating burritos, I'm spending a tremendously slow day at Westward Ink, watching the clock tick down to quitting time so I can get home to Cat.

And yeah... weird that I'm thinking words like "home" and "Cat" almost synonymously, but I can't fucking help it. The more I become embroiled in her affairs, the more intrigued I become by her. The more she starts to blossom and starts to become the confident, take-control woman I know her to be deep inside, the more attracted I become to her. The more I get to know about her and the things she's overcome so far, the more I become attached to her. The more she milks my cock, the more I want her to milk it.

Hard and often.

Haven't even thought about The Silo once since she and I talked about it five nights ago.

My phone dings with a text and I see it's from Cat. Callie said they were going to The Merry Piglets, which always means margaritas with lunch.

It's cute and coy, and I never thought I'd use those words to describe Cat. *Sloane and Callie think I should own my inner kinkiness. And I'm kinda drunk.*

I'm sitting at the front counter, previously bored out of my mind but now fully alert with interest. I immediately write back, *I think you should own it too. And you're a cute drunk.*

It takes a few moments for her to text me back, and I wonder what an inebriated Cat really looks like. Never have I seen her intoxicated. She never once had an alcoholic drink at The Silo, and I've never seen her look to be high or out of control. I bet she's fun though.

Want to know something that really turned me on at The Silo?

And there it is… the first time I've thought about The Silo in five long days. It's a record for sure.

My fingers fly across my phone. *Yes, I do.*

Her reply comes back much faster than the priors, and I go ahead and take that to mean she's eager to let me know her dirty thoughts. This I can get on board with because, for the most part, Cat's sort of taken a backseat in bed and let me control how things go. I'd like to see her start making some demands of her own so I can show her there's someone who really wants to give her that.

I get achingly hard when I read her reply. *Watching you and Logan together.*

My head spins. She liked watching Logan and me together? I can't believe she'd even remember something like that because in The Silo, that stuff's pretty normal.

My cock starts to throb realizing she enjoyed watching *me*.

Sure, with another guy, but that doesn't bother me. What Logan and I do together is hot. We don't mess around with each other without a girl involved, as neither of us is gay. Not even sure we're bisexual.

Maybe.

Who knows?

But we both have no qualms with some guy-on-guy action when we're in the heat of things. Always in a multiples or an orgy-type situation. He's fucked me and I've fucked him, although he prefers to top. I like both.

We've both sucked each other's cock, and let me tell you… he's damn good. Not as good as Cat, but damn near close.

It's not been that long since we did a fantasy together, and a smile comes to my face as I remember that was a four-on-one we did with Bridger, Cain, and Sloane. Logan and I didn't have sex that time, as it was all about Sloane's pleasure, but we did a lot of touching while in the process, and that's just as nice.

I text her back without giving any deep thought to what I'm getting ready to offer. *Want a repeat?*

I hold my breath for what seems like an agonizingly long time, until I get back two words guaranteed to make the rest of this day go slower. *I do.*

We'll be at the apartment by 6:30. Be naked and ready. And sober. I want you fully alert.

After I send that text, I dial Logan's number. He'll be game. I know he'll be well done with work for the day, cleaned up, and ready to go by 6:30 PM. Which is technically a ridiculously early time to get your sexy party on, but fuck if I'm going to wait.

LOGAN'S WAITING AT the top of the stairs that lead up to my apartment, leaning back against the door with one booted foot propped against it, another long leg stretched out. With his arms folded casually across his chest and a bland look on his face, you'd have no idea looking at him that he was vibrating with sexual need right now.

Logan is one of the most sexual creatures I've ever known. Before I knew the real deal about Cat, I would have put them in the same category, almost as if they needed sex to survive. I hang out at The Silo a lot, but Logan is there every single night, for hours at a time. I'm not sure there's a patron there who has as much sex as he does, and it never seems to get old for him.

Maybe he's a sex addict now that I think about it, but whatever. Not my place to judge.

"Can't say I hated getting your call this afternoon," he says with a slow smile as he pushes off the door. "A private night with you and Catherine... fantasy come true."

I smile but hold it for only a moment before I level him with a serious look. "Listen... Cat's in a bit of a rough place. A lot of that stuff at The Silo she did... that was her husband making her do those things."

"What?" Logan asks with his eyebrows drawing inward.

I nod. "But that's not the rough place. Plenty about The Silo she came to like... including apparently watching you and me together... but it's other stuff. She got kicked out of her house, credit cards shut off, and told she was cut out of inheriting anything. Was basically fucking living in her car."

Logan scrubs a hand over his chin, worry in his eyes. He nods at me, and I continue. "She's been staying here for the last week, and well… something's happening between us. I'm not quite sure what it is, but it's something."

"So why am I here?" Logan asks.

"Because despite all that shit she's been through, Cat still has her dirty side. She's apparently owning it. This is by her request tonight."

"What are the boundaries?" he asks, and I know why he's going there. I just told him that something was happening between Cat and me, and he's being respectful of that. Logan and I have both been with committed couples before, and you usually have a talk about what lines can and can't be crossed. Sometimes just an intimate kiss is something a person might not want you to do to their monogamous partner, even if he's okay with you sticking your cock in his wife's pussy. It's complicated at times, but it's best to lay it out.

"Only boundaries are the one's she sets," I say, totally ignoring the slight rumbling of unease over the fact that Cat might very well want to fuck Logan tonight. But if that's what she wants, I'm going to make sure she gets it. "This is all about her fantasy tonight. We'll let her direct."

Logan reaches down, readjusts himself and mutters,

"Let's get started then. I've been sporting this hard-on all afternoon since I took your call."

I turn toward my door and make short work of unlocking it because I've been in the same situation all afternoon too. The apartment is quiet and dark with only a faint spilling of light coming out from my bedroom into the living room.

"Give me just a minute, okay?" I murmur to Logan as he stops by my couch.

"Sure thing."

I walk into the bedroom, immediately assaulted by the vision of Cat exactly how I told her to be.

Naked and in bed.

She's lying on her side, head propped up on her hand and the other laying gracefully along her body. One leg straight, the other slightly bent. It's sexy and provocative and my eyes immediately fall to her breasts, then slide down to check out the rest of her.

"You look gorgeous," I tell her as I walk to edge of the bed, loving the low burn of lust I see in her eyes. I'm thinking this has been a long afternoon for all of us. "Have you touched yourself since you got here?"

She shakes her head.

"Good girl," I say, sitting on the edge of the mattress. I lean over, placing a hand on the bed behind her. My face hovers over hers as she tilts her head to look at me. "Logan's in the living room and will be in here in a minute. But tonight, you're going to tell us what to do and what you want."

She starts to shake her head.

"Yes, Cat," I say firmly. "Your fantasy. We do exactly what you want and there isn't anything you can't ask us to do… to you or to each other, okay?"

Her eyes shine with a mixture of excitement, worry, and a hotter sizzle of lust. "Okay."

"Let me check something out," I tell her as I stand up from the bed. "Turn on your back."

She complies and I push a hand between her legs, pressing two fingers inside of her. Soaking wet.

Pulling them out, I lick them off and start to get undressed, never taking my eyes off Cat. I sense Logan walk in behind me, hear his clothing start to hit the floor, but I keep staring at her. She lets her gaze flick briefly to Logan, but then it's back on me again as I disrobe. Her eyes roam all over me, pinning on my cock once I get my jeans off.

Logan comes up to stand beside me. I give him a brief glance, noting his dick is as hard and straight as mine is. I look back to Cat. "Tell us what to do."

Cat adjusts herself on the bed, pushes up so her back is resting on the pillows, which are stacked against the headboard. She raises her legs, plants her feet on the mattress, and spreads her knees wide. One delicate hand goes between and she starts to play with herself. Soft, tiny strokes… nothing that would get her off, but an indication she's already turned on by what's before her.

Her actions… displaying herself like that and setting herself up to watch us has my cock leaking hard and an unbearable need to crawl on the bed and sink into her.

But then she says, "I want you two to kiss. And touch each other."

Logan turns and starts to place a hand on my shoulder, but I say, "Wait up."

Turning to my nightstand, I open the drawer and pull out a bottle of lube, tossing it on the bed beside Cat. Her eyes go to it and back to me.

"I'm assuming we'll need that at some point," I tell her with a grin.

"I think you will," she whispers, those fingers rubbing slow, lazy circles on herself.

Logan's hand is now at my shoulder and he turns me to him. Then both hands are on my face and he's pulling me to his mouth. Kissing a dude is weird at times, but with Logan, it's always been hot. His lips are soft, his tongue dancing slowly with mine, and our cocks bump against each other, smearing the other with pre-cum.

Logan digs the fingers of one hand into my jaw, pushing through my beard and gripping me tight so he can deepen the kiss. The other drops between us and wraps around my dick.

I can't help the low groan that comes out, and I hear a tiny whisper from Cat, "So hot."

Logan starts to slowly jack me as I let my hands roam over his body. So different from Cat. Hard planes and coarse hair that don't really attract me physically, although I'm generally attracted to Logan. I think it might have more to do with the way his tongue is playing mine or the way his grip is firm on me. Sometimes women go a little too soft, afraid they'll hurt a man down there. Guys know exactly what we can take, so getting jacked or sucked by a guy is many times better.

"Suck his cock," Cat whispers, and I realize my eyes have been closed. They open upon that command, and Logan slowly pulls his mouth away from mine, although his hand still strokes me.

I turn to look at her, but it's kind of a mistake. She has a finger pumping in and out of her pussy, and again... have to restrain the urge to tear myself away from Logan and jump right onto Cat.

She looks to Logan and nods at me. "Suck Rand's dick."

Logan gives her a cocky grin, and I know exactly what that means. He intends to drop me to my knees if he can do it to show Cat exactly how good he is.

I brace.

Spreading and locking my legs as Logan sinks to the carpeted floor and grins up at me with almost a taunt of what's to come. I get ready to bite down on my tongue because I know how fucking talented he is.

But fuck it... if I come right away, I'll get back in the game soon enough.

I'm standing close enough to the bed that Cat could reach out and touch my hip. Just a slight turn of my head and I see that her hand has stilled. She watches us while holding her breath.

"Let me show you a trick that all guys love if they're

man enough to admit it," Logan says to Cat, but he's looking up at me. I know what's coming and I know he's not going to give me any mercy. I decide right then and there not to fight it.

Logan bypasses the lube sitting on the bed and puts his index finger in his mouth where he wets it good. When he pulls it out, he tells me, "Spread 'em."

My head tilts again and I look at Cat, whose eyes are as big as saucers as she watches. I reach my hands back, grab ahold of my ass cheeks, and do exactly as Logan orders me.

Logan pushes his hand between my legs, totally ignoring my dick for the moment, which is straining upward, and runs his finger along the seam between my balls and my asshole. I grit my teeth because it feels amazing to be touched there.

The tip of his wet finger probes me, circling my pucker. I try to breathe in deeply but the anticipation is killing me. I look down at Cat again and she looks up at me before saying to Logan, "Do it."

Logan complies and smoothly pushes his finger into me.

Way in deep all the way to his third knuckle.

"Fuck," I shout out, my hips jerking forward, not to get away from him but for my cock to slap him in the face so he takes a fucking hint and sucks me already.

Logan twists his wrist slightly, pressing right in on my prostate, and my knees do in fact start to buckle. I lock them back tight because I think I could actually come just from him stroking me like that.

I release my hold on my ass and bring one hand to my dick, grabbing it by the base and the other threading my fingers through Logan's hair. Logan doesn't make me wait, giving me a smirk before opening his mouth up and taking me all the way in.

Goddamn, that's good.

Chapter 16
Cat

Never in my entire sexual history have I been as turned on as I am right now. I'm sure it has something to do with the fact that I have two beautiful, built, and sexy men before me, willing to do whatever I want them to do. I can't help myself, pulling my fingers free of my pussy and circling the wet around my clit. Faster and faster while I watch Logan and Rand do their thing.

So empowering.

That's a first feeling too. I'm sure once the flush of lust and impending release washes away, I'm going to be extremely grateful to Rand for giving me this.

I watch and play with myself.

Logan on his knees, pushing himself back and forth on Rand's cock. Cheeks hollowed on the back swing, his eyes closed in bliss. Rand's hands gripping Logan's head tight. White knuckles in an attempt not to start thrusting… fucking Logan's mouth. My fingers circle faster.

My gaze flicks up to Rand and I see he's got his face tilted downward, eyes at half mast, watching Logan work him. Eyes filled with bubbling lust, teeth gritted, jaw locked. He's lost and it's so damn hot. I press harder on my clit as my fingers move faster and faster.

I look back down again, to see what Rand is seeing and focus in on Logan's hand.

In between Rand's legs with his finger pumping in and out of his...

My hips shoot off the bed as I come, a groan rumbling out of me and then floating free. I squeeze my eyes shut briefly, see stars blinking in the darkness, before opening them back up. With hazy and blissful eyes, I see Rand watching me but now his hips are pumping back and forth as he holds Logan's head still.

Yet Logan seems unfazed while Rand fucks his mouth... his throat... with hot eyes pinned on me, Logan's hand is working faster at Rand's ass. My legs snap shut together as an involuntary cramp of need hits me straight in the center.

Then Rand thrusts forward, throws his head back, and roars out a release as he comes with a shudder. I can see the ripple actually run up his spine at the same time Logan's throat works to swallow him down.

It's so damn beautiful.

Rand is so damn beautiful that another cramp of need hits me. I want Rand on the bed with me right now. I want that cock pumping in and out of me, and I want him to be as lost in me as he was just now. But that's not going to happen as I watch him pull his dick out of Logan's mouth, his muscular chest rising and falling in short bursts.

He's spent for now and will need time…

The room is quiet except for the rushing breath of three people in the midst of some crazy sex. Logan rubs his roughened fingers over the corner of his mouth before flexing his jaw. He looks up at Rand with a grin. "Good?"

"The things you can do with that mouth and finger," Rand mutters and then turns to look at me. "What's next, Cat?"

"Next?" I ask, feeling dull witted right now. It was so intense watching that… having that orgasm I can still feel the tingles from… that falling into a deep sleep right now seems like a good idea.

Rand nods down to Logan, who stands from his kneeling position. "Logan needs to come… I'm guessing pretty bad. Your call how we give it to him."

My eyes flare wide, and I shoot Logan an apologetic look. I hadn't even thought about his pleasure, and I feel horribly guilty. Shooting up to my knees, I figure I could give him a blow job, but Rand's hand comes out to grip my shoulder.

He gives a small shake of his head and says with a very pointed look, "Only if you want to do that. But it's *whatever* you want, babe. We're both here to do whatever *you* want us to."

Logan snickers, and I blush with a small smile in his direction. "Sorry."

"No worries," he says with a shrug, but then grabs his cock with his hand, giving it long, slow strokes. "But how about you decide what you want so I can get off. Kind of dying here watching you and Rand come. So fucking hot."

Turning my face to Rand, I move my knees to slide closer to him toward the edge of the bed. He turns his body to face me, one hand coming to my waist where his thumb strokes my skin. "Anything?" I ask him.

"Anything, Cat."

"Do you like…?" I start out, but then my voice trails away. I can feel my cheeks get hot and for a woman who got fucked by seven men while locked in a stockade, I think this hesitancy about my sexuality is truly more of the real Cat starting to come out. Now that I'm in control, I'm just a bit unsure of myself.

So I take a deep breath and let it out.

"Do you like Logan fucking you?" I ask Rand point blank, chin lifted so he can see me owning this. "Because I'd really, really like to see that."

Rand's eyes turn soft, his lips curving up in a gentle smile. "Yeah, babe… I like that a lot."

Leaning in, he kisses me, one hand still gripping my waist, the other coming up to hold the back of my head. His tongue slides into my mouth for a claiming stroke against my tongue before it pulls out and his forehead touches mine. Rand's breath rushes out over his lips onto mine, and he whispers so only I can hear him. "I think I'd do anything you asked me to."

And I melt.

Literally feel my body start to sag and my hands

come to his shoulders to pull him down to the bed with me. Yes, down on the bed with me where I'll stroke him back to life and have him…

Rand's hand at my hip falls away and he lets the strength of his other at the back of my head lower me back down to the mattress. When it hits, he pulls it free and turns to Logan, walking right into the other man's space.

They both crash together in a tangle of arms and legs, mouths fusing together in a deep kiss and hips grinding against each other. I push away the flash of jealousy, focusing instead on the scenes before me. Logan's cock darkened with pre-cum spilling from the top, trapped in between their lower torsos and getting massaged by their bodies undulating. Rand's is half hard, but he ignores it. Instead, he puts his hand in between their bodies and takes his friend in his grip.

Logan jerks and groans over the contact, so much so that their kiss breaks and they stare at each other with hot eyes, faces just inches apart.

"Get on the bed," Logan growls, his hands coming up to Rand's chest and giving him a shove. "On your knees… right beside Cat. Going to fuck you from behind this time."

This time?

Does that mean there will be more tonight? Or is he going to fuck Rand again at some other time? Maybe outside of my presence? I'm not sure how I feel about that, but then my thoughts scatter as Rand climbs right over me, going to his hands and knees. Logan grabs the lube, walks to the end of the bed, and raises one knee up to the mattress while he uncaps the bottle.

"Kiss me," Rand whispers, and my eyes slide to his.

I scramble onto my knees and sidle up to Rand, pressing my lips against his with my hands to his cheeks, flexing into his bristly beard. He sighs into my mouth as we kiss and I close my eyes, giving into it. We kiss and everything else melts away. Just him and me, the smell of his sweat and the mint on his breath. Tongues stroking and rolling against each other. Lips sliding and nipping.

A hiss pushes from his mouth into mine, and Rand's body jerks a bit. My eyes fly open, and I pull away. Rand's head drops down and he moans, back arching. Logan's kneeling right behind him, working two fingers in and out of Rand's ass. A flood of wetness rushes from between my legs and I can feel it dribbling down the inside of my thighs.

I move to the side of Rand so I can see better, placing a tentative hand on his mid back to feel the muscles bunching and flexing as he rounds his back and then arches it again when Logan puts a third finger in.

"Feel good?" I ask softly, my gaze pinned helplessly on Logan's hand and what it's doing between Rand's strong buttocks that are coiled tight.

"Yeah," he grunts as Logan starts to pump, but only a few times before he's pulling his hand away.

More lube, this time dribbled right over Logan's hard cock that I notice is covered with a condom. I'm not sure when that happened… probably while I was kissing Rand, but who cares when. It's the now I'm focused on with Logan lining up to Rand's ass. I slide sideways a bit more, get closer to the action so I can see, still keeping my hand on Rand's back. Logan's a big guy with a lot of girth and for a brief moment, I worry about Rand. But then I watch as he pushes his hips back a little, a silent plea, and I know he'll be all right.

With his hand and hips guiding the way, Logan places the tip of his cock against Rand's ass and flexes forward slightly. The large head slowly disappears as I watch in fascination.

"More," Rand groans. My hand starts stroking the muscles of his back, my other hand coming up to rest on his butt.

"Give him more," I tell Logan softly.

Logan's face is pinched with pleasure, his lower lip between his teeth and digging in hard. He does as I ask and pushes his hips forward even more, sinking inch by inch into Rand. When the trimmed hairs on his pelvis brush against Rand's ass, and I know he's rooted deep, I let my breath out in a wavering gust of longing and excitement.

Rand's head is still hanging low, eyes closed and jaw locked as Logan starts to move. Luxurious pulls of his cock out, with penetratingly slow thrusts back in.

Each time he bottoms out, Rand grunts in pleasure.

Each time Rand grunts in pleasure, an ache throbs between my legs.

Logan picks up the pace, which lends to an almost fevered vibe in the air. Sweat on his forehead, chest heaving and his hands gripping Rand by the hips with this thumbs digging down into the muscle, he mutters an almost endless stream of filth to Rand, "Christ... this feels good. You know I love pussy, man, but this ass... never mind fucking it. Going to come so hard... going to pound you harder. Then when we're all recovered, we're going to fill Cat up. I'll take her pussy... you can have her ass, Rand. Sandwich her right between us and fuck her oh so good."

My gaze slides to Logan, mesmerized by his dirty words. Completely turned on by them as well. He smiles at me as he pumps in and out of Rand, and then nods his head downward with a pointed look that I should take a gander. "Your boy likes dirty talk."

Tilting my head, lowering my eyes, I see Rand with his back rounded, head hanging down and his own hand between his legs, working his cock. Stroking with a tight grip. Quick, furious pumping while he grunts and groans.

He's rock hard again.

He's. Hard. Again.

"Stop," I blurt out, my hand on Rand's ass moving to Logan's chest. He doesn't stop his movements immediately, but slows them down, finally pulling out and then pressing back in deep where he holds still. Both men, with heaving chests, look at me curiously and with a little frustration.

"I want you inside of me," I say as my gaze snaps to Rand's. "Want you to come inside of me."

Total silence. Rand's face strained with the need to come. Logan's not looking much different.

"While he's fucking you," I add on to clarify my wishes.

"Figured that much, Cat," Rand says with his lips tipped upward. While still looking at me but clearly talking to Logan, he says, "Pull out, man."

Logan does as requested, both he and Rand not able to hold back a wistful moan at the friction caused from the exit, and then Rand pushes off the bed coming just to his knees. "You want on your back or knees, Cat?"

"Whatever's best," I breathe out, my heart racing and my skin flushed warm with the thought of what we're about to do.

"On your back," he says in a low voice as he reaches out to graze his knuckles over one of my nipples. "So I can watch your face."

And I melt again, immediately sagging to the bed and positioning myself on my back. Rand maneuvers, comes in between my legs, and lowers himself onto me so he can give me a kiss. His chest presses onto mine, his dick hard and pulsing as it bears down against my pubic mound and his arms slipping under me so he puts me in a full-body hug as his tongue slides into my mouth.

Pure bliss.

My arms go over his shoulders, wrapping around the back of his neck, and I hold him tight to me as we make out, the only movement of our bodies being our tongues and lips.

Finally, he breaks contact, lifting his face from mine and giving me a smile bright with repletion. Eyes holding mine, he pushes off me, grabbing my legs and spreading me wide. Hands to the backs of my thighs, he swivels his hips and as if his dick knows exactly where to go, it pushes into me.

Sinking in like it belongs, every nerve ending firing in welcome relief that he's there. "That's it," he whispers as he claims my pussy. "Taking every inch of me and loving it."

"Yes," I whisper back, my eyes rolling into the back of my head and lids lowering to full darkness. If I watch Rand and see the same expressions I saw on his face when he was fucking Logan's mouth, I know I'm going to burst apart so violently, I'm afraid I won't be put back together.

Rand starts moving, an animalistic sound of need and urgency rising from his chest. He thrusts in and out of me a few times, and my head starts to spin. I become lost to the sensation of him.

But then he stops, and my eyes open slowly. He spreads his legs, thighs on the mattress, and I watch over his shoulder as Logan crawls in between Rand's legs. Using his hand, he guides the head of his cock to Rand's ass, and with nothing more than a lowering of his entire lower body, he fills him up again.

Rand hisses as he's pushed deeper into me, sandwiched in between Logan and me. His elbows go to the mattress, his muscles bulging and straining to keep most of his weight off me. We're all still for just a moment, but then I can feel the outsides of Rand's thigh muscles flex as he raises his hips, pulling out of me.

Just to the tip where he holds still, allowing Logan to pull out of his ass a bit.

Logan pauses… a brief moment in time where I wonder what's going to happen next, before I scream out in pleasure when Logan slams into Rand, who then slams into me. Rand lets out a hoarse bark of surprise, and Logan groans as if he's dying of pleasure.

"Oh, let's do that again," I murmur, trying to unclench my toes that had just previously been curled.

Logan gives a dark laugh, and Rand's eyes glitter as he stares down at me with equal measures of naked desire and fulfilment.

The tilt of his head. The soft smile. The intent stare.

Fulfilment that he's given me what I wanted.

And I melt again.

Then Logan starts fucking Rand, who starts fucking me again, and I come so hard, I feel obliterated. I have no doubt I can put myself back together again, but I'm just wondering what a reassembled Catherine Lyons will look like compared to the old one.

Chapter 17
Rand

"ARE YOU EXCITED about starting work today?" I ask Cat as she leans in toward my small bathroom mirror and puts on mascara.

She gives a soft, "Uh-huh" as she feathers the black goo onto her eyelashes.

I'm fascinated by everything she does to make herself up. Not to make herself more beautiful, because I don't think the makeup and perfect hair does that. It just makes her beautiful in a different way. She could wear nothing on her face, as I've seen her do at night before she goes to bed, and still be just as lovely.

But I watch because she lets me and because I could watch her for hours doing nothing. Pish was already pissed at me for ditching work last Friday, as well as missing Monday and Tuesday of this week. But I pointed out to him that I never take vacation—which is true because there's nowhere I want to be—and that shut him up. I also told him I was taking Wednesday too.

Which I did and enjoyed thoroughly. That was the day after the spectacular fuck-fest that occurred between Cat, Logan, and me. Whereas I thought the three of us would go all night, turns out we all fell into an exhausted heap because of the massive orgasms that ripped through our little group. I think I dozed with my head on Cat's chest and her playing with my hair. When I woke up, Cat was sound asleep and Logan was gone. I noted the way Cat was curled into me and I was spooned around her, and I figure if Logan saw that, he was being the good guy and jetted out of there so we could be alone.

So yesterday… Cat and I did nothing but relax and recover from the events of the last few days. She wasn't going to start with Callie and Sloane until the next day as Callie was having a bunch of shit moved from a warehouse over to the campaign headquarters for them to organize.

Cat and I hung at the apartment all day, wore sweatpants, ordered Chinese takeout, and binged on Netflix. The only sign of energy either of us exhibited was while we were watching *Jessica Jones*. I was sitting on the couch, my legs propped on the coffee table. Cat was lying on her side, her head on my thigh.

Just as Jessica and Cage were getting it on for the first time, Cat shifted, rolled, and came up on her knees beside me. With her face still turned toward the TV screen and watching Cage take Jessica up against the wall, she palmed my crotch with her hand and started rubbing.

My breath froze and I held still.

Deliriously happy she initiated not only because my cock was about to feel really good, but also because Cat was embracing her sexuality in a natural manner. She was doing something she wanted to do with no one prodding her or expecting anything.

So she blew me right there while I watched *Jessica Jones*. Well, fuck... couldn't watch it. Couldn't concentrate on anything but her wet mouth on me, so we had to rewind.

"What's the smile for?" Cat asks.

I blink away the memory, coming back to focus on her watching me in the bathroom mirror as I lean against the doorjamb. Not sure why I'm still loitering because I could have left for work already, but like I said... very much enjoying the view.

"Just thinking about that blow job you gave me yesterday on the couch," I tell her truthfully.

She beams back at me in the mirror as she puts the cap back on her mascara. "It *was* really good, wasn't it?"

"Best ever," I murmur, and I think it was. But then again, each encounter with this woman just keeps getting better and better.

She turns, placing the mascara in a black, quilted bag laying on my cramped vanity. Resting her butt against the counter ledge, she places her palms to either side and says, "Listen... I want to reach out to Kevin and demand a copy of the signed will he says supposedly exists."

"I thought we were going to wait for Bridger—"

"I'm tired of waiting, Rand," she interrupts. "I'm sorry... but this is my life and I want to get this settled so I can move on."

"Move on from here?" I ask her quietly, my throat aching just pushing those words out.

She gives a quick shake of her head. "No. Not from here, here… I mean like move on from Samuel, his family, and everything that was my life."

I instantly inflate with relief and wonder if subconsciously I hadn't been pushing the will aside because I was afraid she would leave after it was worked out. But I can't keep her here against her wishes to move on, whether it be from my apartment or from a bad life, and I swore to myself that I'd help her out as best I could.

"Let me call Bridger really quick and see if he's got anything to offer before you call, okay?" I ask her as I pull my phone out of my pocket.

She nods and I dial Bridger's cell, putting it on speakerphone so Cat can hear when he answers, "What's up?"

"Just checking in to see if you got to look over the copy of that trust agreement I brought you?"

"Sorry man," he says with true apology in his voice. "I've had a bit of an issue going on at The Silo and just haven't been able to get to it."

"What's going on?" I ask, completely feeling a bit guilty I haven't been there in so long. Bridger hasn't said a word, and I wasn't poking the bear on that.

He sighs into the phone. "I don't even know if issue is the right word or not, but I accepted a new patron into the club upon a recommendation of a few of our more established members. In fact, he bought himself a platinum membership, as well as memberships for his harem... four of them in all."

My head snaps over to Cat, and she has the same raised eyebrow look that I do.

"Did you say harem?" I ask with a laugh.

"I don't know what the fuck you call it, but the man has four women he brings in with him, and they all sort of... belong to him, I guess. It's fucking weird, but hey... you know our motto... no judgment."

"Then what's the issue?"

"He's got this girl... woman, really, but young. Twenty years old and supposedly a virgin. Won't let anyone fuck her. They can do other things do her, but not fuck her. Rumor is going around he's going to auction off her virginity and everyone's in an uproar, wanting it for themselves. I've been at The Silo every night just making sure I keep an eye on things. But seriously, reviewing that document just slipped my mind."

"It's cool," I tell him, but inside, I wish he'd have some better advice.

"Listen," Bridger says, his voice coming through the speakerphone in that slightly tinny way, "mind if I give it to Jenna to look at? She's good and it will be a professional eye on it."

Jenna's a former college classmate of Woolf and Bridger's who went on to law school, and she's also Bridger's attorney for the business. She plays at The Silo too—quite well I know from personal experience—and if

Bridger trusts her to review it, then so do I.

I look at Cat and give a nod, telling Bridger, "Yeah, that's fine. Cat's going to go ahead and reach out to Kevin to ask for a signed copy of the will that supposedly cuts her out."

"Sure that's a good play?" Bridger asks.

"I have to," Cat pipes up, and I give her a smile. "I need to move this forward."

"Hi Cat," Bridger says, his voice softening. He always had a soft spot for her and I wonder if he's fucked her. I've never seen him do so and he rarely participates at The Silo. But still, plenty of times Cat and Bridger were there and I wasn't, so it's conceivable.

"Hi, Bridger," she says back, smiling at me. "And thank you for helping."

"My pleasure, darling. Now I've got to get to work."

We disconnect. Cat pushes off from the counter and moves past me to get out of the bathroom. She does this with a hand coming to my waist where it rests softly for a brief moment, and I like to imagine that she did it for no other reason than she wanted to touch me.

I follow her out, through the living room and to the kitchen where she pulls her phone out of her purse.

"I'm calling Kevin right now."

I wordlessly come to stand beside her, my hand going automatically to her lower back where I rest it lightly. A sign of support. A way to give her strength.

She taps her finger on the screen, pulls up Kevin's number and poises her finger above it. "I've got both

Kevin and Richard's contact information in case something happened to their father."

I nod because I can't imagine any other reason she'd have to call them, but I see her eyes filled with unease. It hits me all of a sudden why she would even bother to tell me that.

My hand covers hers, and I pull it back from the phone slightly. "Cat," I say, my tone soft but censuring. "I'd never think you'd do that."

Call up one of those brothers.
Sons to your husband.
Because you wanted to fuck them.

She gives me somewhat of an apologetic grimace. "I just… you don't know me, Rand, and I didn't want you to ever think there was anything—"

"Just stop," I say roughly as I squeeze her hand in mine. "I *do* know you, Cat. Now make the damn call."

She studies me for a moment, and I stare back at her. She finally gives me a nod and pulls her hand free so she can tap on Kevin's name. She hits the speakerphone button, affording me the same courtesy I just gave her during my call to Bridger.

It makes me feel like we're a team.

Unit.

Couple.

Really, Rand? You're letting your head go there?

The phone rings twice and then Kevin is answering. I expected his voice to be higher, maybe even effeminate, because I can't help but view him as a little pussy for fucking his father's wife. I expect he's ugly, small, and weasely.

Instead, his voice is vibrantly deep, and I know in an instant that he's none of the things I expected.

"Catherine," he says smoothly, as if he'd just greased his throat with melted butter. "I thought you'd be calling me. Please tell me you've reconsidered my offer to stay here in Jackson."

Both of our gazes rise from the phone to focus on each other. Cat rolls her eyes in exaggerated fashion, and I grin at her.

"Kevin," Cat says in her most regal, sophisticated voice. I expect she learned to talk this way being married to Samuel and running in wealthy circles. "I want a copy of the will you claim has cut me out of my inheritance as your father's wife."

"So you're not considering my offer?" he asks, sounding almost hurt.

"Kevin," Cat snaps to focus him. "I want a copy of the signed will and I want it immediately. When can you get it to me?"

"Sorry, love," he says, and I can hear the smirk through the phone. I hope I get to wipe it off him one day. "But it's in my father's home office in Vegas and of course, I'm here in Jackson. Once I return, I'll be glad to get you a copy."

"Wrong, Kevin," Cat sneers at the phone, and I can actually feel the rage vibrating off her. "I was in Vegas this weekend. In *my* home… *your* dad's office… and the will you purport he signed isn't there."

She stops, and I'm surprised she had the fortitude to do so. I thought she might blurt out that we saw the original trust agreement and pour-over will signed not long after the wedding, but she didn't. She holds that close to the vest, and I think that's smart. No sense in him knowing exactly how fired up she is or that she has a copy of what is probably the one and only estate document in existence. It's best to let him think she's just a girl poking around... not someone to be reckoned with.

Kevin's silent. For a moment, I think he's disconnected. Cat and I look at each other, and I give a slight shrug to my shoulders. Finally, he asks in a voice filled with icy disdain, "What is it exactly that you want?"

Cat takes a deep breath. "I want a copy of the signed document that governs Samuel's estate, so I know what my rights are. And until such time as we can resolve this, I want you to turn my credit cards back on so I have something to live off until that occurs."

My eyebrows shoot up because I didn't see that coming. Cat glances at me with a questioning look, and I nod at her in agreement of what she just asked for. My hand comes out, and I hit the "mute" button on the phone so he can't hear us. "Ask for the house. Tell him you want back in and him out."

She shakes her head immediately in denial and whispers, even though he can't hear us. "I don't want to go there."

Yeah... that's a big fucking smile taking up residence

on my face right now. I lean forward, kiss her quickly, and then unmute the call.

"Tell me where you are," Kevin asks. "I'll bring it to you."

Yeah, he isn't getting within twenty feet of Cat again. I lean toward the phone slightly and say, "You can send it with a courier to 263 W. Karns Ave, but you're not welcome here."

"And who is this, if I may ask?" he says in an amused voice. "Cat find herself a man or something?"

"I'm your worst nightmare if you fuck her over," I growl into the phone, my eyes flicking up to see Cat watching me with wide eyes.

Kevin makes a scoffing sound and laughs. "Brave man… hiding behind a phone and won't give his name."

"It's Rand Bishop, you asshole. I just gave you my home address, and I work at Westward Ink. You feel free to come see me whenever you want to, and I'll show you exactly the lengths I'm willing to go to make sure you won't fuck Cat over anymore."

A moment of silence while Kevin digests my words, and I'm sure they've pissed him off royally. But he surprises me when he says, "I'll send a copy of the signed document over tomorrow."

"Bring it to Westward Ink," I command because it just hit me… neither Cat nor I will be here during the day, and besides… I don't want him anywhere near her.

"Understood," he says crisply. The phone then beeps twice to indicate he's hung up on the other end.

"Was that okay?" Cat asks me hesitantly, dropping the phone back in her purse.

"You were perfect," I say, sliding my hand from her lower back to her ass and giving it a small smack. I don't do more than that, although I'd love nothing more to drag her back to the bedroom and muss up that perfect makeup and hair. At the least, I want to kiss her, but not sure it's appropriate given the nature of the conversation that was just had.

So I keep it cool and give her a wink. "Well, I better get to work before Pish fires me."

Cat snorts. I spent the many, many hours on the road to and from Vegas telling her all kinds of gory details about Pish. Hell, she probably knows more about my friends and family than anyone as much as we'd talked during that road trip, but she definitely knows what I know about Pish.

That he's a pushover.

I pat my front pocket for my keys, feel the small bulge, and turn toward the door.

"Hey," she says softly.

Turning back to her, I tilt my head to wait for whatever it is she wants to say.

Please be something good. Please be something that lets me know that I'm not imagining some of these feelings or worse yet, that they're one-sided.

"I meant what I said a minute ago," she says, her eyes lasered onto mine so I know she's talking straight.

"What's that?" I ask, since a lot was said in the last

minute or so.

"That I don't want to go back to the Jackson house," she says bluntly. "I really don't want anything he has, but in particular, I don't want to go back there."

"Bad memories and all," I hazard a guess, remembering just how good that felt to hear her say she didn't want to go back the first time.

It's even better the second.

"No," she says simply and picks up her purse. "Just better memories here. Much, much better, and I don't want to give that up."

"Then don't," I tell her leaning forward, grazing my lips on her cheek. "You have a place here as long as you want it."

I hope she reads between the lines. I'm not just talking a bed to sleep in, but I'm certainly not ready to tell her that yet. While Cat's opened up to me in amazing ways, I can still tell that deep down, she's going to be leery of anything that resembles a commitment and I'm not about to scare her off.

Chapter 18
Cat

"THERE'S WAY MORE paper than I thought there'd be," I tell Sloane as I pull several thick folders out of a banker's box.

It's one of about forty banker's boxes that are stacked against the wall in the large conference room of Governor Hayes' campaign headquarters. Sloane and I have been diligently unpacking and organizing it all as best we can. It's the materials from his last campaign for governor when he won the office in a very heated and close race. That was three years ago, and in just over a year from now, the citizens will be voting again on whether to keep him in office.

And this is the extent of my knowledge of how elections are run by a candidate. Sloane's been filling me in a bit. She told me that her father used to be an elected U.S. Senator, so she's done campaign work before. She also told me her dad's a douche and she didn't like to talk about him, but she hoped he had perpetual sunburn from spending all his time on a beach in Brazil with his new and much younger wife.

I didn't press her for any details given the acid in her

voice when she said that.

Callie was in Cheyenne, meeting with her father to start putting together a formalized kick off for the campaign. For my first day of work, she left instructions for me to just help Sloane with organizing the materials, and that seemed easy enough. I wish I had dressed a little differently, choosing a black and white zebra-print Diane Von Furstenberg wrap dress with nude heels. Those have been long since kicked off and my sleeves rolled up as we pull out mailing lists, copies of speeches, policy summaries, advertising campaigns, glossy mailers and signs that were used. We lay them in stacks according to subject on the large table that takes up most of the room and chatter about inane stuff, mostly an attempt to get to know one another.

I had an amazing time with Callie and Sloane at lunch two days ago. The margaritas absolutely helped break the ice, but the fact that these women were so accepting of me says so much about them, that I feel relatively comfortable now despite my sordid past with the two men in their lives.

"So you and Rand, huh?" Sloane says while sitting on the floor before an open box. She's not looking at me but rather pulling out manila envelopes and checking out the contents.

Just casual conversation.

"Yeah," I say a little uncertainly since I really have no clue what the nature of our relationship is. "He's a great guy."

"Hung like a horse too," Sloane says, just as casually and still focusing on her work. She seems intent on what she's doing and as if her statement wasn't anything more than an afterthought.

"Excuse me?" I ask, stunned by her knowledge of Rand's body parts.

She looks up at me with a sheepish grin. "You're not the only one who had experience with all things wicked at The Silo."

"You and Rand?"

"Me, Rand, Logan, Bridger, and Cain," she says, her grin getting bigger with a slightly wistful look on her face. "All at the same time."

My jaw drops wide open, and I make no move to close it. I just stare at her, my eyes probably as big as an owl's. I can't believe it. No way. Sloane looks like the poster girl for innocence with her sweetly rounded face and cute as pie blonde waves coming to just above her shoulder.

Just... no way.

"Yup," she says with a chuckle, completely amused at my shock. "Cain arranged it. I'm sure Rand told you all about how I was an undercover reporter investigating The Silo and Governor Hayes. I was playing ignorant of The Silo with Cain and he was showing me a part of it but not really. Took me to one of the fantasy cabins and had the guys waiting there for me."

"Wow," I say as I lower myself slowly into one of the chairs that surround the conference room tables. I'm not sure how I feel about this. There's a weird, low bubbling feeling that I can't quite place. Like my favorite toy got stolen from me on the playground by another girl. And yet, there's no way that's jealousy. I have no right or claim to be such.

"I tell you that only to make you more at ease with me," Sloane says. "I know it really bothered you at lunch the other day… making friendships with us… not sure how we'd look at you or if we'd judge you. I hope Callie and I have both shown that we don't care about what happened in the past. I just told you about Rand so you know I've got dirty stuff in my closet too, but it doesn't mean anything more than just an experience."

I nod in understanding. She's right… the knowledge that she was with Rand helps to obviate my guilt over being with her man.

"I saw you at The Silo once," Sloane says, now leaning back and placing her hands flat on the carpet behind her.

"You did?" I cringe internally wondering exactly what she saw me doing. While Sloane walks a bit on the wild side, I'm betting the four-on-one she had was the wildest thing she's ever done. She'd probably be sick if she knew some of the things I've done.

"It was after your husband died," Sloane says with a nod of her head. "I was there with Cain and Bridger had told us. You were in one of the rooms… locked in a stockade."

A small smile comes to my lips and my fingers come

up to inadvertently touch them in remembrance. That was a good night. It was the night I first got to make my own choices about who I let into my body.

"You were beautiful," Sloane says softly, and my gaze slides to her. She doesn't say that in a "come on" type of way, but rather in a respectfully deferent way. "I remember being amazed at what strength and confidence you must have had to do that."

"Insanity more like it," I mutter as I push out of the chair and walk over to the boxes again.

"No," Sloane says. "I saw your face. There was pride there. And pleasure. You owned it. It was exquisitely erotic but beautifully inspiring. I envy you a bit."

I turn, startled to hear her say that. "Don't envy me. What you saw was a rarity. Most of my Silo experiences are not good."

"I suspected as much," Sloane says with a sympathetic smile. "And I'm really sorry for that."

Turning back around, I grab the next banker's box and haul it down. "Well, it's all in the past."

"You say that as if you almost believe it," she says, and my eyes snap to her.

"What do you mean?" I ask curiously. She acts like she has insight into me that I don't have about myself.

"You're holding back with Rand."

"I'm not—"

"You most definitely are," she reprimands. "I ask about Rand and you're like, 'He's a great guy'. I call bullshit on that."

My eyes narrow on her. "What would you know?"

"I know he's taken you in, given you shelter, provided safety, and shielded you from judgment. Arranged for a job, took you to Vegas, and I bet he's handing you orgasms like they're candy every night, right?"

Not sure how she knows all that, but I'm going to guess it's through Bridger to Woolf to Callie to her, but regardless… she's right about all those things. She's so right about them, and it makes me feel horrible that I refuse to give them the recognition they deserve.

"Rand deserves way better than me," I tell her, finally voicing a fear I've had from the moment he held me after I told him about all the ways in which Samuel abused me.

Sloane cocks her head. "How do you figure?"

"I've got nothing to offer. I'm just a woman who is good for one thing, and I've been too well used for there to be anything special about me."

I hope that didn't sound too whiny because I'm just trying to call it as I see it. But now that I've told her that, I stiffen my spine and hold her gaze, knowing in my heart of hearts I just shared with her my secret fear that's holding me back from Rand.

He's much too good for me.

And I know I can't keep him. Once I figure out what I'm entitled to—or not—I'm going to have to move on and let him have his life back. Until then, I'm going to keep accepting what he's offering me because I guess that's just me being selfish. I like the feelings he provokes in me too much. I like the safety and security and the way he makes me laugh. I'll take it for a bit longer, which only confirms I'm no good. I'll end up using him up and leaving him behind at some point.

But it's what's best for him, I'm sure of it.

Sloane looks at me skeptically. "You totally don't even see yourself, do you?"

"Sure I do," I mutter, pulling the lid off the box I just set down on the conference room table.

I see myself in the mirror every day, and I know exactly the kind of person looking back at me.

My phone starts ringing from inside my purse, and I pull it out to check Caller ID. I try to push down the measure of annoyance that starts to rise when I see "Trish Lyons" on the screen.

I don't have her under the beloved title of "Mom" because she doesn't hold that honor. I stopped considering her my mom long ago.

Little liar.

Swatting my conscience away, I reject the phone call, sending it to voice mail. I start to drop it back in my purse, but it starts ringing again.

Trish Lyons.

"You can answer it if you need to," Sloane says from her seat on the ground. "Callie's really laid back about personal calls."

I don't want to answer it, but I recognize my mom's antics and she's escalating. This isn't the first time it's happened. Something is prompting her to reach out, and she's following the normal pattern.

First, it starts with little texts. *Just checking in, baby. How are you?*

When I ignore them, she turns on the "mom" act a bit more. *Please call me. Really worried about you.*

Yeah, bullshit.

Then the calls start. She starts to give more away on the voice mails she leaves. *Just trying to reach you. I'm in sort of a pickle and could use some help.*

Followed by, *I need some cash pretty quick, Catherine. They're going to turn my electricity off if not. Can you wire it to me?*

And when that goes unanswered, she gets nasty. *If you don't send me some money, I'm going to keep calling and calling. I'm not going away so just send the fucking money. You don't want me showing up on your doorstep.*

And I so don't want her showing up on my doorstep. She did it once and made a huge scene, which embarrassed the hell out of me in front of Samuel.

So when I finally give her the money, it's so I can have a little bit of peace. It is usually short lived because once she learned I was married to a billionaire, the requests came more frequently. I never had the guts to tell Samuel what I was doing, so I just took some cash advances off my card and would send them to my mom when she asked. It kept her happy for a bit until it didn't anymore.

We've been through the ignored texts, which she's been sending me for almost a week now. She called and left voice mails yesterday and the day before. Today would be about the time she started to threaten me.

Normally, I would ignore this call too but something in me is a bit different today than it was even yesterday. This morning, I stood up to Kevin and demanded something for myself.

That was something I'm not sure I've ever done before, and I don't pretend otherwise, probably would have never happened but for Rand taking me in and putting me under his wing.

But still… I can do this.

I can stand up to my mother.

I connect the call and say, "Hello Trish."

She doesn't even attempt to be offended because she's not. She's never minded if I called her Mom or not. "I'm surprised you actually answered. I have a better relationship with your voice mail."

"Because we have no relationship at all," I remind her in a tired voice, my eyes sliding down to Sloane to see she's got her head bent back over the box, trying to be unobtrusive. But I don't care if she hears this. Hell, she's watched me gang banged before, so why hide my wretched mom at this point? "What can I do for you?"

She launches right into her tale of woe. "Well, I've had a major leak in the roof and I have to get it replaced. It's going to be pricey, and you know I just don't have that type of savings. Probably at least ten grand."

My mom isn't the brightest bulb in the bunch, and I'm going to have to assume any intellect I have at all was handed down from my dad. She knew her daughter was married to a billionaire. She might not know exactly how many zeroes that is, but she knows it's a lot. The few times I've seen her in in the past three years, she's seen the jewelry I sport, the Mercedes I drive, and the designer clothing. I even had her over for dinner once to my palatial house, maybe hoping to rub her face in the fact that I landed well despite the things she did to screw me up.

Trish Lyons saw all of that and yet she never asked for more than a few hundred dollars at a time. Hell, I'd drop five-hundred dollars on a haircut every six weeks, so it was nothing to me. She would hit me up for the same amount every few months, so in reality, it wasn't that bad. Not sure why I dragged things out… ignoring her texts and calls until she turned nasty, then I'd eventually give in and hand the money over.

No, wait… I do know why I did that.

I did that because there was a small part of me that still considered her to be my mother. Some remote part of my heart that perhaps pitied her for her shortcomings and lack of love. Maybe I even did it in gratitude for the life of luxury that had been bestowed upon me.

But regardless, all those years, poor, intellectually challenged Trish Lyons never asked for more than a pittance. I suspected it was maybe to buy some dope or something.

Now she's asking for ten grand and that's quite the jump.

And I know exactly why.

"You heard Samuel died," I guess as I pace alongside the conference room table.

"Just terrible news, sweetie," she coos at me in such a fake, syrupy voice that my teeth start aching. "Are you okay?"

"I'm fine," I say in a clipped voice. "And I don't have the money."

"Well, of course you do," she says as if I'm the silliest person in the world. "Your husband was rich. He's dead. So you're rich."

If only life were that simple.

"Samuel cut me out of the will," I tell my mother, which is not something I believe at all. In fact, I suspect I'm due a big chunk of change and can buy a new trailer for my mom, not just a roof, if I wanted. But I'll never tell her that. She doesn't deserve to know.

Because if I'm cutting out the poisonous past and refusing to be owned anymore, I'll be damned if I'm going to let my mom maintain any type of hold on me. At the most, I might give her a tiny bit of money once the estate gets settled, but then I'm done with her.

"I don't believe it," Trish says, scoffing. "He wouldn't."

"Well, he did," I snap.

"I'm coming over. We can talk about this," my mom says in a brusque voice.

"I'm not in Vegas."

Small pause. Can hear the wheels turning. "Where are you?" she asks.

"Look… I'm at work and can't talk," I say, ignoring her question. She doesn't deserve to know where I am.

"But what am I supposed—?"

"Take care of yourself," I say softly and disconnect the phone.

Is that the last I'll hear of Trish Lyons?

Nope. There'll be another day, another dollar asked for.

The one good thing about not having a pot to piss in right now is that it makes my conversations with my mom a lot shorter.

Chapter 19
Rand

I NOTE CAT dressed a lot differently for work today as she walks into the Snake River Brewery to meet me for dinner in a pair of dark jeans and a form-fitted plaid shirt with expensive leather boots that come up over her knees.

Yesterday, she was all polished sophistication when she left. She came back to the apartment tired, sweaty, and with dirt smudges all over her dress. Over frozen pizza because neither one of us wanted to cook, she told me about her day, which apparently included unloading and sorting dirty boxes filled with old campaign stuff, Sloane telling Cat all about our encounter together, as well as a call from her loser mother. It was a full day for her.

Cat didn't seem bent out of shape that I have carnal knowledge of Sloane, but I expect that's because Cat has carnal knowledge of Sloane's man, Cain. Ordinary people would never understand the dynamics of this type of sexual freedom, but hell... sometimes it seems a little weird to me as well.

But no more weird I suppose than the fact that I

seem to fall more for Cat each day… hell, each moment we're together… and I can't seem to figure out if these feelings are real or fanned perhaps brighter by an unexpressed desire to be a hero to her.

She walks toward me, hips swaying, and every man in the bar turns his head to look at her. Her eyes are only for me as I stand up from my stool to greet her. Cat steps into me, her hands to my waist and she goes to tiptoes to press her lips to the lower side of my jaw. "Hey," she says softly.

"Good day at work, honey?" I ask playfully as I drop my hand to her ass and cop a quick feel.

She laughs and steps past me, plopping down on the stool I had been saving for her. I take my seat beside her, and she takes a grateful swig of the Snake River Pale Ale I'd had poured for her by the bartender when I'd arrived about fifteen minutes ago. I call out to one of the bartenders who has his back to me, counting money from the cash drawer. "Ryan… go ahead and put in a barbeque chicken quesadilla and a bison burger."

He looks over his head and says, "Sure thing, Rand."

"How'd you know I wanted a burger?" Cat asks. She knows I ordered the burger for her since I know she doesn't like chicken, which is strange because I thought everyone likes chicken. Still, it's a unique fact about her that's hard to forget.

"Lucky guess," I say with a smirk. "So seriously… how was your second day of work?"

"More of the same unpacking boxes, but Callie was

there today and she started educating me on what the process will be like over the next year."

"Sounds fun," I say with trademark snark.

She smiles, but the light doesn't last long before her eyes turn serious. "Did he ever show?"

She's talking about Kevin who had agreed to deliver the purported current and signed estate paperwork of Samuel Vaughn. I expected him or someone on his behalf to come to Westward Ink today and hand it off.

Well, that's not true. I actually expected him not to bring it but at the least figured he'd call Cat with some bullshit excuse. Instead, there wasn't a peep from him all day.

Cat knows this because she texted me about every hour for an update.

> *Did he show?*
> *Do you have it?*
> *Where do you think he is?*
> *He's not going to show, right?*

I shake my head in the negative to her original question. "I ran by the apartment right after work to see if perhaps someone left it in my mailbox. No one ever came by the shop."

"Fuck, he's an asshole," she mutters as she reaches for her beer. "Should have known he wouldn't follow through. My credit cards didn't get turned on either."

"It's not because he's an asshole, Cat," I tell her, and she turns to blink at me in surprise. "It's because he doesn't have it. It doesn't exist."

"You think?"

"I more than think," I say confidently.

I'd been thinking about it all day. If she was truly cut out of the will, there was no reason to keep a signed copy from her. Kevin Vaughn was bluffing to cut her out of his life with minimum fuss, and he was banking on the fact that she was going to be the pliant and subservient woman she was when Samuel was alive.

"Should I call him?" she asks, her finger absently stroking up and down the glass wet with condensation.

I shrug. "What's the point? He probably won't answer, and if he does, he'll give you a round of bullshit. The fact of the matter is, you have a copy of a valid trust agreement that leaves you money and a house. It's time to turn this over to an attorney and get this shit sorted."

Cat raises her gaze to me, and she gives me a nod of agreement. "You're right. It's time and I've got the money from my jewelry I can use to hire an attorney now."

"We'll call Bridger later and ask him if Jenna will handle it," I tell her as I lean sideways on my stool and bump my shoulder against hers. "I'm sure she'll give you a discount too."

"Sounds good," she says, her voice sounding as relaxed and happy as I've ever heard it.

"So, let's play 'What If'," I say as I turn on my stool to face her a bit. "What if you ultimately find out you get nothing from Samuel's estate?"

Cat turns, her knees brushing against my thigh. She rests a forearm on the bar, the other on the back of my stool. "I guess I'd have to be a better roommate and start paying you rent, huh?"

"You'd want to stay here?"

"I think so," she says hesitantly. "I know exactly what's waiting for me in Vegas. I think I'd like to explore the opportunities here. And I will pay you rent as soon as I get my first paycheck."

Hmmmmm... that tells me exactly shit.

"You know you're not a roommate to me, right?" I tell her, deciding that maybe we need a little plain talk between us. "I've had roommates before and they were nothing like you. We're different. What we have between us is different."

Her arm shifts and her hand goes from the back of my stool to brush against my shoulder. Her eyes stare at her hand as she strokes me, almost in confusion. "I'm not sure what we are."

"Well, I think we're a little north of roommates, a little east of friendship, and probably a little south of fuck buddies."

Her gaze slides from my shoulder to meet mine as her lips turn upward. "I'm lost."

I laugh and slide my hand around the back of her neck, pulling her to me for a kiss. "I'm lost too. But I'm glad you're right here beside me now."

"Me too," she admits, and that makes me smile. I release my hold on her neck, turning to grab my beer as she says, "But you know I'm afraid to believe in this, right? You know I've never had a relationship before. I have no clue what to do, no clue if I'm any good at anything. I'm afraid you're expecting something of me I can't give, and that one day, you're going to wake up and realize I'm really not someone you'd want to give the time of day to and that your hero talents are wasted on me."

A dull, cramping sensation starts in the center of my chest and squeezes tighter as I absorb her words… take in the solemnity of her gaze upon me. God, she's fucked in the head and I can't imagine being so lost and unaware of your own potential.

"Cat," I say as I ignore my beer and turn fully to her. My hands go to her knees but before I can say anything further, my phone rings in my back pocket, and it startles me for a moment. I would normally ignore it because this is a fucking serious issue we need to discuss, but I asked Pish to call me if someone dropped the will off after I left. I give a squeeze to her knees and a hold a finger up. "Just a minute."

I fish in the back pocket of my jeans and pull the phone out, looking at the number. It's not from Westward Ink, but it's not one I recognize either. I have a moment of indecision if I should answer or ignore, but then choose to connect the call in case it's perhaps one of the other artists at the shop calling me on a cell phone I don't have programmed in my contacts. I don't know all of them well enough to call them friends.

"Hello," I say into phone after bringing it to my ear.

"Is this Rand Bishop?" A young woman... definitely not someone from the shop.

"It is."

"This is Amy Felgar, a patient care rep at St. John's Medical Center. Tarryn Stoker is apparently being admitted and her nurse asked me to call you."

My stomach drops so hard and fast that I feel nauseated. "Is she okay?"

She doesn't answer right away, and I can hear some clacking on a computer. "I'm sorry, I don't have much info in the system. They might not have it all entered, but it does say she's being scheduled for surgery."

No clue what my face looks like, but I feel Cat's hand on my thigh with the weight of warm assurance. I look at her, and she returns a worried stare. "I'm on my way."

Hanging up, I put the phone back in my pocket and stand up from the stool. "Tarryn's had some sort of accident. Getting ready to go into surgery. She asked them to call me so it must be pretty serious."

"Yeah... okay," Cat says immediately as I open my wallet up and take some money out. I lay it on the bar so she can pay for the tab. Her eyes glance to the money, and then flick back to me. "I'll bring your food home. Call me once you know something."

"I will," I murmur as I lean in to brush my lips against her temple. "And I'm sorry... this was bad timing. We'll continue the talk when I get back to the apartment."

"It's fine," she reassures me with an understanding smile. "I hope she's okay."

"Me too." I absolutely hate leaving Cat right now, especially on the heels of her revealing the terribly low opinion she has of herself. She needs affirmation of her strengths, not to have me abandon her. But shit… it's not like I can't not go to the hospital. If anything happened to Tarryn and I didn't go, I'd never forgive myself for being so callous.

So I have to go.

Another kiss, this time on Cat's lips, and I leave the Snake River Brewery.

The drive to St. John's takes no more than fifteen minutes as it sits only about ten blocks east and I manage to catch almost every green light. It's a small medical facility but given the amount of ski injuries in this area, they've got an excellent trauma unit.

It takes no time at all to park and make my way back to the surgical suite that the front receptionist directs me to. A nurse greets me at the door and leads me back to a curtained room where I find Tarryn. My eyes quickly roam over her, taking in pale skin but no other outward signs of injury other than an elevated leg wrapped in a temporary splint and bandages.

"What happened?" I ask as I walk up to the side of the bed opposite the IV pole that she's hooked to.

"Stupid really," she says as she reaches a hand toward mine. I take it and give a supportive squeeze. "I was stepping off the sidewalk, crossing right there at Cache and Pearl, and I just stepped down wrong. Ankle buckled and snapped."

"You're kidding?" I say in disbelief that something so simple could cause a break that needs surgery. Rotten fucking luck.

"I knew I could count on you to come," she says as she looks up at me with an adoring smile as the nurse walks into the cubicle room and hangs something else up on the IV stand.

"How soon before she goes back?" I ask the nurse.

"It won't be tonight. Probably first thing in the morning, around six or so," the nurse says briskly. "They want to make sure all the alcohol is out of her system, and the X-rays show the break is fairly clean and stable."

"I was out with Laney and Gayle for some cocktails," Tarryn says with a laugh. "You know how it goes."

"Did that have anything to do with why you fell?" I ask.

She shrugs and moves a thumb over the top of my hand to stroke it. "I don't know. I doubt it. I really just stepped down wrong off the curb."

The nurse writes something in her chart and then walks out of the curtained area. I pull my hand from Tarryn's and try to ignore the hurt look on your face. "Why did you have them call me?"

"Well, because I'm having surgery. Who else would I call?" she responds seriously, as if this was the most common sense thing in the world. Despite the fact we've been broken up for four years.

"Oh, I don't know," I say sarcastically. "How about your roommate and best friend Laney? Or your next best friend Gayle? You know, the girls who were with you when this happened and who you spend almost every day with."

Tarryn still doesn't get it. She waves an impatient hand at me. "Laney will be back. She was going to go handle a few things first, pack me a bag and stuff. She'll be back later. But I knew you'd want to be here too."

Taking a deep breath as the anger rises, I try to remember that she's lying in a hospital bed with a broken ankle and facing surgery. I try to retain a measure of sympathy, but I still can't help it when I say, "Tarryn… I *don't* want to be here. We are not together. There shouldn't be any expectation on your part that I would be here. Now, while I care for you because of things we've shared in the past, we don't have anything past a casual friendship. And when you do stuff like this, you're making it harder on me to want to even maintain that."

She blinks at me several times, eyes wide with surprise. As if this is the first time she's heard this line from me. But it's not. It's just the first time she's heard it while lying in a hospital with a broken ankle and facing surgery. The other time was when she got a flat tire and called me to change it. Or when she got drunk on her birthday and called me at midnight to come out and celebrate with her. Or let's not forget the time she found mouse droppings under her sink and called me to come over and set traps.

"Tarryn," I say gently as I squat beside the bed and put my hand on her shoulder. "It is over with us. Totally over, and I think to make the boundaries clearer, I really need you to just stop reaching out to me."

"No communication whatsoever?" she whispers after a hard swallow.

I don't want to hurt her, but I still say it anyway. "None. I'll stay here with you until Laney gets here, but then that's it, Tarryn."

"I don't understand how you couldn't want to continue our friendship," she says in a small voice.

"Because you want more than that," I tell her simply. "Despite you just calling it a friendship, you want more."

"And you don't?" she asks with her head tilted. "Not ever?"

How can she keep such hope alive? Maybe because I still did stupid shit like change her tire or set her mousetraps, although I didn't go celebrate her birthday with her. I was pissed she woke me up on a work night. Still, I'm just as much at fault because I would usually drop what I was doing to help her out when she called. I was a sap that way. While I'd always make it clear to her I was doing these things out of friendship, I can see why she'd have continued hope. It's because I was still always there for her.

But as I just told her, that all has to stop.

"There's someone else," I tell her softly, and I watch her face fall. "And I really want it to work, so my focus and attention is going to be there. One-hundred percent. In fact, it should be there right now, and that's why I'm leaving as soon as Laney gets here."

Her eyes mist up and she closes them against the sting and my stare, but she gives me a small nod of acknowledgment.

I hope it's also of acceptance, but only time will tell.

Now all I have to do is wait for Laney to show up, so I can get back to Cat and we can continue our conversation. It's time for her to start realizing the potential of what she has within, as well as what we have between us.

Chapter 20
Cat

I PULL MY Mercedes curbside in front of Jake and Lorelei's house, just on the other side of their small driveway. Rand will park his Suburban on the adjacent side, with us leaving plenty of room for their cars when they get home. The house is dark except for the porch light and the driveway is currently empty.

I manage to juggle the takeout containers—which are still quite hot since I had them just package our food up to go rather than eat mine there—along with my purse and keys as I get out of my car and hit the lock button. The driveway is lit up by two sconce lights on either side of the double car garage, but the side of the house is fairly dark as I walk toward the stairway that will lead up to the apartment. I know there's a motion sensor that will turn on a security light there as soon as I reach the end of the driveway and veer off on the small path to the side, so I have no hesitation as I walk toward the house.

Just as I step onto the cement pavers that lead to the wooden staircase, two things hit me at once.

The light isn't working because it doesn't come on, and something is rushing at me in the dark.

I don't have time to scream. Hell, I don't even have time to comprehend I should be fearful.

Instead, something barrels into me, catching at my shoulder and driving me up underneath the staircase and into the side of the house where I slam hard into the wall. My purse and the food goes flying, as do the keys in my hand.

Before I can even take in a breath, which is difficult since it was just knocked out of me, a large, sweaty hand clamps over my mouth, while a beefy arm wraps around my chest. I immediately smell stale beer, cigarettes, and what might possibly be hot dogs, along with the unmistakable scent of motor oil.

I try to take in air but the hand over my mouth is partially obstructing my nose, making it difficult. I'm seized with panic that I might suffocate and can't control my body as it starts to flail.

"You better calm the fuck down, bitch," the man snarls in my ear and his mouth is so close, I can feel the brush of a beard against my skin and the spittle that hits my cheek. To reiterate his point, the arm falls away from my chest, only to come back moments later with a switchblade held expertly in his hands. While I can't see much, he has me turned toward the street, so the glow from the garage sconces causes the blade to glimmer. I can't help the small moan of terror that slips free.

Before I can even try to think of something to save myself, he's spinning me fast, shoving me backward into the wall. My head slams into it with a jarring thud that rattles me, but not enough I don't feel the press of the blade against the base of my throat. It's so dark that I can't make out a damn thing other than the outline of his form.

"Orders were clear," he mumbles, and it almost sounds slurred. "But no reason I can't have a little fun."

Orders? Fun?

Before I can figure it all out, his free hand comes to my blouse, paws at the opening at the top of my chest and manages to get a few fingers lodged in so he can rip it open. Buttons go flying as the white camisole I wear underneath is revealed to the cool night air. It is then I realize what the hell he means by fun.

My body starts to react again, and my hands go to his wrist that holds the knife to my throat as I scream, "No."

Kicking a leg out, I catch him in the shin, and he curses at me before pressing the blade harder against me. I feel the skin open up, and it stings terribly.

"I will cut your motherfucking throat wide open if you don't quiet the fuck up and hold still," he yells at me, completely oblivious that he's making as much noise as I am right now. The alcohol fumes coming off him and the way his words come out less than clear leads me to believe he's definitely drunk or close to it.

Drunk or not, he's incredibly strong and he's cut into the bottom of my neck, so my body goes absolutely still.

"That's better," he praises, then his hand starts pawing at the bottom of my camisole again, trying to inch his way up underneath of it. I take in a deep breath through my nose, trying to think of a way to fight back without getting my throat slit open.

Maybe a knee to his nuts? Surely that will hurt him bad enough he won't be able to control the knife.

Another scream to distract him?

His rough fingers touch my stomach, and panic starts to seize me again. I can't help it. My hands try to push him away from me, thinking a sliced throat would be better than experiencing the "fun" he wants to have.

My body locks tight and I try to figure out exactly where his crotch might be in the gloom, intent to launch my kick, when light suddenly floods the driveway and the side of the house, illuminating my attacker.

Dark, greasy hair that comes down to his shoulders and parts in the middle. A long, wiry beard. Dirty face smudged with oil and sweat. The light surprises him and his eyes flare wide as they turn toward the source, which I know is a car that's just pulled into the driveway.

Either Lorelei or Jake, but I can't tell because I can't turn my head without causing the blade to go in deeper.

I have no clue if they can see us, but my attacker must not think so, even though I can see his eyes are pale blue from the shimmer of the light on him. He presses the blade in tighter and doesn't say a word, seemingly unsure of what to do. For the first time, I feel a small trickle of blood that rolls down past my collarbone to my chest.

The engine is cut off, and I hear the ticking of the motor. The lights don't go out and the car door opens.

All of this happens in just seconds, and without any thought as to whether it's the right thing to do or not, I open my mouth and let out the most piercing shriek I can muster. It startles the man so much that he actually jerks backward from me, my neck suddenly free from the knife. I turn and see Lorelei standing beside her car with the door still open, not even fifteen feet away. She's staring straight at us, the headlights showing her exactly what the situation is. I haven't met her yet, but I did see her getting in her car one morning from the upper window in the garage apartment. I wonder if she knows who I am.

Because she's standing in the glow of the sconce lights, I see clearly the look of shock cross her face, then her eyes narrow in recognition of me and a scary, greasy man standing there with a knife.

Oh, fuck… what was I thinking? Lorelei is pregnant. She might even have her daughter in the backseat. She's now in as much danger as I am.

"Lorelei… run," I scream, my back still pinned against the wall, not by my attacker but merely by my terror.

But she doesn't. Instead, she calmly reaches into her purse and pulls a gun out. My gaze goes to the man, watching his eyes widen in surprise. I'm sure mine look the same.

"You get the hell away from her," Lorelei says as she

holds the gun aimed at him in a sure, two-handed grip. She looks completely confident in her abilities, and I think that might be because everyone in Wyoming owns guns and knows how to shoot.

The man doesn't move one way or the other. He stands frozen to the spot, his eyes riveted on Lorelei and the gun, his hand holding the knife loosely by his side. My gut instinct—no, my internal sense of self-preservation—tells me to run—but I stand frozen to the spot as well, afraid any movement from me might provoke him to attack.

"Only going to say this one more time," Lorelei says, and I hear the unmistakable snick of the gun cocking. "Get the hell away from her."

He only hesitates for one, maybe two seconds before he bolts off into the darkness, the sound of his feet thumping on the hard ground and eventually receding into the distance.

"Get over here, Cat," Lorelei says, her gun now swung slightly toward the way in which my attacker just ran. Well, that answers the question… she knows who I am.

I bend to grab my purse, but Lorelei barks at me, "Over here now. I can't see much past you and I don't know if he's still out there."

There's no hesitation because the thought he might be back propels me as much as Lorelei's commanding voice. I run straight at her, confident she won't shoot me.

She nods at her car and says, "Get in the back with Amber."

I don't argue but do exactly as she says. When the door is closed, she slowly backs into the driver's seat and shuts the door. With amazing efficiency, she sets the gun on the dashboard, reaches into her purse to grab her phone, and manages to start the car. Handing the phone to me, she says, "Call 911. Tell them what happened and the address. Tell them I'm leaving and going to drive the block until they get here."

"Why?" I ask as I take the phone.

"Because I have no clue if there are others, possibly in the house or apartment," she says as she shifts the car into reverse.

Brilliant. Would have never thought of that.

I turn to look at Amber sitting beside me in the car seat. Beautiful little girl with golden blonde hair pulled into a ponytail, clutching a teddy bear. I give her a tremulous smile. "Hi."

She looks at me with solemn eyes, understanding that something scary is going on here.

Then I turn back to Lorelei's phone to call the police.

⬢

"Can you remember anything else?" Detective Blanton asks as he sits beside me on the couch in Lorelei and Jake's living room, typing notes on an iPad. He's a nice-looking man… tall with dark hair peppered lightly with gray, which tells me he's been a cop for a while.

"I think that's it," I say, my brain trying to sift through all the details, but I feel they're all muddied from the fear and adrenaline. It took me no more than five minutes to recount to him what happened the first time, and that's only because the entire thing couldn't have lasted more than two minutes, although it felt like twenty.

He had me go through my story three more times, each time managing to pull out some other detail I had forgotten. It makes me wonder what else I've failed to tell him.

He doesn't say anything, just continues to type in some notes.

The front door opens, but I don't flinch as police officers have been coming in and out as they search for evidence, making sure that no one was inside the house. I turn my head, surprised to see Rand standing there, his face pale and his jaw locked. He sidesteps a cop, rounds the loveseat, and heads straight toward me. I stand up, shuffle to the side of the coffee table, and meet him at mid-room where his arms are around me and he's pushing my face into his chest.

"Jesus," he growls as he squeezes me breathlessly. "Thank fuck for Lorelei."

I nod, because yes… thank fuck. As soon as we returned to the house, only after Lorelei saw the first cruiser pull into the driveway, she called Rand and Jake to let them know what happened. I had no idea what she said because I was immediately pulled into an interview to try to get my statement while details were fresh and untainted. Three other cars pulled up within moments, with two officers heading off into the darkness to see if they'd luck out and find the guy who attacked me. An ambulance arrived moments later.

But here Rand is now with his arms banded around me tightly and for the first time since the man grabbed me, I feel a measure of safety.

Rand pulls back slightly and looks down at me. "Are you okay? Do you need to go to the hospital?"

Hospital?

Hospital!

"How's Tarryn?" I blurt out, my hand coming to his chest. "Is she alright?"

Rand rolls his eyes and glares at me, pulling me back to the couch where he pushes me down and then squats in front of me.

"Forget about her," he says as his fingers come to flutter over the white bandage on my throat that the paramedic put on me. He said it wasn't deep at all and should heal up fine, so I refused a trip to the hospital. "He cut you?"

"I'm fine," I say, rather than confirm the obvious. It turns out he didn't cut me all that bad. A thin slice… more a scratch really, that produced a single large bead of blood that trickled down my chest.

Lorelei walks out of the back hallway and smiles at Rand and me. "I just put Amber down. Can I get anyone coffee?"

The detective looks up from his iPad and says, "I'd actually like to get your statement, Mrs. Gearhart."

Lorelei nods and sits down on the loveseat while Rand pushes up off the floor to pace while she tells her story. He mutters and curses to himself as he listens, and I'm thankful he wasn't here when I told the cop what happened, as it was far more unpleasant than Lorelei valiantly chasing him off with a gun.

"Give me as detailed a description as you can," the detective prods her.

"He was about fifteen feet from me and my headlights illuminated him pretty well. Five-nine, maybe hundred and sixty pounds. Dark brown hair to shoulder, full beard and mustache. Jeans, black boots, and a long-sleeved dark t-shirt. Leather cut with an MC patch on the front that I couldn't see all that well, but I saw a larger one on the back when he turned to run. Had a skull on the back. Oh, and he had a teardrop tattoo under his right eye, at least I'm pretty sure that's what it was, but it all happened so fast. I'm not sure how much that helps."

I stare at Lorelei, my mouth agape. How did she get all that in the few seconds she saw him? How in the hell did she see that tattoo when I was almost face to face with him and didn't notice it. Or maybe I did notice it but it just didn't register. Or perhaps it registered but I've forgotten it because I was more worried about not getting my throat slit.

Let's face it... I'm practically useless at this eyewitness stuff. All I had was greasy hair and a preference for beer and hot dogs, which granted... if they had tracking dogs, they might be able to sniff him out based on that.

Detective Blanton nods as he types the information in, his mouth moving silently as he talks to himself at the same time. When he finishes, he looks up at me. "Did he say anything at all? Have a distinct accent? Anything else you can remember?"

Shit! He did talk to me and I didn't even remember it until he asked. Absolutely fucking useless, and I'm thinking there's even more I've forgotten and he's going to need to interview me several more times to get the entire story.

I nod effusively. "He said he had orders, but that he was going to have fun first."

"Orders?' the detective asks with raised eyebrows, and Rand comes to a standstill. I can feel the shock and anger vibrating off him, but I don't dare look. I know what he's thinking.

"Yeah... he said something like 'orders were clear' but that he wanted to have some fun first," I confirm.

"Son of a bitch," Rand says as he comes to the same conclusion I just did.

"Did someone have motive to hurt you?" the cop asks as he looks at me but cuts a quick glance at Rand.

I nod, but Rand answers for me. "Her late husband's oldest son, Kevin Vaughn. Cat's owed some money from the estate and he's claiming there's another will cutting her out. We've asked for a signed copy and he was supposed to deliver it today, but he never showed."

"What kind of money are we talking about?" the detective asks, now very interested in this turn of events.

"Five million and a house here in Jackson," I provide.

"And what is the estate worth?" he asks.

I shrug. "I don't know. Samuel was a billionaire. But a lot."

"And you think five million out of a billion plus is worth killing you over?"

It's a fair question and it's something I've thought about to the extent I never understood why Kevin wouldn't just let me have that. It was nominal in the grand scheme of things. "No, I don't think that's something that should cause someone to want to kill me," I tell him with a measure of confusion. "But he kicked me out of my house, shut all my access to money off, claiming there was this new will that cut me out completely. He's not been able to produce that, and he made an offer to buy me off a few days ago."

"Buy you off?" Detective Blanton asks.

Squaring my shoulders, I tell him bluntly, "Five thousand dollars or I could move into the Jackson house and be his mistress."

If this surprises the detective, he doesn't let it show, merely bows his head over the iPad and notes that. He asks for contact info for Kevin as well as Richard, confirming where he can get up with me for more questions if needed and so he can keep me updated.

With Lorelei and I both assuring him that's all we can remember, he goes outside to oversee the other cops in searching around the house for evidence.

Rand walks up to me and holds his hand out. I take it, and he pulls me from the couch. "Come on, let's get you upstairs, fed, and then ready for bed."

I nod with a tired smile and turn to Lorelei as she stands from the love seat. "I know we haven't been formally introduced, but thank you for saving my life tonight. And seriously… all that stuff you remembered about what he looked like… you, madam, are a fucking legend."

She grins and leans in to give me a hug. "My pleasure. I'm just glad you're okay."

Rand leads me out of the living room and to the front door, Lorelei following behind us. Food sounds good, but a hot shower sounds better as I can't get the smell of hot dogs and beer out of my head.

Twisting the knob, Rand pulls the door open and I see both Jake and Bridger standing at the bottom of the porch talking to Detective Blanton. Both their heads turn our way, Jake's eyes going to Lorelei's, where he does a quick up and down to ensure she's fine and then gives her a transparent look that says, *I'm so proud of you, glad you're safe, and I'm going to kill that asshole if I find him for even coming on to my property, but before that, I'm going to take you inside and fuck you because I love you so much.*

Bridger looks straight at me, his eyes also roaming

over me quickly and coming to stop at the bandage on my neck. His lips flatten out in a grimace, his eyes coming back to mine where he gives me a sad look. He turns back to Jake, claps him on the shoulder, and then turns to Rand as he leads me down the porch steps.

When my feet hit the bottom, Bridger reaches a hand out and grips my chin. "You okay?"

"Yeah… I'm fine."

He nods and then looks to Rand, nodding upward to his apartment. "We need to talk."

Chapter 21
Rand

I DIDN'T THINK I could be strung any tighter.

Cat was attacked on the doorstep of our home and it was nothing more than a fortuitous moment that Lorelei happened to come home at that exact time. I shudder thinking about the alternative because that means I'd have to imagine Cat laying broken, raped, and dead for us to find when we got home later, and that's not something I can handle.

But when Bridger says we need to talk, my body tightens even more and my teeth slam together so hard I think they may have cracked.

"Come on up," I tell Bridger as I grip Cat's hand tighter and lead her to the stairwell. Bridger follows behind, and we easily navigate our way as the police have a large ground lamp set up on the driveway as they look at footprints and comb the area for anything that can assist them in the investigation. I'm assuming that whoever attacked Cat knocked out the security light because it's not on.

The wooden porch at the top of the stairs is empty, but there were some technicians up there when I arrived a bit ago dusting for prints on the door. They had confirmed it was still locked and the apartment was secure, but they figured the attacker could have tried to get inside first before Cat arrived. Black dust smudges the doorknob, but I ignore it as I release Cat's hand to pull my keys out and open the door.

We're all silent as we walk in, and I quickly turn on lights in the living room and kitchen. Cat goes to the couch and sits on it with a sigh. Her plaid blouse is still open, the white camisole underneath demurely hiding everything, but I don't miss the fact the buttons are missing with pieces of thread hanging from the places they were once secured.

My teeth clamp down harder and my jaw starts to hurt from the force of it. I want to kill someone... well, Kevin to be exact because I know damn well he's behind this. Then I want just a few minutes with the guy who dared to attack Cat because he's going to regret the day his sorry, piece-of-shit mother ever gave birth to him because he'd rather have not been born than what I intend to do to him.

I go to the cabinet to the right of the sink and pull out a can of chicken noodle soup. It's the best I can manage for Cat at this moment, and I go about making it silently because I'm afraid if I open my mouth to talk about the events of the last hour I'm going to lose my shit. Bridger comes into the kitchen, takes a seat at the table, and watches me silently. He said we need to talk and I'm not sure what he's waiting for, but I wait all the same. Not sure if he means he wants to talk to me privately or if he's just waiting until I can feed Cat.

While the soup heats, I pull an open bottle of white wine from the fridge that Cat had put there. I also grab two beers for Bridger and me. Cat gets up from the couch, walks into the kitchen, and accepts a glass of wine from me as she sits down at the other chair I have at my tiny table.

"Why are you here?" she asks Bridger bluntly after taking a sip of the wine and setting it down before her. "How did you know this was going on?"

"I didn't," he says. "Shocked the shit out of me when I pulled up and saw the circus. Jake and that cop filled me in."

Pouring the soup into a bowl, I set it before Cat with a large spoon. I almost expect her to push it away, but instead, she starts eating it, taking the time to blow on each spoonful she brings to her mouth.

"So what's up?" I say as I lean back against the counter, crossing my arms over my chest. I want Bridger to hurry up, say whatever he needs, and then get the fuck gone. I have a woman who was attacked and I need to check her over. I need to see with my eyes that she's okay, and I need to feel with my hands the same. I need to give her the opportunity to tell me how fucking scared she was, and then I need to reassure her she's safe and that will never fucking happen again. And then… if she's still not exhausted and ready to go to sleep, I need to take the time to let her know how valued she is and that I want something more.

That was made abundantly clear to me the minute Lorelei called me at the hospital to tell me what happened. I always knew Cat might leave the area and go back to Vegas, but tonight I came very close to losing her and it made me prioritize a bit.

Made me realize she's my top priority.

"Jenna went through the entire trust agreement you gave me," Bridger says while tapping his index finger on the table. Cat pauses with a spoon of soup halfway to her mouth. "Cat stands to inherit a bit more than just five million and a house. That's why I came here."

"What?" Cat says, dropping the spoon back down.

"Yeah… the five million and the house was an immediate bequest to get you set up, but later on in the document, he also gives you ten percent of all profits from the hotels and subsidiary businesses under them for the remainder of your life, and then that reverts to his kids if you die before them."

My mind quickly calculates. Ten percent of a billion is one hundred million, and that's just estimating Samuel's worth. It's probably more.

"Holy fuck," I say as I turn my gaze upon Bridger and he's watching me carefully. "Now *that* is something Kevin would kill over."

"Yup," Bridger agrees and cuts a glance at Cat. "Did you know that?"

"No," she says in astonishment. "I mean… Samuel said he'd take care of me, but I thought the five million and a house was more in line with what he meant."

I don't say it, but all I can think is, *Yeah… that fucker must be showing his appreciation for all the times his wife took someone else's cock so he could humiliate her.*

"I don't want that money," Cat says bitterly, and I know she's thinking the same thing. What that money really represents.

But fuck if I'm going to let her walk away from her due. "Yes, you do."

"No—"

I cut her off with a sharp, "Yes, Cat. It's yours under the law and you are not turning your nose up at it. Your husband may have been the ultimate prick, but in the end, he was looking out for you."

Her mouth snaps shut and she glares at me. I know there's more argument there, but we'll worry about that later. Turning to Bridger I say, "We need to go down, grab that detective, and tell him this."

"Already did that when he walked out. He wants a copy of the trust agreement."

"I'll get it to him tomorrow," I say, but my mind is already racing ahead, trying to figure out how Kevin could be connected to the attacker.

But as usual, Bridger is uncannily ahead of me. "Cop told me a description of the guy that attacked Cat. Sounds like he could be a member of Mayhem's Mission."

I nod because that's what I had been thinking. While plenty of people ride bikes in this area, there's a huge motorcycle club—Mayhem's Mission—and they are definitely shady. Without a doubt, Kevin would get someone to do his dirty work, and I could see him being stupid enough to approach a biker to do it.

"I'm going to call my buddy, Kyle Sommerville, tonight. He rides with them. I'll see if he's heard anything." Bridger stands from the table indicating that's all the information he has to share.

"Think he'll know something?" Cat asks him as she stands up too.

He turns to her. "Maybe, and if he does, he still might not tell me anything, but I figure it's worth a shot."

"Well, thank you," Cat says as she steps into Bridger, wrapping her hands around his waist. He seems surprised for a moment. The man is not the huggy-feely type. But then his face softens, his arms come around her upper back, and he gives her a quick squeeze before releasing her.

I walk Bridger to the door, noting that Cat sits back down to continue eating her soup. Still, to make sure she can't hear, I step out onto the small porch behind him and pull the door shut behind me. He turns, knowing I'm here seeking a private word.

"You think it was Kevin behind this?" I ask to make sure we're on the same page.

"Yup. Same as you."

"Then I'm going to pay him a visit after Cat goes to sleep tonight," I say with a nod. "I'll get the truth."

"Yeah, you are absolutely *not* going to do that," Bridger says gruffly and steps into me. "You're going to let the police handle this."

I might not have his bulk but I stand eye to eye with him, so I lean into him rather than back. "That fucker hired someone to kill Cat. Someone who didn't intend to just do it easily. He was going to rape her first. Not going to let that slide."

Bridger doesn't physically back away, but his voice softens a bit. "I get it, man. You care for her and you want vengeance. But it's not going to make anything better for her. If you go there tonight and beat the shit out of him, the only one who that is making feel better is you. Trust me… you're best served to go back in there and hold that girl tonight. She needs that more than you running off on a fool's errand."

In that moment, I hate him for being right, calm, and wise. I hate he can take the high road and still be able to sleep tonight, but if I do as he asks and take the high road, I'm going to burn from the inside-out with my failure to protect her.

Still, I can't disagree with him that at least for tonight, Cat needs me by her side, not running off to avenge her. So, I nod at him curtly and turn to head back inside.

Before my hand touches the knob, Bridger asks in a low voice that's sure not to filter down to the cops pacing around the yard with their flashlights. "You ever coming back to The Silo?"

I look over my shoulder at him.

His face is inscrutable.

I shrug and say, "No immediate plans, but if I do, it will be with Cat."

Bridger lets out a deep chuckle of understanding as I walk back into the apartment where I find Cat at the sink, washing out her bowl. She doesn't turn to face me but instead asks, "Everything okay?"

"I'm the one who should be asking you that," I say as I walk up behind her. Reaching around with my hands, I take the bowl from her and place it in the sink, then turn her around to face me. She does so easily, looking up at me with curiosity. Her eyes are wan, but still she smiles at me.

My eyes drop to the bandage and with slightly shaky hands, I peel the tape and gauze back so I can see for myself.

A thin, red line about three inches long, about two inches above her left collarbone. The air wheezes out of my chest as I realize just how much worse it could be. Placing the bandage back in place, I press the tape onto her skin and look up at her with an encouraging smile that takes all my willpower to give her.

"Not bad at all," I say. Her eyes shine with amusement at me that I'm trying to downplay what happened, just to take the weight and magnitude off her shoulders a bit.

"You need to eat," she says, hands sliding up to my chest. "And you still haven't told me if Tarryn's okay?"

My hands capture hers, and I hold them in place right over my heart. "Tarryn's fine. She's having surgery tomorrow on her ankle, and I've asked her to stop contacting me."

"Rand," Cat says in a censuring tone.

"Don't, Cat," I warn her, still trying to gentle my words as she's had a shittier day than I have. "You let me handle Tarryn and trust I'm doing what's right and I'm doing it in a way that's not intentionally hurtful, okay?"

Immediately, her cheeks turn pink and her gaze drops. "I'm sorry… I shouldn't have…"

"Cat," I say softly but firmly to cut her off, and she looks back up. "Let's talk about you, okay?"

"Me?"

"Yeah… and me."

"And you?" she asks hesitantly.

"Let's talk about us and if there's a concept of us," I clarify with a smile, taking her by the hand and walking her into the living room. My desire is to walk her right into the bedroom so I can undress her, examine her fully to make sure I'm not missing anything, and then pull her into bed where I'd also really like to fuck her but know that I'll ultimately just end up holding her.

But this conversation needs some boundaries, so it's to the couch I lead us. She takes a seat and rather than sit beside her, I plop my butt on the coffee table instead where our knees bump together.

She frowns and says, "Uh-oh… this is serious."

"Yeah," I admit.

"You want me to leave?" she asks softly, her eyes shining at me with some understanding she thinks I need but totally don't want.

"No, I don't want you to leave," I tell her with exasperation as I take her hands. "I want to talk about you staying… forever, if you want."

"Staying?" she asks carefully. "You mean more than just here at the apartment with you?"

I don't answer her directly but rather turn back to where we had left things at the Snake River Brewery before I'd got called away by Tarryn. "You told me tonight that you were afraid that I was going to wake up one day and realize you're not the person I'd want to give the time of day to."

She nods, lips pursed in an ashamed grimace.

"Well, my fears are a little different," I tell her as I press forward. "I'm afraid I'm going to wake up one day and you'll be gone because I didn't make the bold move to tell you how I'm feeling. I know you said you're afraid you can't give me what I'm expecting, and the ironic thing is, you already give me that and so much more, and you don't even realize it."

"Rand," she says, and she sounds desperate. Her face is pale and she looks decidedly uncomfortable, but I decide to push forward.

"I'm crazy about you, Cat," I tell her firmly, looking her dead in the eye. "That call tonight from Lorelei was my wake-up call and I realized I was not ready to lose you in any fashion. I'm falling in love with you and I'm sorry if that makes you uncomfortable, but you need to know for a woman who doesn't think she amounts to much, you're pretty much amounting to my everything."

Cat blinks at me, her eyes getting shiny. "You don't mean that."

"I do and one day, you'll believe it too," I tell her with utter confidence.

"I don't know if I can love," she whispers fearfully. "I mean... look at what I know of it. A cold, derelict mother who only wants to use me and a dead husband who got off on humiliating me... a father who abandoned me. I don't know what it even means to care for someone."

"That's bullshit, Cat, and you know it," I tell her. "The mere fact you're worried about not giving me what I need tells me you care for me. Hell, the fact that you were more worried about how Tarryn was tonight than yourself tells me that you've got a heart the size of this state."

She blinks at me again, and I can see she's confused. She even shakes her head in silent denial, opens her mouth to do the same, and then seems to reconsider because she closes it just as quickly. Her gaze slides over to my bookshelf that holds photographs of me competing and with my family. It tells of a happy, fulfilled life surrounded by people who love and care for me.

And then she totally changes the subject.

At least I think it's a change of subject.

"If Kevin did this... hired someone to kill me, do

you think that's something within his very makeup or was it learned behavior from maybe his father… to sort of take what you want?"

Well, shit. That's a deep as hell question and I don't know much about Kevin or Samuel. She has to have a reason for asking it, but I'm not sure what she's looking for, so I'm a little hesitant when I say, "I have to believe that his father's influence played a role. His father pretty much taught him he could have what he wanted without working for it. You're the example of that. He let that shit have you… someone beautiful, amazing, and totally beyond his reach, and he just handed you over without his son even earning the right to breathe the same air as you."

She nods, gaze coming back to me. "I think that's probably true. Although Richard doesn't seem to have that same entitlement."

"Or maybe he's involved in this with Kevin and we just don't know it," I point out.

"Also true," she says softly, and then changes subjects again. "I wonder what type of influence my father would have been on me. You know, if he'd have stuck around… been involved in my life."

"You don't know that he abandoned you," I say carefully, so she's not making conclusions about a situation she truly knows nothing about.

"That's what my mom says," she says bitterly. "But I can never trust what she says, so who knows?"

"Well, you didn't have very good role models in your

life," I tell her, as this is something I am sure about. "And yet, you're still an incredibly caring and empathetic woman, so I'm going to have to say that part is inside of you somehow. Maybe that's part of your dad."

Her smile softens, lips curved in a wistful arc while her eyes get dreamy. "You know… if I get money from Samuel's estate, I think I'm going to try to find my dad. It may be a chase after nothing, but it seems the right thing to do if I were to have a windfall of some sort."

"That inheritance is not a windfall," I remind her. "It's your due under the law as his wife. And we're going to make sure you get every penny."

She nods with another smile, and then yawns. It's my cue that this deep conversation is over for now. While that part of me that is dying for her to admit her feelings for me wants to bully her into it, I think enough has been said tonight to at least make her think. She knows that this is more than just casual for me, so now I really just need to sit back and let her try to figure things out.

Chapter 22
Cat

I WALK INTO The Silo with my head held high but my palms sweating fiercely. While my head tells me this is a good idea, my heart is already hurting in anticipation of what Rand will think.

It's been four days since I was attacked and things have not gotten any clearer to me. In fact, I feel like I'm struggling to stay afloat in muddied waters.

Detective Blanton brought Kevin in for questioning the very next morning. According to the detective, Kevin acted shocked he was being questioned in relation to the attack and of course, denied any involvement. He was released after two hours of being grilled and maintaining a consistent refusal to admit to hiring someone to kill me.

This was frustrating, especially because the detective told me he didn't buy Kevin's innocent act for a moment. He had asked Kevin about the supposed will he claimed cut me out, and after a lot of hemming and hawing on his part, he did finally admit there wasn't another will. He said he didn't believe I deserved anything and that's the reason why he said there was. He didn't even act abashed that he kicked me out of my home on a lie.

This of course raised a huge, red flag to the detective and has motivated him to push harder to find my attacker, who could then possibly turn on Kevin.

The other thing that happened was Richard called me that evening, as apparently he'd been questioned by the detective via telephone immediately after Kevin was. If I can believe him, and I think I can, Richard was appalled that Kevin claimed there was another will and used that to kick me out of the house. He confirmed for me what Bridger had revealed just four days ago.

I was going to get five million dollars, the Jackson house, and apparently yearly profits in the amount of ten percent. Richard didn't seem put out in the slightest. The best thing that happened was he assured me Kevin had vacated the house today to return to Vegas and I could move back immediately if I wanted. He also opened up a bank account in my name and transferred some immediate funds until he could get a larger transfer done, as well as turned my credit cards back on, not that it mattered. I had cut those cards up days ago, as I didn't want anything reminding me that I was once Catherine Vaughn. I even went and got a new Wyoming driver's license with my maiden name of Lyons, although I hadn't decided whether or not to stay here.

About the only thing I have decided is that Rand has become important enough to me that I've decided to cut him loose.

I know he has faith in me.

I know he sees something within me that I just can't seem to recognize myself.

I know, without a doubt, that he believes we could have something solid and long lasting between us.

Unfortunately, I just don't believe that.

While it warmed me down to my toes when he told me that he was crazy about me and was falling in love with me, cold reality soon settled in as I lay in his arms that night. I thought about all the things that make me a wretched human being and felt myself growing colder on the inside, a slithering cloud of blackness filling me up.

I'm a woman who let dozens of men fuck me.

Defile me.

Humiliate me.

I let my husband force me to have sex with people who were as vile and disgusting as he was.

I let him make me have sex with his own son, for God's sake.

I sat there like a doormat and took that abuse for years, and why did I do it?

Because the money and having a place to live was more important than my self-respect. At any time, I could have walked out that door and gone back to stripping. It may not have been the best life, but it was an honest one, and I could have gotten right back up on that stage and been able to support myself just fine.

But if I'm being absolutely honest with myself, and reflecting on the true nature of myself so I can decide what to do about Rand, then I have to admit I was perfectly willing to let myself be defiled and humiliated so I could keep the fancy house, Mercedes, and designer clothing. I whored myself out for a cushy life and that right there tells me all I need to know about my true character.

And that is not someone who would ever be worthy of Rand Bishop.

The only problem was that I didn't know how to go about breaking it off. We spent the weekend together just hanging out in the apartment, fucking constantly. It was desperately pathetic on my part because I wanted to hold onto the physical pleasure with him just a little bit longer, knowing that there would never be another man comparable to him in my bed. It goes without saying there will never be another who is comparable in my heart either. Since I'm being honest about all the terrible things that make up Cat Lyons, I can also be truthful and admit I do love Rand. I love him enough to make sure he does far better than me.

All weekend, Rand was careful in his words with me, preferring to take more of a backseat when it came to talking about the future or feelings. I think he was giving me "space" to come to the same conclusions he did, but all I realized is that while I cared for him more than anything in this world, I was nowhere near good enough for him.

I simply don't deserve him.

He absolutely doesn't deserve a woman like me.

We both went back to work on Monday as usual—him to the tattoo shop and me to the Hayes' campaign headquarters—and it killed me to come home last night to find he made dinner for us. It was the perfect picture of domesticity, and it made me realize I could not let his hope continue to build.

So when I got up this morning for work, I knew I needed to send a decisive message to him that I was most certainly not the one for him. The note on the kitchen table telling him I was spending the evening at The Silo should do the trick, even though I'm sick to my stomach about it.

I need to stay strong. This is the best way… to remind him of who I am deep down so he can realize his heart is being wasted on someone like me.

Walking up to the bar, I glance around at the patrons. I should just choose someone, fuck him fast, and get it over with. That will, for me at least, cut the ties to Rand. Once I'm with someone else, I know it's over.

Instead, I decide to order a drink to calm my nerves. I take a seat at the bar and order a glass of wine, sipping on it while contemplating how much my life sucks at this moment. Two men approach me, but I decline the invitation. I tell myself I'm enjoying my wine and want to finish it first, although truthfully, I don't even know what kind I'm sipping.

"Odd… seeing you here," I hear from behind me and recognize the gravel-like timber to Bridger's voice. I don't even bother to look at him as he takes the seat next to me.

"Why's that?" I ask blandly.

"You've been absent for a while… you and Rand wrapped up in each other. It's just odd you're here now. Without him."

I shrug and still don't look at him.

A sip of wine.

Staring blankly at the bar top.

"I talked to my buddy, Kyle," Bridger says in a low voice, thankfully leaving the subject of Rand and me alone. "He was noncommittal on whether he could identify the guy based on the description. I sort of got the impression he was going to poke around and find out what he could before he decides if he's going to help."

"What does that mean?" I ask as I swivel my stool so I'm facing Bridger.

"It means that if the hit on you was brought before the club and sanctioned, Kyle won't tell me shit. But if this was a rogue act, he might give us a tip in the right direction."

"Oh," I say in disappointment as I swivel back to face the bar. I know Kevin's not going to roll over on anything, and that the only way to pin him to this is by finding the guy who tried to carry out the order, hoping he gives Kevin up for a plea deal or something. It sounds to me as if that's probably not going to happen, which is a cause for concern. It means I'm still vulnerable and although Richard has given me assurances, I think Kevin is a bit on the sociopathic side. I wouldn't put it past him to continue to come after me.

"So this is it, huh?" he prods. "You're making the break from him?"

So much for him leaving the subject of Rand and me alone. Gaze goes to my wine... wish I had about three of these in me right now. "It's the right thing to do. He deserves better than me."

"If you say so," Bridger says mildly.

I turn to him in surprise, finally looking at the man who most people look upon as some sort of god around here. He's been nothing short of nice and supportive of me, and I've always had the distinct impression he takes care of those he calls friends. I don't necessarily think I'm in that category, but I know damn well Rand is. So, I thought he might try to persuade me otherwise.

For Rand's benefit.

"You're not going to try to talk me out of this?" I ask, my eyes narrowing on him.

"Nope," he says with a confident smile. "You're a big girl and can make your own decisions. You're also a smart girl. I've got confidence in you."

Huh?

I think this just affirms for me that Bridger probably recognizes those same god-awful qualities that I see in myself. He probably knows this is the best thing. This should be affirmation to me of my decision but instead it hurts me deep down to know that I must be right about myself.

"Besides," Bridger says as almost an afterthought.

"Rand just pulled into the parking lot as I was walking in. Figured he'll have plenty to say to get you to change your mind."

"Rand's here?" I spin swiftly on my chair, looking back at the door. And sure enough, he's standing there just at the end of the short hall that leads into the main room. His gaze is pinned on me with an absolutely unreadable expression on his face.

He stalks across the room, not looking anywhere else but at me. As he gets closer—when I can see the green of his eyes—I note they're filled with disappointment.

When he reaches me, he spares a quick look to Bridger and lifts his chin in greeting before turning back to me. He just stares and I don't know what to say. Should I apologize? Explain my actions? Or maybe I should just own them to make the break easier.

Before I can utter a word though, Bridger stands up and claps a hand on Rand's shoulder I'm assuming in commiseration. He gives me a guarded look and turns to head back across the room. Rand and I both watch him walk out of The Silo.

"Why are you doing this, Cat?" Rand asks softly, and I slide my gaze back to him.

I lay open my heart and tell him the truth. "Because I'm not good enough for you."

I expect him to scoff, roll his eyes, and lay into me with a speech about all my fine qualities. But he doesn't. He just stares at me with the look of a man who knows the ride will be bumpy but who is prepared to hold on tight.

"If this is what you need to do," Rand says in a neutral voice, "then you do it. Just so you know—it's not going to change my feelings about you."

My mouth falls open as I realize he's deadly serious. "You'd sincerely be okay with me fucking someone else here tonight?"

"No, I won't be okay with it," he says with a touch of anger in his voice and his eyes firing a little hot. "If you're going to play around with others, I want to be involved. But if you feel this is what you need to do to because you can't deal with my feelings, or maybe the feelings you have for me, then you need to do it."

"I need to do it?" I whisper back in question since he seems to think he knows what I need.

"You need to do it," he reiterates. "But I'm here to tell you, Cat. You won't feel better. You'll feel worse because you'll know it hurts me. It won't make the break any easier for either of us."

This angers me because I know he's right and I don't want him to be. I also don't want to fuck someone else, so maybe I should just really lay it on the line so we can end things on words rather than actions.

I lean toward him, keeping my voice just above a whisper. "Do you know how much strange cock I've had in me? Multitudes of men who I didn't even know their name? Fucking me in my mouth… my pussy… my ass. I never said no. I never thought to have a tiny bit of self-respect and tell my asshole, evil husband that I wasn't doing those nasty things. I took it over and over again, and you know why? Because I liked the money and the lifestyle. I didn't want to go back to a dirty, cockroach-infested apartment or a sticky stage with a stripper pole. I whored myself out to be a wealthy woman, and I did it without regrets. Is that the type of person you could fall in love with?"

"I know all of that," Rand says back in a low voice, and I don't detect a trace of bitterness over my "used goods" status. Instead, his voice is gentle as he reiterates, "I know all that and I don't care. But you are wrong about one thing… you do have regrets. If you didn't, it wouldn't bother you so much right now."

I blink at him, unsure of what to say.

He's so right.

I regret everything I've ever done from the moment I met Samuel Vaughn. I regret marrying someone without love, for choosing money over respect, and for hurting Rand in any way.

He leans in closer, lips hovering just inches away from mine. I breathe in, and he smells so good…

"You do what you have to do, Cat," Rand says softly. "It's not chasing me away."

He kisses me. Nothing but a tender kiss on the corner of my mouth.

Then he turns away from me and walks out of The Silo.

Chapter 23
Rand

I'm not a fan of Vegas. Been a handful of times, usually for a bachelor party. Not big on gambling, definitely don't want to see Cirque de Soleil or Celine, and all-you-can-eat buffets are overrated.

This part of Vegas isn't much better. No glitzy lights. No throng of people walking around with stars in their eyes.

Nope. Cat's mom lives in a small trailer park on the outskirts of town with nothing but flat desert as far as the eye can see. When I pull my Suburban onto the dirt path that leads into the entrance, dust kicks up and swirls all around.

I left Cat in The Silo going on almost twenty-four hours ago.

I left her behind and told her she needed to do what she needed to do, and I don't regret that. I can't make Cat into something she doesn't want to be. I have to let her figure things out so she accepts them.

She has to be in control of her destiny. Of that, I'm absolutely certain.

So I went home, packed a duffle bag with a few days'

worth of clothing, and hopped in my SUV. I drove straight out of town and headed south, intent on doing something for Cat that might help her regain her identity. It's a long shot, but I don't have anything but time on my hands.

I thought about flying because I hate long drives, but then immediately discounted it for two reasons. First, I needed space from Cat and I needed it at that moment. Probably couldn't have caught a flight out last night and that would mean a potential run in with her at the apartment. She needed the space to figure things out as well, so I knew driving the ten-plus hours would do the trick. Secondly though, and most important, it gave Bridger time to do what he needed to do.

As soon as I hit the road, I called him and told him I was going to find Cat's father. He seemed neither surprised nor skeptical of my actions, but just asked what he could do to help. I told him I needed to first find Cat's mom because she was the only one who knew who he was. Cat told me her mother said he abandoned them and she didn't even put the name on the birth certificate.

No clue if that's true or not, but I'm going to find out.

Bridger also showed me why he's got the respect of everyone in The Silo, and why people turn to him when their troubles get too much to handle.

"I'm heading back over to The Silo now," he'd told me last night. "I'll keep an eye on her for you."

"Let her do what she wants to do," I told him, even

though the thought of her fucking someone there made my stomach knot up.

"You got it, brother," he replied. "And for what it's worth, you're doing the right thing."

"Going to find her father?"

"No," he said solemnly. "Letting her figure herself out. Only way it's going to work between you two."

The words were a small comfort as I traveled mile after mile to Nevada. But even his wise words started to dull when I saw Vegas come into view around eight AM. I went straight to the Bellagio and checked in.

Pulled my clothes off and fell on the bed in an exhausted heap.

Sleep came easily despite my worries.

When I woke up around five, Bridger had sent me a text with Trish Lyons' address and two additional words, *Good luck*.

After a quick shower and a room service meal, I got my Suburban from the valet and headed out of town to hopefully get the information I need.

I navigate the neat rows of trailers, all fairly well-kept with underpinning and permanent decks built on although they all have some age on them. As I pull up to Trish's home, I see a silver sedan parked perpendicular to the porch steps, and I hope it's hers. I'm prepared to camp out and wait if it's not, but I'd sure like to get this over with because I doubt it's going to be pleasant.

I park behind the silver car and shut my engine off. As I open the driver's door, I see a flutter of movement at the window so I know someone's definitely in there.

By the time I exit my SUV and hit the top porch step, the front door is opening, leaving the screen door in place as a barrier. I assume that's Cat's mom staring out at me, but I can't be sure as they look nothing alike. This woman is shorter than Cat by several inches and has thinning blonde hair that's pulled back into a bun. Her skin is overly tan and although she can't be more than mid-forties, the damage from the sun creates an almost leather-like look that adds hard years onto her.

"Can I help you?" she asks in a voice that's unfriendly and brusque.

"Trish Lyons?" I counter.

She could deny it, but I can tell by the look on her face that it's her. Still, she plays dumb. "Depends who's asking."

I don't have time for this shit. "My name is Rand Bishop. I'm a friend of your daughter's. I want to find her father, and I want you to tell me his name. I'm prepared to pay well for the information."

Her face morphs from skepticism to interest the minute I mention money. Her hand shoots out, and she pushes the screen door open. "Come on inside and we'll talk."

I step inside, pleased to find the interior cool. Her house is well kept but a little worn. Carpet and furniture looking as if it dated back to Cat's childhood days. I glance around and don't see a single picture of Cat and while it doesn't necessarily surprise me, it does sadden me. This woman hasn't minded taking money from Cat over the last several years but she doesn't care enough about her to even have her photograph on display.

"Would you like something to drink?" she asks me as I follow her into the kitchen that sits right beside the living room with a short, half-wall divider between the spaces.

"No thanks," I say.

She sits at the small, round table in the center, nodding at the chair opposite of her. I take a seat, lean back, and clasp my hands on the table.

"How much money are you willing to pay me for the name of Cat's father?" she asks, her eyes now gleaming with the possibilities.

"Ten thousand," I say, ready to haggle with this woman. She's going to try to squeeze everything out of me, no doubt.

"That won't do it," she says and rubs a finger over her chin thoughtfully. "But twenty-five would."

I know I can get her down more because I recognize the lust for the money in her gaze. But I want something more than just the name of Cat's father from her, so I tell her, "Done. However, after this, you don't ever ask your daughter for another dime. You can contact her to inquire as to how she's doing, wish her happy birthday, or just in general try to be a mother. But you don't squeeze her for money ever again."

Rather than respond to my offer, she says, "That husband of hers is dead. I expect she's inherited a ton of money. Seems like I'm selling out short at twenty-five now that I think about it."

I could lie to this woman, tell her that Cat didn't get any inheritance, but that doesn't necessarily sit right with me. So I hedge a little and tell her the truth as it stands today. "Cat doesn't have anything other than a little bit of money she got from pawning her jewelry. She was kicked out of her home and told she'd been cut out of the will. She's working a job right now making fifteen bucks an hour. She's got nothing to give you."

That was all truth. Her eyes are calculating as she considers what I've said.

"But I do have money… lots of it, and twenty-five thousand is more than fair to pay for a name and a final payoff for you to leave Cat alone."

"What does she hope to gain by finding him?" she asks, not because she cares for Cat but because she's trying to see if there's another angle to exploit.

I ignore the question because she doesn't deserve to hear anything about Cat's need to find herself. It's partly this woman's fault that her daughter is so lost. Instead, I say, "I'll give you half now for the name and the other half when I find him."

"What if you don't find him?" she asks, leaning forward with shrewd eyes.

"If I don't find him, then you don't get the rest of the money." I lean forward and hold her stare.

"That doesn't seem fair," she pouts.

"Take it or leave it." I was done negotiating and I knew she was going to take it. No way she was turning her nose up at $12,500 in cash right now.

Trish stands up from the table and walks back into the living room. I don't follow but watch her pull a small box out of a rattan chest on one end of the couch. She opens it up, riffles through, and comes back to me, sullenly handing me a piece of paper.

I take it from her and see it's a computer printout of a news article dated February 3, 2003. There's a grainy picture of a man wearing a military uniform with a beret. The title says, "Fort Bragg Soldier Awarded Bronze Star".

"I would Google him every now and then," she says, nodding down to the paper in my hand. "Found that a few years ago, but not really sure why I kept it. Was just curiosity, I guess."

My eyes move back and forth as I read the short article:

Fort Bragg, NC (AP): Sergeant Major Allen Henning with the 82nd Airborne Division was awarded the Bronze Star with Valor for selfless actions he undertook in Afghanistan that saved the lives of numerous soldiers. Sergeant Major Henning, along with fourteen other soldiers, came under enemy fire while stationed at Forward Operating Base Eagle in the Balad district of Afghanistan. After identifying the shooter in an Afghani uniform, who had already shot two soldiers under Henning's command, Sergeant Major Henning managed to return cover fire to enable others to get to safety. He then managed to wound the assailant, effectively disarming him and ensuring his quick capture by U.S. Forces.

The article goes on to say that Allen Henning is from Green Bay, Wisconsin and had joined the Army in 1990 at the age of eighteen. I know Cat is twenty-four, born in 1991, so if this is her father, that would have made him nineteen at the time.

I look up to Trish, who doesn't hold an ounce of fondness on her face for the man who gave her a daughter.

"What's the story with you two?" I ask bluntly.

She grimaces and sits back down at the table. "I was living with a friend in Fayetteville, North Carolina and met Allen there. He'd been in the Army only a few months stationed at Ft. Bragg. We had a brief affair and then I came back to Vegas. He apparently went on to do quite well for himself."

"Define brief affair," I push at her.

She shrugs. "We were together maybe four months. Because we were young and stupid, we were fucking like rabbits with no protection. I got pregnant and never told him."

"Why not?" I ask, trying not to let my lip curl up in disdain at her.

"He was gung ho about the Army, and I sure as shit didn't want to lead that type of life. He got sent to some school at a base in Alabama. He wanted me to wait for him back at Fort Bragg but as soon as he left, I used that opportunity to come back home to Vegas."

"You just left without telling him you were leaving?"

"Knew he'd try to talk me out of it. If he'd known I

was pregnant, he would have followed me to Vegas. Allen was just one of those upstanding people, always doing the right thing. Was kind of dull actually."

Man, this woman is cracked in the head.

"If you didn't want to be tied down, why in the world would you even keep the baby?" I have to ask her. Because in the few minutes I've been in this woman's presence, I can tell she has no business being a mother.

"I didn't have the funds to get back to Vegas. Told my mom I was pregnant and abandoned, which wasn't the entire truth, but she wired me money to get home. She made me promise to keep the baby though as she didn't believe in abortion. So I had Catherine and lived with my mom for about three years. She pretty much took care of the baby until she died from a sudden brain aneurysm, then I had to step up to the plate and become a mom."

Yeah, lady… you most certainly didn't step up to the plate.

"Why didn't you just give Cat to her father if you didn't want her?" I ask, unable to hold the derision out of my voice.

"Because she had her uses," she says without an ounce of shame, still looking me in the face. "Tax breaks and government assistance."

"You have got to be fucking kidding me," I growl at her from across the table, pushing my chair back and standing up. "You kept a child because she helped you with taxes and food stamps? What the hell is wrong with you?"

Trish's face flushes red as she tries to defend herself. "I did the best I could. I never beat her or abused her."

"You neglected her," I spit at her. "You kept her from a parent who might have wanted to give her love and devotion. The only thing you love about your daughter is the money she gives you."

She shrugs again, not willing to engage me in a debate over her mothering skills. Instead, she says, "Look... how about I just get my money and you go on your fool's errand trying to chase Allen down? Not sure what you hope to accomplish with that, but that was the easiest twenty-five thousand made in the history of the world."

"Twelve-thousand-five hundred," I correct her as I pull my checkbook out of my back pocket. "You don't get the other half until I find her dad."

THE DISDAINFUL TASK of handing money over to that woman complete, I jump in my Suburban and head back to the Bellagio, calling Bridger on the way through the hands-free Bluetooth.

"Fruitful discussion?" is how Bridger answers.

"Yeah... got the name of Cat's father. Allen Henning. Was in the Army, at least as of 2003 when he won a Bronze Star. Originally from Green Bay and was stationed at Fort Bragg. That's all I got."

"Piece of cake," Bridger says, and I will have to take

his word on it. The man has dozens of contacts that provide all sorts of useful information, and I'm grateful he's helping me on this. "I'll have something for you by morning."

"Thanks, man," I say as I rub the back of neck, which is aching from the tension of having to actually be in Trish Lyons' presence.

"Sure thing," he says. "And your girl went home alone last night. Sat at the bar and drank water the rest of the night after that one glass of wine. Left around midnight. I'm assuming she went back to your place."

I wonder what Cat thought when she got to the apartment and I wasn't there. I left a note, intentionally vague, that just said I was going to be out of town for a few days and would call her when I could. That must have sufficed for her, as she hasn't attempted to reach out to me.

"Also got something on Cat's attacker," Bridger says, causing me to sit up straight in my seat, my aching neck forgotten. "Kyle identified him… says he's a member of the club but her attack was something he did on his own. It wasn't brought before the president and sanctioned. Sounds like he got a nice chunk of change that he kept all to himself, so the club wasn't happy at all about having heat brought down on them with no pay in return."

I grimace because just a minute change of circumstances—Kevin approaching the head honcho instead of some rogue member—would have meant we'd never get this information.

"What's that mean?" I ask.

"It means Kyle was authorized to tip the cops to where they can find the dude. Hopefully, he'll roll on Kevin or they'll find some evidence connecting them."

Hopefully.

Because until Kevin was behind bars, Cat wasn't truly safe. I hadn't liked the thought of leaving town, but Bridger confirmed Kevin had gone back to Vegas and that he'd keep an eye on Cat for me.

Knowing that fuckwad is here in Vegas and that I could do some serious damage if I could track him down has me vibrating with adrenaline. Wouldn't be hard to get his address. Bet Bridger could whip it up for me in no time at all.

Shaking my head, I force myself to leave those thoughts by the wayside. If I'm lucky, I'm going to have Cat's father's location tomorrow morning and I'll be heading out to talk to him. I can't let Kevin waylay me just because I want the pleasure of breaking his face.

That's going to have to wait until I can get Cat's father back for her.

Chapter 24
Cat

I WALK THROUGH the cavernous house made of logs and slate that will soon be transferred to me in name once Samuel's estate is settled. Until then, and with Kevin back in Vegas according to Richard, I decided to move out of Rand's apartment and back into the home I shared with my late husband when we visited Jackson.

The entire place is furnished and decorated in typical western flair with heavy pine furniture covered in leather and silk throw pillows in Native American palettes to soften up the look. Typical stuffed and mounted game trophies on the wall. Accent lamps done in cowhide and elk antlers.

It's unoriginal but homey, and if it were not the house I shared with Samuel Vaughn, I'd find it charming.

But instead, I hate this place because it's only purpose was to have a place to sleep when he brought me to The Silo. I have no intention of keeping it. Once things get settled, I'll sell and bank the money. Once I figure out what I want to be now that I've been forced to grow up, I'll have the financial freedom to chase new dreams, but I won't be doing it near anything that remotely reminds me of Samuel Vaughn. That means the Jackson house has to go at some point.

For now though, I'll take the refuge, as there's no way I could stay at Rand's place after how we left things four nights ago. I spent the rest of the night he left me at The Silo brooding and sipping at bottled water. He told me to do what I needed to do.

He essentially said I should fuck someone else if I needed to do that.

That was confusing to me at first because it almost sounded like he didn't care, but when I really thought about it, that's not what was going on at all. Rand was telling me to do what *I needed to do*, whatever that may be, to figure out what I want. He was hoping I'd figure out I wanted him, of course.

And, of course, I absolutely want him.

It's just that I don't think I deserve him.

So that night, I sipped at my water, brooded, and I thought about life, choices, consequences, and regret. I thought about love and lust, security and comfort. I didn't need anyone to paint me a clearer picture.

I know now that Rand Bishop is it for me. I'll never find another like him, and I'll never want anything more in the world than him.

I just had to talk myself into truly believing I could have it and not stain him at the same time.

So I went to the apartment, maybe in the hopes of letting him try to knock some sense into me, only to find him gone.

Nothing but a simple note:

Cat,

Be gone for a few days. Please stay—don't feel like you need to leave. Will try to call soon.

Rand

I must have stared at that note for twenty minutes, trying to glean something out of it to help me figure out what was in Rand's mind. Did he take off because he assumed I would indeed fuck someone else at The Silo? Was that his way of "accepting" my feelings that I'm not good enough?

Is he agreeing with me about that?'

The unmistakable and emphatic answer comes to me as clear as a bell.

No.

No way would Rand think that about me.

He's been my one true champion from that day he pulled me out of my car and brought me to his apartment. He's spent countless energy on validating and affirming me. He's never judged me once for my choices, and despite knowing the worst about me, he still desires me on both a physical and emotional level.

Which begs the question… if Rand can be that stubbornly set on seeing me as a good person, why can't I? I mean… I admire Rand. He's a smart guy. Well rounded, kind, and empathetic. He has good business sense and isn't a fool. So why in the hell would I even think to discount what he sees about me?

Why would I ever think that's not the entire truth?

Walking past the overstuffed couch in the living room, I reach out and straighten a throw pillow. My life has been reduced to fluffing pillows because there's nothing else to do but sit around and wait for Rand to come back.

No idea where he could have gone. I went to Westward Ink two days ago, but Pish didn't know where he was or when he'd be back. I considered going to the Wicked Horse and asking Bridger, but for some reason, I didn't think I could look him in the eye and admit I may have made a very big mistake by going to The Silo that night, which in turn, drove Rand away.

My doorbell rings, startling me with a shock of adrenaline because there's no reason for anyone to be at my door. I have no friends and my heart refuses to believe it would be Rand.

For a split second, I think about ignoring it because if it is Rand, then I'll be forced to make a decision on how I choose to view myself and what I believe I'm entitled to. Scary prospect, and I'm not sure I'm ready.

But then I decide to go for it because it could be a courier delivering papers from Richard regarding the transfer of monies, or it could be Detective Blanton with an update on the case.

Instead, when I open the door, I'm greeted by the smiling face of Callie Hayes.

The woman who hired me out of the goodness of her

heart, only to have me quit on her after three days on the job. Yes, the day after my run in with Rand at The Silo, I went into campaign headquarters and told Callie I couldn't work for her anymore.

She asked why and I told her the truth.

That I now had quite a bit of money coming my way and didn't need the job.

She just smiled at me and nodded politely, not buying for one second that was the reason I was quitting. But because she's a professional, she wished me well and told me I'd be welcome back if I wanted.

I felt like shit leaving her like that, but the truth is, at that point, I had figured my life in Jackson, Wyoming was over. I felt like a fraud, and Rand had left. There was no reason for me to stay and continue to cultivate friendships. In fact, I had intended to hightail it back to Vegas. Even though there's no one there I love, it's still my hometown.

Yet four days later, I'm still here and watching as Callie pushes past me into my home. She looks around as she shrugs out of her jean jacket. It's late afternoon and the temps really start to dip at this time of year, but not enough to warrant a big coat.

"Nice place," she says conversationally.

"Um… thanks," I respond as I follow her into the living room.

She turns, smiling at me brightly.

I smile back, not so bright and with mostly confusion. "What are you doing here?"

"Checking in on you, silly," she says with a wave of her hand. "I didn't buy that shit about you having all kinds of money now and moving on with your life. Well, I totally bought the money thing… I mean, hello… your husband was a gazillionaire or something, but I refused to believe you were bailing on Rand."

"Rand bailed on me," I say quietly. I realize for the first time I'm a little hurt he left without any true resolution between us. The way he's left me wondering, mulling, and stewing over my life has me in knots, and I'm doing nothing but obsessing on how to untie those so I can have peace.

Huh?

Maybe that's what Rand intended all along to happen to me?

Shaking my head, I look at Callie. With my most confident voice, I say, "I appreciate you checking on me, but as you can see, I'm fine."

And she snorts at me with a major eye roll, and then just levels one cocked eyebrow at me.

I get a little miffed. "You don't know me so just level that look somewhere else."

"I know what it's like to love someone but they don't give you the same back in return, mainly because they're too stupid to realize it," she murmurs, her head tilted and eyes sympathetic. "I know because Woolf did it to me, and I know how that made me feel. You're running away from Rand, and I can tell you… it's going to hurt him deeply."

My shoulders immediately sag and any thought I had of fighting her on this seeps out of me. I don't want to cause Rand pain. I don't want to be stupid and lose something that could be very good for me. I just don't know how to accept my own worthiness.

I look at Callie with misery-filled eyes. "I don't know how to do this."

"Do what?" she asks, taking a step toward me with hands coming out to grasp mine.

"Accept happiness—feel worthy—trust that Rand is really crazy for me. I don't know how to give credence to all of these amazing things I've never had before. It doesn't feel right… or genuine to me. I feel like a fraud."

"Why?" she asks, her eyes wide with curiosity. "Why would you ever feel that way?"

"Because I'm not the type of woman anyone respects. I sold out. Sold my own fucking self-respect and worth for the almighty dollar. I let myself be treated abominably because I didn't have the fortitude to demand better for myself. And here Rand Bishop is before me, almost perfect in every way a human can be, and he wants me to step off into a happily ever after with him that I'm sure is going to come crumbling down when he realizes the type of person I really am."

Callie stares at me and says, "Phew. That was a mouthful."

"He's too good for me," I say bitterly, pulling my hands from her.

"Does Rand know all your dirty secrets?" she asks me

point blank.

"Well… yeah… I've told him everything."

"And how does he feel about all of that?" she asks, but before I can reply, she says, "I mean… does he berate you for your choices? Look down his nose at you? Mock you? Make you feel inferior? Does he constantly rub your nose in your mistakes and make you feel ashamed of yourself?"

I pull up straight, incensed on Rand's behalf. "Of course he doesn't. He's done nothing but call me a survivor. He's said my past doesn't matter."

"Then why the fuck are you letting it matter?" Callie asks sarcastically, and I feel like she'd love to add a thump onto my forehead for being so dense. "If you trust Rand, then you must believe what he says. If you believe what he says, then your past doesn't have shit to do with your future with him."

I have no words.

No comeback.

Certainly no argument.

My gaze drops to the floor as I can't bear to have Callie see my own mortification at being so stupid.

I do trust Rand. Clearly trust his reasoning better than my own, since my head seems pretty fucked up these days. But more importantly, if I just let go of my notions of inferiority, and for the briefest of moments, suspend my own self-doubt, I can admit to myself that Rand seems to think I'm pretty great as is.

So why shouldn't I?

My eyes snaps up, pinning Callie, who's looking at me expectantly. "I'm a fucking idiot."

She bursts out laughing, throwing her head back and revealing beautifully straight, white teeth. I can't help it... I laugh too. We stare at each other in amusement as our laughs turn to chuckles, and then finally recede into a sheepish smile from me and a happy smile from Callie.

"Okay, my job here is done," she says proudly, leaning in to kiss my cheek. "I expect to hear all the nitty-gritty details about how you and Rand make up, and you can't spare any of the sexy stuff either."

I snort. "He's got to show back up in town for that to happen."

"I'm sure he'll be back soon," she says, and something about the look on her face makes me do a double take.

"Wait a minute... do you know where he is?" I ask suspiciously.

She doesn't say anything for a moment, and I think she might deny it, but then she sighs and shrugs her shoulders at me. "Actually, I do know where he is, I do know when he's coming back and no, I won't tell you. That's for him."

"But—"

"Now, I really have to go. Lots of stuff to do today," she chirps at me, brushing by me to the front door.

"But—"

"Later, Cat."

The door opens and then closes behind her quickly,

and I realize that Callie just came over here to help pave the way for Rand's return. She was gauging the situation and was bound and determined to do her damndest to make sure my head was on straight when he showed up on my doorstep.

Shaking my head and smiling to myself, I walk up to the front door and peek outside the rectangular pane of glass that sits to the side. Callie gets in her car, a sassy little BMW, and pulls out of my driveway.

Damn, I'm glad she came by.

I start to turn away, but movement catches my eye. I watch as another vehicle pulls in. I don't recognize it... a nondescript black four door with a Wyoming plate on the front. The late afternoon sun hits the windshield at just such an angle that I can't see who it is. My gut tells me it's Detective Blanton, and I get excited that he may have news for me.

I'm surprised when after the car comes to a stop, the passenger door opens first. A man gets out and takes a look around the front yard. He's probably in his mid-forties with dark brown hair, tall, fit, and reasonably attractive. The driver's door opens and my jaw drops open when I see Rand get out. He says something to the other man across the top of the car, who nods in return.

Both men close their doors and start walking up to the house, and for the life of me, I have no clue what's going on.

Rand walks up the porch steps first, and just as his foot hits the top landing, I open the door. His gaze snaps to mine and lights up with joy to see me standing there. I have a flood of warmth and happiness course through me as I realize how much I've missed him in the past few days, and how much I just want to throw myself into his arms.

But he brought company and that holds me back.

I look to the older man again, and note he has brown eyes and olive-toned skin. He gives me a cautious smile, and when he does, I note he only has one dimple popping on the left side.

Huh, just like me… only one dimple working.

Just. Like. Me.

I tilt my head, looking at him closer.

It can't be.

It just can't.

I turn my head slowly back to Rand and look at him… my eyes pleading with him to tell me who this man is.

"Cat," Rand says quietly as he nods to the stranger. "I found your father."

Chapter 25
Rand

GODDAMN, SHE LOOKS gorgeous. Wearing a pair of faded jeans ripped at the knee, a sweatshirt, and fuzzy socks. Hair pulled up in a ponytail and not a lick of makeup on her face.

And now she looks woozy, her legs buckling slightly when I reveal that I found her dad.

I step forward quickly, put my arm around her waist, and hold her tightly. Turning her toward Allen, I watch as her eyes roam all over his face.

Slowly… taking in every detail. Probably comparing the arch of her eyebrows to his, or the way their noses tilt slightly upward at the end. I took one look at Allen Henning when I tracked him down to Fayetteville, North Carolina, and I had no doubt he was Cat's father.

That was three days ago. Bridger worked his magic and found out that Sergeant Major Allen Henning retired from the Army just this year after twenty-five years of active duty. He never returned to Green Bay, instead settling in Fayetteville as he'd spent almost as much time there as he had growing up in Wisconsin. Allen had married a local girl and they had two children, a boy age fifteen and a girl, age eleven.

I left my Suburban in Vegas and caught a flight to Raleigh, North Carolina. Once there, I rented a car and drove the hour and a half to Fayetteville. I had no clue how Allen would receive me because I knew very little about the character of this man, but I didn't let that hold me back. I made it to his house at dinnertime as he was just setting down with his family to eat.

He was gracious but didn't invite me in. Instead, he stepped out onto the front porch into the air that was still quite warm and humid in early September.

I didn't hold any punches because I knew I'd found the right man. "Mr. Henning… I'm in love with a woman who I believe is your daughter."

He blinked at me in surprise, but he wasn't pissed, and that started to clue me in to the man's character. "Excuse me?"

"Back in 1990, you briefly dated a woman named Trish Lyons."

His eyebrows furrowed inward as he flipped backward in time and then his nose wrinkled slightly. "Yeah… we were together a few months. She sort of dumped me with no explanation. Hadn't thought about her in years actually."

"Well… she was pregnant when she left and didn't tell you about it. Went back to Vegas and had the baby. A girl named Catherine."

To give the man credit, he stayed upright although his face went ghostly white. "I have a daughter?"

"Yes," I told him with a smile. "She's twenty-four. She's also sweet, amazing, and gorgeous. She had a shitty life. Yet, she still turned out amazing. She had no one her entire life who she could count on, and her mother always told her you abandoned them. I sought you out to see if that was true, and if it wasn't, to give Cat a little piece of her heritage."

"I never would have abandoned her if I'd known," he whispered roughly.

"I know," I told him. "I can just tell you wouldn't."

Allen then invited me in. He called his wife, Marsha, into the living room where he recounted to her what I'd just told him in a quiet voice so the kids wouldn't hear. She had the same stunned look, but then she immediately became concerned about Catherine the way Allen had.

I then got invited to dinner, but we agreed not to say anything to the kids. Allen felt that was a conversation he and Marsha needed to have with them after they learned more about Cat.

So I sat at the dinner table with the Henning family, and I learned all about them.

And they are fucking phenomenal. Cat is getting ready to inherit a dad who is eager to make up for lost time and a stepmother who is ready to dote on her. Allen told me this morning when I picked him up at his house to make the trip here with me that the kids were over the moon to learn they have a sibling.

Today has dragged by so slowly, flying out of Raleigh to Dallas, and then into Jackson. Allen and I have spent plenty of time the last few days talking about Catherine. While I haven't told him any details about her life with Samuel, I told him everything I knew about the way Trish raised her. To say that Allen wanted to make a side trip to Vegas and give the woman a piece of his mind was an understatement.

I also watched Allen grieve today while we sat in Dallas on our layover. It hit him all at once... he missed twenty-four years of his daughter's life. Missed changing her diapers and her first steps. Teaching her to read and how to drive a car. Missed threatening the first boy to take her on a date, and while Cat ultimately married poorly, he missed his opportunity to give his daughter away. I have to say, it's awkward watching a grown man get emotional, and mainly because my fucking eyes misted up too as he talked about all the shit he missed out on.

And now here we stand with Cat looking like she's about ready to pass out and Allen looking like he's going to vomit if someone doesn't say something fast.

So I step into action, my hand gripping Cat at her waist. "Cat... baby... this is your dad, Allen Henning. Lots to explain, but first, he never knew of your existence until I showed up on his doorstep three days ago."

Cat's head tilts as she looks at him, almost as if she's afraid to ask even the first question for fear of being crushed. So he decides to take matters into his own hand and simply pulls her into his arms for a hug.

She goes willingly, her arms wrapping around his

waist and her cheek pressing into his wide chest. They sway back and forth, gripping each other tightly. Cat with her eyes closed but tears still dribbling out and flowing down her cheeks. Allen with this temple resting on top of her head, his eyes also closed, and the happiest, most peaceful and serene smile gracing his lips.

I could stand there all afternoon and watch Cat just hugging her father, but she's the first to pull back. She looks up at her dad, who gently wipes her tears and then turns her gaze to meet mine. "How? How in the world did you find him?"

"I paid your mom a visit," I say simply, but there's no way in hell I'll admit I paid the woman for the information unless Cat asks me point blank.

"She'd never give that information up," Cat says as she narrows her eyes at me. "How much did you pay her?"

Well, fuck.

I duck my head, think about lying, and then finally look back at her with a grimace. "A lot, and it was worth every penny. Let's leave it at that."

She nods, but I know she's not letting it go. She's merely deferring the discussion until she can get me alone, not wanting any unpleasantness to ruin this moment. I take the opportunity to fill her in as succinctly as I can, figuring Allen can do the rest.

"Your mom told me that she dated Allen briefly in 1990 while she lived in Fayetteville, North Carolina with a friend," I begin.

Cat's eyebrows jump upward. "She lived in North Carolina?"

I nod. "Briefly. Dated Allen and got pregnant. Left and went back to Vegas without telling him."

Cat's gaze swings back to her father's. "You never knew about me?"

"Never," he says fiercely. "And if I did, I would have never let you go. Never."

Fuck... okay, that's getting to me.

Getting to me even more to see Cat's eyes fill up with bright, shining tears of joy. Time to lighten the mood just a bit.

"So, okay... how about you two move the party inside and get to know each other?" I say, taking Cat's arm and turning her toward the door. I clap Allen on the shoulder and pull him along.

Cat opens the front door, steps into the foyer, and turns to welcome us both in. Allen crosses the threshold as she smiles at him with absolute eternal hope on her face. Her eyes slide to me and she motions with her hand to invite me in.

I shake my head. "Uh-uh. You two need alone time. You have lots to talk about."

She cocks her head at me, but I don't stick around. I nod at Cat's father with a smile before turning to jog down the porch steps. Allen and Cat have a lot of catching up to do. I've come to learn a lot about this man and his family the last two days, and Cat needs to hear it all from him as well. She also needs to decide how much of her past she wants to share with him, and that's a private matter that I don't need to impede on.

As I reach the rental car—my mind suddenly trying to figure out if I should fly to Vegas tomorrow to get my Suburban, which means I'd incur the wrath of Pish if I don't get my ass back to work—I hear Cat call out, "Hey... Rand... wait up?"

I turn to see her coming down the porch steps, her dad standing in the doorway with his hands tucked in his pockets, watching us carefully. I didn't hold anything back from Allen. He knows I love the hell out of Cat.

"What's up?" I say casually, not really knowing where Cat's head is at. Bridger told me she left my apartment and moved back in the house. He told me all about Cat quitting her job with Callie and the police suspecting Kevin but not able to do a damn thing until they find the attacker.

Cat comes to a stop a few feet from me, looking uncertain. I hate that. I want her to feel free to jump in my arms, but she's just been given a shock, and things between us are unstable at best. So I give her a friendly smile to encourage her to speak.

"Looks like there wasn't a will that cut me out," she tells me as she sticks her hands into the back pockets of her jeans and rocks on her feet nervously. "Richard called me... told me to move back in here and that Kevin was going back to Vegas."

My gaze flicks to the large house and then back to her. "I get it... who wouldn't want to live in that?"

She winces slightly but doesn't engage in the very awkward conversation that would ensue about her moving out of my apartment while I was gone. Instead, she says, "Detective Blanton interviewed Kevin. He thinks he was involved with my attack, but Kevin won't admit anything."

I nod. Bridger had kept me in the loop. "Bridger's buddy, Kyle, came through. Identified the guy who attacked you. It wasn't sanctioned by the MC, so they're going to share that info with the police. They'll put a warrant out for his arrest."

Cat's gorgeous mouth forms into an "O" of surprise. "I didn't know that."

"Well, hopefully, they'll find the guy quickly and he'll roll on Kevin. Then you can put all of this behind you."

She nods, gaze dropping to the ground… clearly indecisive about what to say. When her face lifts, she turns to look at her dad standing in the doorway waiting for her, and then back to me.

"I can't believe you went to all that trouble for me," she says quietly and with such earnest gratitude, I actually feel a little hot under the collar.

My gut says to play it cool with her, but fuck that… I missed her too much and I want her to know that this isn't over between us. "I'd do anything for you, Cat. Come find me when you're ready, but for now… go get to know your dad. He's a great guy."

Her eyes shimmer as she smiles at me brilliantly. She

inclines her head to me… a silent gesture of acceptance and pleasure over my words… and turns to race back to the house like a little girl who is having her first Christmas. I watch until she hits the porch. Her dad moves to the side to allow her to come through, and they link arms as they turn to go inside. When the door shuts, I get in the rental car and head home.

Chapter 26
Cat

IT'S BEEN A week since Rand brought my father to me. Since that amazing man went out and tracked down the missing puzzle piece in my life. I didn't realize how badly I needed that piece until it was presented to me.

I'm not sure I'll ever be able to adequately convey to Rand what that means to me.

Did to me.

The way it changed me.

Not many people can really understand my background. It's hard to comprehend what it does to the human spirit... the belief that someone doesn't want you. I knew my mom didn't want me, and I only had her telling me my father abandoned me to complete my familial unit.

I told my father everything during his visit.

And I mean everything, even down to telling him about Samuel and how he used me. I didn't give him vivid details, but I gave him enough that my dad started crying, which made me cry too. He then assured me that he wants me. That even when he didn't know I existed, he wanted me. That was lovely, and I cried harder.

My dad then pointed out that given my history and not having the most important people to depend upon—that being parents—he said it was no wonder I accepted what Samuel wanted of me as his wife. He thought it spoke to perhaps my inherent need to be wanted, even as vile as the circumstances were. He reiterated to me something that Rand has said on more than one occasion… that I was a survivor.

The five days I had with my dad were not nearly enough. We spent every moment together, just talking endlessly. We had twenty-four years of catching up to do. While my life's details were not easy for him to take, I reveled in hearing about his. He was a career Army man and a true hero. I apparently have amazing grandparents back in Green Bay that cannot wait to meet me. His wife, Marsha—my new stepmom, so weird to say that—is the freakin' bomb. We've talked several times by phone and she's everything that my mother was not. I also had a tentative talk on the phone with my new siblings. My brother, Jared, is fifteen and really into soccer. This was an awkward conversation because I know nothing about soccer or fifteen-year-old boys, but in the end, it was okay because he said, "I can't wait to meet you, Cat," and that made my day.

Now my sister, Natasha, is a spitfire at age eleven. I do know something about eleven-year-old girls so we talked about music, Snapchat, fingernail polish, and boys, not necessarily in that order, and well… mostly about boys. I did this while my dad listened in on my end of the conversation and rolled his eyes, muttering, "I don't want to know about this stuff."

It was a perfect five days.

I was completely reborn, and I say completely because the process started before my dad came back into my life. I realize now that process started the night Rand found me in my car and made me start believing in a better life.

And now I stand outside Rand's apartment, wondering how I can take this last piece of my life's puzzle and snap it into place so that my existence will be as close to perfect as a person can hope for. I wipe my hands on my skirt because they're sweaty from nerves and take a deep breath, trying to will my heart to slow the hell down.

Rapping my knuckles against the door twice, I listen intently. I can hear him walking, hear the creaking of the floor on the other side of the door, and then he's standing there in front of me, looking better than ever. Blond hair falling over his forehead and he pushes it back, giving me a lazy smile. He stretches his other hand out high to grab onto the doorjamb, which raises his t-shirt up slightly so I get a peek of his stomach. I can't help it... my eyes fall and stare, and when my tongue pops out to lick my lower lip, Rand gives a husky laugh.

Cheeks red and warm, my gaze snaps back up to his. Amusement shining in his eyes, he says, "Took you long enough to come see me."

"Well, with my dad visiting and all—"

"He flew out two days ago," he points out to me, and

this is something I know well. It's taken me two days to get my nerve up to come see Rand after my dad left for North Carolina.

Two days where I tried to prepare the best speech ever to let him know what he means to me, and as I stand here now, I can't remember a damn word.

It's gone. Blank. All the pretty poetic words about what he's done for me and the realizations I've come to… just… gone.

So I blurt out, "I think I love you."

The amusement drains out of Rand's eyes and his stare becomes very intent, his body going still.

Was that the wrong thing to say? Shit.

"I mean… what I really meant to say is—"

Rand lunges at me, hands going to either side of my face. With a tight grip, he yanks me into him. Our mouths crash together, our bodies press in tight. My entire being sighs in relief and that last piece of the puzzle snaps in with a resounding click.

Or is that my heart finally settling into place now that it finally knows what love really is?

Not sure.

I'm being lifted, his hands moving from my face to my ass, where he pulls me up his body and my legs lock around him. We don't stop that delicious kiss for even a moment as Rand turns into the apartment and kicks the door shut behind him. My arms circle around his entire head, fingers in his hair as our tongues duel and our teeth scrape against each other.

Then I'm flying… free for a moment until my back hits his bed and his body covers me from the top. Mouth back on mine as hands start to roam.

My fingers slip under the back of his t-shirt, pressing into his muscles. Rand grinds his pelvis against me, and we both groan over the sensation.

His hand slides under my skirt and goes straight to my hip. He starts to yank at my panties, trying to get them off me.

"I really need to fuck you," he mutters as he rears up and puts both hands to the task.

"Wait," I say, my arms rising and my palms going to his chest. "That night at The Silo… when I went there… I didn't—"

"I know," he says brusquely, eyes pinned to the job at hand, which is now currently sliding my panties past my knees.

Okay, that conversation clearly doesn't need to happen. But there's so much to say and I can't concentrate when he's stripping me.

"But we need to talk about—"

"Cat," Rand practically barks at me with amused frustration as he pulls my underwear free and tosses it over his shoulder. "We can talk about how much we love each other, spiritual awakenings, and all that other foo-foo shit that occurs when you're in a relationship later, but right now… it's been a long damn time since I've been inside this pussy and I'm not about to wait so we can hash all this crap out."

I know I should be offended, but I'm not. He's adorable.

"You love me?" I ask, knowing that's really the only important thing I need to know.

"Yes," he says as his smile softens. He presses the palm of one hand against my mound, turns his wrist, and then slips a finger inside of me. "And you're wet as hell right now, so I'm going to fuck you and then we'll talk later, okay?"

"Okay," I sigh as my hips undulate against the sensations.

"Good girl," he commends me as he works to free his cock from his jeans.

His hands go under my knees after he does, raising and spreading me wide, and then he's sinking in deep and it's the best feeling in the world. Totally different from any time before since there are true emotions involved now.

Because now I know who I am and I understand my worthiness to be happy.

Because he loves me and I love him, and that makes all the difference.

⊛

RAND'S HAND STROKES my lower back in wide circles while I lay on top of him, lulling me to the edge of sleep. My heart rate is finally back to normal but what is still going full tilt is the happiness coursing through me.

Let's think about all the reasons why.

I have a wonderful man who loves me and thinks I'm perfect, warts and all.

I have a family now… a father, a stepmother, a brother, and a sister.

I live in a beautiful place and have real friends.

I have money… lots and lots of money, thanks to Richard transferring the five million dollars to me even though the estate hasn't been settled. He feels absolutely terrible about what Kevin did and is bending over backward to make things right for me.

What Kevin did…

I jerk upright, pressing my hands into Rand's chest and looking down at him. "Kevin," I practically squeal. "I forgot to tell you about Kevin."

"He was arrested day before yesterday," Rand says blandly as his hands go to my butt where they start kneading into my muscles.

"How did you hear that?" I ask, although I can guess.

"Bridger told me," he says, his fingers inching inward… sliding along the crack of my ass and then downward.

I reach back and push his hands away because he's too damn distracting. "So you know all about them arresting my attacker?"

"Yup," he says with a grin. "It's a small town. You hear things."

Small town, my ass. I'm sure Bridger told him what happened, which was essentially that someone from Mayhem's Mission tipped the police toward Jim March, who was my suspected attacker. He fit the description, including the teardrop tattoo, which was apparently the key to identifying him. The police picked him up and grilled him hard with their suspicions he'd been hired to kill me.

The guy wasn't totally stupid because he hired a lawyer, who then turned around and helped him cut a deal with the DA's office. He rolled on Kevin and provided key details to prove he was hired by him. The next day a warrant was issued for Kevin's arrest and sent to the Vegas police. He was in custody within a few hours and will be extradited back to Wyoming within the next few days.

"It's finally over," Rand says quietly, his arms now coming up to wrap around my lower back.

"Or a wiser person would say it's really just beginning," I counter with a grin.

"Who are you and what have you done with the pessimist formerly known as Cat Lyons?" he chuckles.

I snicker before leaning my face down to kiss him. "Well, she found a guy who's pretty amazing and who taught her to see the good in herself."

"Oh, yeah?" he asks slyly. "Tell me more about this dude."

"Well, he's incredibly hot, fantastic in bed, and he happens to be one of the kindest, wisest, and most caring people Cat Lyons has ever met. He made her sort of look at life from a new perspective."

"She should totally give him a blow job for that,"

Rand says to me earnestly. "He so deserves that, don't you think?"

I laugh, kiss him again on his lips, and say, "Yes… he totally deserves it."

I push against his chest so that I start to slide down his body. His arms loosen to allow my descent, and I can feel his cock start to twitch against me as my breasts drag down his abdomen.

"Hey," Rand whispers, and I halt… looking up at him.

He brings a hand to my face, pushes my hair behind my ear, and says, "I love you. I mean, I really, really love you, and I cannot wait to show you how fantastic that can be."

I smile, bending forward to kiss his chest before looking back up at him. "I already know how fantastic it is. And I love you too."

"That's my girl," he murmurs before his hands go to my head and he gently pushes on me to get moving again.

Epilogue
Logan

I THINK THIS woman may be the death of me.

A dire prediction, but probably true.

Probably true because she's not mine to have and I'd probably take her, even at the risk to my own safety.

I'm fixated on her... obsessed really. That black-as-midnight hair and huge, blue eyes the color of the Wyoming sky. Her skin pale... almost translucent. She looks otherworldly, in fact, and it's no secret that every man in The Silo is obsessed with her as much as I am.

I have to have her, and maybe tonight will be the night. My dick is already hard and aching with the thought, and if I'm given the pleasure of her company, my cock won't even get to touch her pussy, which I'm betting is sweeter than honey. I try to look nonchalant as her "owner" walks around The Silo, chatting up the various patrons and deciding who gets to play with her tonight. He's passed me by on four other occasions. I expect tonight won't be any different because he knows I don't have the type of bank he'll be asking for when he ultimately auctions her off. So many men slobbering to get a taste of her and only one sweet, virginal girl to go around.

That's right.

She's a virgin.

Twenty years old and looking like a porcelain china doll that would break if not handled carefully. But I also know she's stronger than she looks as I've watched her take a mouth fucking like a champ.

She's a contradiction.

She's most likely my downfall.

Like I said, she'll probably be the death of me, but it's a risk I'm willing to take.

If you enjoyed *Wicked Need* as much as I enjoyed writing it, it would mean a lot for you to give me a review on your favorite retailer's website.

Connect with Sawyer online:

Website: www.sawyerbennett.com

Twitter: www.twitter.com/bennettbooks

Facebook: www.facebook.com/bennettbooks

Other Books by Sawyer Bennett

The Off Series
Off Sides
Off Limits
Off The Record
Off Course
Off Chance
Off Season
Off Duty

The Last Call Series
On The Rocks
Make It A Double
Sugar On The Edge
With A Twist
Shaken Not Stirred

The Legal Affairs Series
Legal Affairs Sneak Peek (FREE)
Legal Affairs
Confessions of a Litigation God
Clash: A Legal Affairs Story (Book #1 of Cal and Macy's Story)
Grind: A Legal Affairs Story (Book #2 of Cal and Macy's Story)
Yield: A Legal Affairs Story (Book #3 of Cal and Macy's Story)
Friction: A Legal Affairs Novel

Stand Alone Titles
If I Return
Uncivilized
Love: Uncivilized

The Sugar Bowl Series
Sugar Daddy

**The Cold Fury Hockey Series
(Random House / Loveswept)**
Alex
Garrett
Zack
Ryker
Hawke
4 Book Bundle – Alex, Garrett, Zack, Ryker

The Wicked Horse Series
Wicked Fall
Wicked Lust
Wicked Need

The Forever Land Chronicles
Forever Young

About the Author

New York Times and USA Today Bestselling Author, Sawyer Bennett is a snarky southern woman and reformed trial lawyer who decided to finally start putting on paper all of the stories that were floating in her head. Her husband works for a Fortune 100 company which lets him fly all over the world while she stays at home with their daughter and three big, furry dogs who hog the bed. Sawyer would like to report she doesn't have many weaknesses but can be bribed with a nominal amount of milk chocolate.

Sawyer is the author of several contemporary romances including the popular Off Series, the Legal Affairs Series, The Carolina Cold Fury Hockey Series and the Last Call Series.

www.ingramcontent.com/pod-product-compliance
Lightning Source LLC
Chambersburg PA
CBHW082245120525
26596CB00010B/515